PRAISE FOR THE CAIT MORGAN MYSTERIES

"In the finest tradition of Agatha Christie . . . Ace brings us the closed-room drama, with a dollop of romantic suspense and historical intrigue." —*Library Journal*

"Touches of Christie or Marsh but with a bouquet of Kinsey Millhone." —*Globe and Mail*

"A sparkling, well-plotted, and quite devious mystery in the cozy tradition." —*Hamilton Spectator*

"Perfect comfort reading. You could call it Agatha Christie set in the modern world, with great dollops of lovingly described food and drink." —CrimeFictionLover.com

"A delight for fans of the classic mystery . . . Cait Morgan . . . and her husband make a pair of believable and very real sleuths." —Vicky Delany, national bestselling author of the Lighthouse Library mystery series

"Unique and original, this engaging treasure hunt through the art world—and one family's secrets—sets an endearing, smart, and contemporary couple on a compelling quest. Intelligent, touching, and more than a mystery, this page-turner is a revealing insight into love and loyalty." —Hank Phillippi Ryan, Agatha, Anthony, and Mary Higgins Clark award-winning author

THE CAIT MORGAN MYSTERY SERIES

The Corpse with the Silver Tongue
The Corpse with the Golden Nose
The Corpse with the Emerald Thumb
The Corpse with the Platinum Hair
The Corpse with the Sapphire Eyes
The Corpse with the Diamond Hand
The Corpse with the Garnet Face
The Corpse with the Ruby Lips

ALSO BY CATHY ACE

The Case of the Dotty Dowager
The Case of the Missing Morris Dancer
The Curious Cook

THE Corpse WITH THE Ruby Lips

CATHY ACE

TouchWood
Editions

Designed by Pete Kohut
Edited by Frances Thorsen
Proofread by Claire Philipson
Cover image by Krivinis, istockphoto.com

LIBRARY AND ARCHIVES CANADA CATALOGUING IN PUBLICATION
Ace, Cathy, 1960–, author
The corpse with the ruby lips / Cathy Ace.
(A Cait Morgan mystery)

Issued in print and electronic formats.
ISBN 978-1-77151-195-7

I. Title. II. Series: Ace, Cathy, 1960– . Cait Morgan mystery

PS8601.C41C666 2016   C813'.6   C2016-903369-4

We acknowledge the financial support of the Government of Canada through the Canada
Book Fund and the Canada Council for the Arts, and of the province of British Columbia
through the British Columbia Arts Council and the Book Publishing Tax Credit.

Canada Council
for the Arts

Conseil des Arts
du Canada

BRITISH COLUMBIA
ARTS COUNCIL

The interior pages of this book have been printed on 100% post-consumer recycled
paper, processed chlorine free, and printed with vegetable-based inks.

PRINTED IN CANADA AT FRIESENS

20 19 18 17 16   1 2 3 4 5

To Oliver

October 25, 1976

CAMPUS MURDER VICTIM TO BE REMEMBERED

A memorial service for Mrs. Ilona Seszták, the late wife of Professor Kristóf Seszták, will take place at the Great Concourse at 2:00 PM tomorrow, October 26, 1976. All are welcome. In a telephone call to the *UVan Voice* Professor Seszták said, "We ask the entire community to join my family in remembering my dear wife's contributions to our life at this university, and to do whatever they can to help the police find her attacker."

Mrs. Seszták's remains were found on Bike Path West, on campus, at 7:30 AM on Wednesday, October 20, by Sam Gillies. Sam is one of the stars of the UVan swim team. He was on his way to a training session at the pool when he found the remains.

The police are asking for anyone with information about the whereabouts of Mrs. Seszták after 5:00 PM on Tuesday, October 19 (the day of UVan's convocation ceremony) to report to an officer. Investigating officers will be in attendance at the memorial gathering, and are available for private meetings at their temporary inquiry center at the President's Office from 9:00 AM to 5:00 PM every day.

Bike Path West remains closed until further notice, and all female students are requested to adhere to the 8:00 PM curfew imposed by our president.

1976 Calling the Twenty-First Century

I WAS LATE. I HATE being late. I didn't have time for public trans-portation, so I was sitting in a taxi crossing a bridge that spanned the roiling Danube River. As I stared miserably at the impressive Budapest skyline, I tried to talk myself into a happier frame of mind.

Sometimes you think you're about to zig when life throws something in your path, so you have to zag. That's what happened to Bud and me. If Bud hadn't had to stay in Canada tending to his mother after her hip replacement surgery, I'd have felt entirely different about my time in a city that had long beckoned me. As it was, we'd both had to adapt to our changed circumstances, so I'd set off to deliver a month-long course at the Hungarian University of Budapest with as much of a skip in my step as possible. However, the last ten lonely days had knocked the stuffing out of me and I was missing my husband dreadfully. Who knew longing had so many layers? Not me, for one.

Both Bud and I knew he'd done the right thing staying behind to give his father a helping hand with his mother's recuperation, and we agreed we'd focus on looking forward to him joining me at the end of my time in Hungary for a shorter-than-planned week-long visit. There'd been brave tears at the airport, and lots of talk during our Skype conversations since then about what we'd do when he eventually joined me.

But now? Only ten days into my time alone, that glimmer of hope seemed a long way off as I accepted that teaching in a foreign city wasn't so different from teaching at home, and working on a research paper can be equally frustrating whether the view from the window is of the glittering lights of a historic cityscape or the countryside around our home in British Columbia.

"You are happy to be visiting our beautiful Budapest, yes?" asked the cab driver in accented but flawless English.

"Absolutely," I lied.

"You have seen our wonderful monuments? Our architecture?" he continued, smiling at me over his shoulder as we veered too close to a passing tram.

"Not yet, but I'm looking forward to it," I said, pressing my foot on an imaginary brake pedal and trying to steer the cab with my body movements.

"But you must do this."

I tried to focus on the sights around me as I replied, "I certainly will." *If I live through this journey.*

"At least tonight you will enjoy the New York Café," added the driver. "It is known around the world for its decadence and luxury."

"And I hear the food is excellent." I hoped he'd stop chatting and concentrate on the knots of traffic.

"I hear this too," he agreed.

"There it is," I said, relieved we'd arrived safely. I emerged in front of the lavishly decorated Austro-Hungarian building and steeled myself. The dinner I was about to attend would place me at a table with my temporary colleagues from the psychology department at the HUB, as the university was affectionately known, as well as two deans of schools—and would likely demand my contribution to learned conversation.

As I handed my coat to an elderly attendant, I was surprised to be greeted by one of my students, who was checking her lipstick in a mirror placed beside the cavernous cloakroom (already half-filled with heavy coats).

"Professor Morgan," exclaimed Zsófia Takács, sounding as

surprised as I felt to find ourselves standing next to each other. "I didn't know you'd be here tonight."

"And I'm surprised to see you here. Are you a part of the HUB group attending the musical evening?"

The girl laughed. "No, I am part of the musical evening itself. See the lady over there in pink?" She turned and waved toward a wizened but fiercely upright, overdressed woman. Sitting across the restaurant beside a small dais, she wiggled her fingers in our direction. "That's my great-aunt Klara. She taught me a lot of old songs, and I sometimes get the chance to sing them. For free, of course, like tonight. They said I can perform two. It's a great honor to sing here. Usually I only have the chance to get up on stage in bars and clubs. I hope you enjoy it."

Sweat was beading on her upper lip. Despite her immaculate makeup and splendid outfit, the twenty-year-old looked more like a young girl playing dress-up than a confident performer about to wow an audience. I felt a bit of encouragement was needed. "You look the part, and I'm sure you'll do yourself and your great-aunt proud."

Zsófia looked apprehensive. "I hope so. I shall sing as she has taught me, and I am wearing clothes she has loaned me. To make my family proud is all I want."

It was hard to believe the elderly Klara's desiccated figure could once have filled out the black fifties-style velvet dress with cinched waist and full skirt that now hugged Zsófia's curves. "The black works well with your hair and lip color. Their fire-engine red will look good on stage," I said cheerily. Having been somewhat Junoesque my entire life, I knew how few and far between compliments could be. "So, your great-aunt was a singer too?"

"She still is," said Zsófia, smiling warmly. "Sometimes it's difficult to get her to stop." Her tone communicated love, respect, and indulgence. "I hope I have that much spirit when I'm almost ninety."

3

Having only met the girl in a classroom setting before then, I took the opportunity to study her in a different light. I'd pegged her as sharply intelligent, hardworking, and one of the few taking my course because she wanted the knowledge, not merely a good grade. She was confident in lectures and willing to take a leadership role in group discussions. I found her surprisingly easy to warm to. Indeed, Bud and I had spoken about her a few times during our Skype chats, and he reckoned I liked her because she reminded me of myself when I was her age. As she fussed with her retro hairdo in the mirrored area beside the coat check, I reapplied the lip gloss I'd smeared when I'd slapped my hand over my mouth as my driver swung his cab around a corner.

Seeing her there, looking so different—so grown up, yet vulnerable and nervous—I asked myself again what it was about her, rather than just any twenty-year-old, that I found appealing, and silently admitted that maybe it was the way her insecurities peeped through the shell she'd built about herself with costume and bravado. I knew I'd done much the same my whole life, until Bud came along and gave me the confidence I needed to accept I could only be me and I didn't have to build walls to protect myself.

"I'd better join Klara," said Zsófia, acknowledging the beckoning of a man in a tail suit. "They want me to be seated next to the stage. Enjoy dinner—the food's amazing." There was a long pause. "Can I talk to you about something afterward? It's a personal thing, and I want it to be kept away from the HUB. I've tried to think about how to ask you this favor since you arrived, but I haven't known what to say. Tonight would be ideal."

I imagined she wanted to ask for an extension to a report deadline, or for an agreed-upon late arrival the next day, so I answered breezily, "But of course. I'll hold back at the end of our dinner and we can have a chat then. Okay?" I wasn't going to make it difficult for her; she was diligent, and I'm fine with cutting a hardworking student a little slack. It's the lazy ones who need to fear my wrath.

I found my party in the busy restaurant and threw myself into conversation with the senior faculty members as I took in my surroundings. Ceiling vaults painted with cherubs and bucolic idylls, marble columns carved to writhing perfection, and everywhere the glint from ornate chandeliers shining upon gold leaf. The sound of chatter bounced about, and I tried to imagine the conversations that had taken place in this very room when the clientele had been the greatest philosophers, writers, and artists of the day, and the fashion had been to sip a coffee for several hours.

The chitchat at my table wasn't going to change the world, but at least it progressed politely, accompanied by the gentle yet atmospheric sounds of a trio of local musicians, all sporting white tie and tails. One was playing the cimbalom, which reminded me of the movie *The Third Man* with its brittle, haunting zither music—almost a character in its own right.

Dinner was, as I'd hoped, spectacular. Since Budapest is pretty much the foie gras capital of the world, I began with that. Once I'd finished savoring the velvety, meltingly rich treat I faced something I wasn't at all sure about when I'd ordered it—"pork throttle." My tablemates had pointed to various parts of their anatomies when I'd asked what it was, but I'd decided to be brave. When it arrived I was relieved to see it was pork knuckle, with crisply roasted skin and meat literally falling off the bone as I sliced into it.

Needless to say I was completely stuffed by the time I'd eaten my main course, and I could practically feel my arteries clogging as I simply read the dessert menu. On the advice of my colleagues I selected the New York chocolate cake—something of a signature dish at the place, I gathered. I was delighted to see it was quite small, and it melted in my mouth with the texture of a rich mousse.

As coffee and some delicious, but frankly unnecessary, petit fours were served, the musicians took a break. I noticed Zsófia had left her great-aunt's table and was moving toward the dais. I felt apprehensive for the poor girl, and hoped nerves wouldn't mar her performance.

As the cimbalom player introduced Zsófia by name, I hoped the conversation would die down, but the chattering masses didn't miss a beat until the girl began to sing. Her voice was magnificent—smoky and passionate. It was perfect for the eighteenth-century Hungarian *verbunkos* (dance-inspired) song she began with. She quickly won the attention of the entire dining room, and heads popped up over the gold balustrades of the balcony above us as people tried to see who was singing. The applause at the end of her first song was more than polite and she thanked her great-aunt for having taught it to her. She began to sing again in Hungarian with a little of the Roma language here and there. She stared, transfixed, and her eyes even filled with tears as she worked her way to the crescendo, garnering rapturous applause. Even the servers clapped. I wondered if that was usual.

Leaving the little dais, Zsófia returned to her great-aunt's table. The elderly woman wrapped her rose-brocaded arms about her great-niece's waist, hugging her tight. I suspected tears were involved, and both women looked sad and happy in equal measure—pretty normal for Hungarians, by all accounts.

Finally, after a round of polite goodnights, I remained at my table and waited for my student to join me. I didn't have to sit alone for long. Leaving her great-aunt Klara sipping a large snifter of brandy, Zsófia wafted between the emptying tables and came to sit beside me.

"Was I all right?" she asked hesitantly.

"So much more than all right, Zsófia. Have you thought of singing as a career?"

Zsófia's porcelain-pale cheeks flushed, then she spluttered, "Mama wants me to get my degree, then a real job for a few years. Then, maybe, I can try, she said. It's not a secure life, I understand that. She is thinking only of me."

I could tell she was saying what was expected.

"Have your parents ever seen you perform?" I asked.

"Papa died many years ago. Now there is only Mama. This is the first time anyone in my family has seen me sing in public. Klara came because she knows the violinist and asked him if I could sing these songs tonight. She said it was a test for me. She thought I did reasonably well." Zsófia leaned in and said quietly, "She didn't think I was quite as good as she was when she was younger, but she said I might be one day." She winked at me, and it was clear she felt pride at her performance.

"Well, for what it's worth, I don't think many people who heard you tonight would think you should give it up—but I'm not a mother, let alone *yours*, so maybe you'd better do as she says. Now—what was it you wanted to talk to me about? You'd better not keep Klara waiting too long."

Zsófia shifted uncomfortably on her seat. "It's difficult, and it's a big favor," she began.

"Sometimes it's best to just say these things, and get it over with," I urged.

"Very well," she replied, sitting upright, "I'd like you to help me find out who murdered my grandmother."

I was so taken aback by this that I didn't speak for at least five seconds, which is a long time for me.

"Your grandmother was murdered?" She nodded. "I'm terribly sorry to hear it, Zsófia, but I don't think that's something I can help with. Surely it's a matter for the police." I was puzzled.

The girl sighed heavily and glanced toward her great-aunt, who was holding an empty glass in the air. "Oh dear, this isn't the time to talk properly. I've done this all wrong. I have to put Klara into a taxi, and get back home myself." She rummaged around in her purse—her everyday tote, which didn't match the rest of her elegant outfit. "I wonder if it's in here." She pulled out a thumb drive and pressed it into my hand. "It's a start. In among all of my HUB assignments, there's a folder called 'Ilona Overview,' which will give you just that. I hope you'll at least read it. It won't take you long; there's not much there." She leaned toward me and moved as though to hug me, then clearly thought better of it. Her microexpressions told a tale of great inner turmoil, and her eyes hunted mine for some sort of reassurance.

I knew I had to gain control of the situation. "With the greatest respect, Zsófia, I don't think I can grant your request. I don't know what's on this," I held up the tiny device, "but I do know it's not something I should, or could, become involved with. An ongoing murder inquiry is—"

"It's not a current inquiry," whispered Zsófia. "The case was dropped back in the 1970s. And I know you can't help right now, while you're here. I'm not asking you to do anything but read this information for now. I am asking you to help when you get back to Canada. That's where it happened, you see. It is a cold case now, but I need to know what happened. My mother, she will not speak to me about it." She furtively glanced around the grand room. "There are eyes and ears everywhere, I cannot say more."

I, too, glanced about—but couldn't see anything except a pretty normal-looking smattering of restaurant patrons. I was having trouble piecing together the information she was giving me in a way that made sense. "Your grandmother was murdered in Canada?" She nodded. "And the case has been shelved since the seventies?" More nodding. "So why do you want me to look into it, now? Wouldn't it be easier to sit down with your family and speak to them about it?"

The girl's eyes filled with tears. "Mama can't speak of it. It hurts her so much. And there's no one else I can really speak to about it. Uncle was there too, but he—he can't be relied upon."

"In what way can't he be relied upon?"

"His recollection of those times is not good. And poor Mama is not capable of doing it. Please help me? You are a professional in criminology. You teach where my grandmother was killed. When you return to Canada you will be on the spot where it happened. Maybe you can talk to the local police and ask them to help too? I think today cold cases are sometimes worked upon, this is correct?"

I nodded. I knew they were, though I had no insights into exactly why certain cases were selected for renewed attention versus others. "I can understand this must mean a great deal to you, but I'm really not sure what I can do to help. I have no special connections that would allow me to gain access to a cold case file." As I said the words I knew I wasn't being exactly truthful; there were certainly some steps I could take, like asking my ex-cop husband to pull a few strings, but I wasn't sure I wanted to get involved.

Zsófia leaned even closer to my ear. "When a member of your family dies, and you don't know why, it is difficult to bear. Maybe you cannot understand this, but to me, it is always on my mind. Now more than ever—because you are here, and you come from there, where it happened."

As the girl's tears flowed I felt the tightening in my tummy I always get when I think of my mother and father being killed in an utterly senseless car wreck. *It was just an accident* are the words that haunt me. Something that happened without reason, without intention. A chance occurrence that robbed me of my parents. How much worse it must be to know that an intended act, a murder, has robbed you of a family member, and to not be able to understand the reason for it.

Wiping away her tears, and her sophisticated makeup, Zsófia appeared before me as a young girl looking for answers. I know in my heart what it feels like to never be able to get any, and my sympathy for her welled up with my own recollections of a funeral held at a church in Wales where neither I nor my sister had been able to sing a single word of our parents' favorite hymns because of our uncontrollable sobbing.

Pushing a tissue up her sleeve, Zsófia whispered, "Please, will you just look at the file that's on there? I've studied everything you've ever written and I admire your work a great deal. You have an amazing brain—you're so clever. There isn't much to read through. All I've managed to gather together is a few newspaper clippings from the times. Because you know the area where it happened, you might have a different perspective on the case. I would value your opinion a great deal." Her eyes begged me with more emotion than any words could have mustered.

Of course I was flattered—who wouldn't be?—and it seemed she wasn't asking me to do very much, just read a little information and give an opinion. Given that I'd been sent by my university to Hungary in a sort of interuniversity ambassadorial role I reckoned I couldn't really refuse. I relented. "Very well. I'll try to read it before tomorrow's lecture. How about you come to my office immediately afterward, and we'll talk then. Okay?"

Zsófia stood, her eyes still hunting our surroundings, and answered sharply, "No, not your office. It won't be private. They're everywhere. Let's go for coffee. I know a place that's good and loud. My treat. Thanks so much, Professor Morgan. Goodnight."

As she left I called after her, "You know I have my own office? I don't share with anyone."

"Still not private." She darted away.

As Zsófia Takács collected her great-aunt Klara, I remained seated at my empty table wondering what I'd let myself in for. I rationalized that once I'd read the file on the thumb drive, I'd be clearer about what the girl was talking about, and would be able to decline her request to help from a position of knowledge, not just give a knee-jerk reaction. I supposed I owed her at least the politeness of that much attention.

While making my way to retrieve my coat from the cloakroom, I returned Zsófia's parting wave as she and Klara left the restaurant. As I did so, I noticed a man about twenty yards away from them swivel his head in my direction. He stared at me for several seconds, then returned his attention to the exit, immediately rushing toward it as though on a mission to catch up with someone who'd left. Maybe he knew Zsófia and was curious to see who she'd been waving at? Or might he be following her? I shook my head and pulled on my coat. *Too much rich food, talk of being listened to, and haunting zither music for you, Cait Morgan,* I told myself.

A Word in My Ear

I KNOW MYSELF PRETTY WELL, so as I made my way toward the exit I spotted the danger signs: a murder that had taken place decades ago in Canada sounded a good deal more interesting than poring over data for a research paper for the umpteenth time. The next thing that occurred to me was that I didn't want to spend forty-five minutes on public transportation getting back to my apartment to be able to discover what was on the thumb drive. I decided to splash out on yet another a taxi, which the maître d' graciously arranged for me.

When I walked out through the grand portal of the New York Café onto the slick streets, I knew I'd made the right choice; my students kept telling me it was unusually mild and wet for the time of year in Budapest, but I guessed the temperature had plummeted to close to freezing while we'd all been dining. I knew my trusty mac with a hood wouldn't have kept me snug on my tram and bus journey over the river and up the hill to my digs, so I relished the speed and ease with which I made the trip in the cab.

Bud and I had agreed I would text him when I arrived home from the evening's event, then we'd connect on Skype when we could. I checked my watch as I climbed the marble staircase to my temporary apartment. The nine-hour time difference meant it was just gone noon in BC, so probably Bud would be doing something with, or for, his mum. I decided to text him after I'd had a quick look at the files on the thumb drive, so I popped the kettle on, got into my comfy wrap, and opened up my laptop.

It seemed as though it was just a few minutes later that my cellphone buzzed, startling me. It was a text from Bud, asking if I was okay.

I checked my watch. Where had all the time gone? I texted back asking if I should I call him . . . but the next thing I knew, the familiar little beeps of Skype were ringing from my keyboard. I clicked, and there he was.

"Where have you been?" he snapped. "I've been worried to death. You said you'd be home by ten your time. It's after eleven. What happened? Why didn't you text me to say you'd be later than you thought?"

Bud's face told me he was truly upset. I thought it best to tell the truth-*ish*. "Sorry. I got caught up talking to a student who was there, and didn't realize you'd be so worried." I adopted my "sweet puppy" face and threw myself at his mercy. Apparently my husband wasn't feeling particularly merciful.

"Look, it's bad enough you're all the way over there without me. I know the sorts of situations you can get yourself into—and don't make that face; you know exactly what I'm talking about. I was at my wits' end. You know I can't let Mom and Dad see me worried; they feel guilty enough I've stayed here to be with them as it is. Mom keeps bringing it up all the time—how if she'd only been more careful on the back step and hadn't fallen she wouldn't have needed the surgery and you and I could be together now. It's beginning to get to me, Cait. You should have texted me. It's not much to ask."

I felt guilty and could sense myself flushing. "I'm really, truly sorry. I didn't mean to make you worry. How's your mum doing, anyway? Making good progress?"

"If you can call criticizing absolutely everything I try to do for her 'progress' then yes, she's coming along just fine." *Ah.* "She should know I'm doing my best, shouldn't she? Dad too. But neither of us seems to be able to even *breathe* the right way at the moment."

"She's probably frustrated." I used my most soothing voice.

"*She's* frustrated?" Bud cursed quietly. "She has no idea what Dad and I are going through."

I watched as Bud all but pulled out his hair by raking his hands through it. I could tell he was more than a little stressed. Then he shook himself, just like Marty does when he's been in the pond, and said, "I'm sorry, Cait. I shouldn't dump on you. She's getting on, she's had major surgery, Dad's feeling useless, and I am too. We're all in the same boat, and we each think the other two are trying to sink it. Don't worry, I'll pull myself together, and we'll get through this. If it's not frustration, it's boredom. It's all 'hurry up and wait' here. I miss you, and I miss Marty, and I miss our home—I'm sure my old room was bigger when I used to live here before—and, let's be honest, I just miss the ability to have some control over my own life." He sighed so heavily I thought he would run out of air. "But enough about me—what have you been up to, and why was there a student at this thing? I thought you were out at some swank place with the equivalent of your own dean back here. That's what you said, right? That *was* tonight?"

We both leaned back in our chairs, thousands of miles apart, and started our conversation afresh. I wanted to hug my husband, but I couldn't, so I did the next best thing—I decided to tell him a tale of an unsolved murder and ask for his help.

Bud listened silently as I talked for some time, then he leaned forward and interrupted, "I knew it. I knew you'd get yourself mixed up in something questionable."

"I'm not 'mixed up' in anything, Bud. All I've done is read some files and begin to tell you about them. I've told the girl I can't help her, but . . . well . . . you know . . ."

Bud leaned back and beamed, a sight that warmed my heart. "Can't resist, can you?"

I shook my head.

"And this is the girl we've spoken about before—the bright spark with the ample hips and engagingly vulnerable edge? The one who's just like you?"

"She's not like me, Bud. Well, not much. But you're right, that's the one."

"And why's she asking you to take on her case?"

I felt my right eyebrow arch toward my hairline as I replied, "Oh, let me think for a minute. Other than that the murder took place on the campus in Canada where I work, and she sees me as an academic authority figure with a pretty well-known, and some might even say highly regarded, specialism in victim profiling, I cannot imagine."

Bud chuckled, then puffed out his cheeks and replied, "So let me get this straight, my ever-so-well-thought-of wife: in 1976 the grandfather of this student of yours was a professor at the University of Vancouver, right?"

"Yes, he arrived there in 1957, when my university invited the thirteen faculty members and almost one hundred students from the psychology faculty of the Hungarian University of Budapest to join them in Canada."

"And why did it do that? The University of Vancouver, I mean."

"As I'm sure you know, the Hungarians had been living through extremely difficult times here in Budapest. After the Germans left their city at the end of the Second World War, the Russians rolled in. In 1956 there was the hope of the Hungarian Uprising, but it seems Professor Kristóf Seszták saw the writing on the wall. He managed to get some of his faculty and students to a 'study retreat' in the forests of Sopron, about a hundred miles away from Budapest. Once word reached them about the Russians throwing everything they had at quelling the uprising, the group fled across the border to Austria on foot, with almost nothing except their lives and their freedom. Canada, in the shape of UVan, reached out and welcomed the whole lot of them in—they got visas, arrived in 1957, and stayed. UVan's administrators allowed all of the students to complete their studies in Hungarian, trusting the faculty that had arrived from Hungary enough to back the final grades given with the university's own academic weight. Seszták remained as a professor, later a professor emeritus, at UVan until 1992, when he returned to Hungary."

"And his wife, Zsófia's grandmother, was killed on the University of Vancouver's campus in 1976, right?"

"Yes. According to the newspaper reports Zsófia sourced, Mrs. Ilona Seszták was found with her head smashed in on one of the bike paths, but there were no strong leads in the case."

"And that's all you know?"

"Well, no, I know more. But not much. From the clippings, I know the Sesztáks had two children, a daughter and a son. The daughter is Alexa, and the fact that Zsófia's surname is Takács suggests to me she's the daughter's child. The son is Valentin. The newspapers say the Burnaby detachment of the RCMP handled the case. No one saw the murdered woman after five in the evening the day before her body was found. A student found her remains as he cycled to swimming practice around seven thirty the next morning, so she was killed sometime between those hours. Also, the day she disappeared was the day that year's graduation ceremonies were held. I can tell you, therefore, that on the day of her death the campus would have been flooded with visiting parents and families. Maybe the upheaval of convocation in 1976 wouldn't have been as significant as it is these days, but it would have been busy enough for strangers to not have been remarked upon. They found no weapon; she had no known enemies and was involved in no known disputes. That's about it. I'm guessing it's still an open case."

"You're guessing?" Bud's eyes narrowed.

"Well, I wondered if that might be something you could clarify? Maybe you could make a phone call or two?" I leaned into the camera and beamed my goofiest smile.

"What a wife you are," said Bud, shaking his head. "You just use me, don't you? That's all I'm good for. Really? You want me to, what, just check on the case and, who knows, maybe even find out who worked on it, and where the files might be?"

"Well, you did say you were bored," I dared. Bud glared at me. "Besides, I don't need you to find out who worked the case. I already know Jack White did, among others. His name was mentioned in the notes I read. You'll be proud to know he refused to comment when quizzed by a reporter, but he was clearly on the scene. He was pretty junior at the time, but I'm sure he'd remember it. Jack's our friend, the man who mentored you, and he's currently boarding Marty while you're at your mum and dad's place. So probably one phone call would do it. You know Jack would do anything for you. Maybe you could run out to his place in Hatzic to check on Marty for an hour or so tomorrow, and have a coffee with him to talk it over?"

"You've really thought it all through, haven't you? Before I commit myself, given that I am supposed to be delivering constant care and devotion to my ailing mother at this end of things," he winked at me, "I have a question of my own. Your university is in Burnaby, so I understand why the Burnaby RCMP investigated the homicide, rather than it falling to the Vancouver Police Department. But why is it called the University of Vancouver if it's in Burnaby? Don't laugh—I know I've lived here my whole life but it's never occurred to me before. So?"

Just like the little girl who sits at the front of the classroom—which I'd always been—I allowed my hand to shoot up. "Please, sir. I know that one, sir."

Bud's face creased into a broad grin. "Coles Notes version, okay?"

"In 1935, when the University of Vancouver first opened its doors, it was housed in a building in downtown Vancouver that has long since been demolished to make way for one of those glittering high-rises. The executives quickly realized they would need to expand, but couldn't do it where they were. The City of Burnaby offered them a great deal on some land, so they took it. The beginnings of the campus where I work opened in 1946, and, as you know, they've been building there pretty much constantly ever since, with a big bump in activity in the past ten years. Because of various political sensitivities, the name University of Vancouver was retained, even though the buildings are in Burnaby. The weird postscript to my tale is that, in 2010, we opened a satellite campus in downtown Vancouver, so the part-time MBA students could make it to evening classes more easily. The circle has been completed."

Bud smiled gratefully. "One mystery solved, at least. Thanks."

"You're welcome. So, will you do it? We both know you could."

Bud shook his head in mock disbelief. "Got it all worked out, haven't you?"

I smiled sweetly. "I try. And you do seem terribly bored."

Bud leaned toward the camera. "Okay, I give up. You've got me. I've noted all the names and dates, and, yes, I'll grab the excuse to get out of here for a few hours to see Marty—but it might not be tomorrow. And don't hold your breath, there might be nothing Jack can do to help; he has been retired for a good deal longer than me. But tell me one thing—why are you so keen to help *this* girl?"

I could feel my brow furrowing as I gave his question the consideration it deserved. "Other than hating to see justice go unserved, I'll admit I'm intrigued. The reason she was there tonight was because she was singing—performing with a small ensemble. She was excellent. Could be the next Adele, she has that sort of voice. To be honest, it reminded me a bit of my mum's voice when she used to sing me to sleep—soft and round." I knew the sadness I felt for the loss of my mother must have been showing on my face, because it sat so heavily in my heart. "And that's the other thing—Mum and Dad . . . I know their deaths were accidental, and I struggle to come to terms with that every day. This girl? There might be some chance we can help her get answers. Something she can grasp onto when she's grappling with her grandmother not being a part of her life. Even before tonight, you know I'd warmed to Zsófia in class. She's bright, lively, and embraces a unique personal style in a beguiling way. She's bursting with promise and seems both talented and driven. I like her." I decided to not mention my hint of a suspicion she might have had someone following her that evening—in any case, upon further reflection, I'd all but discounted the sense of unease I'd felt when I'd seen the man sprint out of the restaurant after her.

"You realize you hardly ever say you *like* a person, right?"

"I do."

"Okay then, I'll find out what I can. So, are you off to bed now?"

I stretched my arms above my head. "Better had. Got an early start."

"Night, night then. Love you lots."

"Love you more."

"Love you most. Until tomorrow."

I let him win, blew a kiss, switched everything off, and then flopped into bed.

All Talk

AS I DELIVERED MY LECTURE the next morning, and the class worked through interactive exercises, I felt a strange tension whenever I looked at Zsófia—not healthy or normal for a professor and student. Her request to look into her grandmother's death, and my simple act of reading the files she'd prepared, had shifted the axis of our relationship. I knew I'd have to handle the matter with care.

My students scattered at the close of our session, but Zsófia and her "puppy"—a boy named Laszlo who followed her everywhere—hung back. Zsófia approached me, while wriggling her arms into her coat sleeves, and hissed beside my ear, "I must go home. My uncle is not well today. I must help my mother. Can we meet on Monday instead? Unless you would like to meet me at the Gellért Spa at 11:00 AM on Sunday. I teach water aerobics there until then."

I hesitated. "Maybe Monday would be better," I replied quietly. I didn't want to sacrifice the little free time I had.

Glancing toward the hovering Laszlo, Zsófia asked, "Did you read the files I gave you?" I told her I had. Her face softened. "Thank you so much, Professor. Don't say anything, to anyone. Promise?"

"I promise."

As she left with her admirer in tow, I spotted her trying to swat him away with her tote bag, but he continued to shuffle behind her as she all but ran out the door. I wondered briefly what might be wrong with her uncle, but realized I had work to get on with, and moved to gather up my papers.

"Ah, Professor Morgan, I'm glad I caught you."

At the sound of the reedy voice my head popped up. It was Patrik Matyas. He'd tracked me down. *Rats!*

"Hello, Professor Matyas. I'm afraid you've caught me at a busy moment. I must get back to my office to sort out some grading."

"But surely you'll have to eat something for lunch?" He walked across the room toward me, grinning. His long neck and protruding teeth made me think of a llama, and I don't care much for llamas; they kick and spit, even when they look like they're smiling.

I checked my watch. "It's a bit early for lunch, don't you think."

Matyas checked his own timepiece. "But no. The best time to eat lunch is before it is busy. I know an excellent place for a delicious, warming, and inexpensive meal. Allow me to show you. Be my guest."

He was beside me—so close I could tell he lacked any sense of personal space and had possibly used half a bottle of sharply scented cologne five minutes earlier.

"I see Zsófia Takács is in your group. She's an interesting girl. Dangerous, too," he whispered.

I bit. "Dangerous? What do you mean?"

"I could tell you over lunch," he said conspiratorially.

I gave in, grabbed my coat and bags, and allowed him to steer me out of the HUB toward what he promised would be a gastronomic delight. *It had better be*, I thought.

The streets were awash with rain. In the little park beside the HUB bare trees stood stark against the gray skies, and everyone seemed to be dressed in various hues of sludge. I felt as though I'd stepped into a black and white movie as we hurried along the narrow streets of Budapest toward what turned out to be a butcher shop.

"They serve food?" I was surprised.

"Oh yes," replied Patrik, his rosebud-mouthed smirk and fluttering hands exuding excitement, "the best blood sausage in town, and pickles to die for."

21

I suspected a lunch of blood sausage and pickles might, indeed, kill me, but I allowed him to open the door for me, and I was transported into an unexpected world where the welcoming smell of roasting meat and paprika was overwhelming. My saliva glands kicked in before I'd even reached the display cabinets at the rear of the shop. Patrik wriggled, giggling, into the tiny space beside me at the counter and explained the various cuts on offer, then suggested I try his favorites, which I agreed was a good idea, hoping it was.

It was clear many of the dishes on offer had taken hours to prepare, but the service was fast; within five minutes we were seated, and I was enjoying my first mouthful of Hungarian blood sausage.

"How is it?" asked Patrik too eagerly.

"It's different," I began, playing him along a little.

"How?" The glint in his eye gave him away.

"I'm used to blood pudding being made just from blood and a few spices, but this has meat in it, and cereal of some sort, as well as the blood. It's good. The paprika isn't overwhelming. Thanks for suggesting it." He looked disappointed; I suspected he'd been hoping for a display of disgust, and I wondered how many other visiting professors before me he'd urged to eat at the butcher shop. His idea of sport? It struck me he might be the type to enjoy such a game.

The tables in the shop were close together, and I quickly became convinced most Hungarians were incapable of speaking quietly. I couldn't help but overhear several loud conversations at once, all seemingly good-humored and covering a range of topics befitting an eatery within easy walking distance of two universities, and not far from several government buildings.

Upon my arrival at the HUB, Patrik had shown me around the building where my lectures would be held, then helped me navigate the necessary journey to find the photocopiers and office supplies, and obtain my security clearances. He'd done it all with a prissy smile

I found unsettling. He hadn't been assigned to me, as such, but he'd made it clear he should be my first point of contact as he was the informal liaison between the dean's office and visiting lecturers.

He'd immediately struck me as the gossipy type; not something I care for. Over our lunch he merrily chattered on, asking how I was settling in, if I was enjoying the city, and if I wanted any guidance about what to see and where to go. I did my best to make noncommittal replies; all I really wanted to do was get through the month until Bud could join me, and get my research paper finished. As soon as I mentioned the dinner at the New York Café the night before, he did a creditable impersonation of a clam, and I suspected he was hurt he hadn't been invited.

I decided it was high time I grasped the subject he'd raised back in the lecture room, so I asked, "Why did you say Zsófia Takács is dangerous? What did you mean?" I wanted to add that it was quite an inappropriate thing to say about a student, but managed to stop myself.

Patrik elaborately scanned the place before replying, "I think she's just managed to get a good junior professor kicked out."

"How on earth did she do that?" I kept my voice low, because I reckoned whatever was about to be said wasn't something that should be overheard.

"Someone accused him of suggesting a better grade was available if certain . . . favors were granted. You know what I mean?" His little black eyes glittered with scandal behind his heavily framed rectangular spectacles.

"I assume you mean of a sexual nature?"

He nodded excitedly, with his mouth pursed prudishly.

"And Zsófia Takács made that allegation? And he's been fired because of it?"

Patrik shrugged slightly. "No one has confirmed the name of the female student, but I believe it was her. Many people do."

I weighed what he'd said. Did Zsófia strike me as the sort of girl who'd report wrongdoings to the proper authorities? Yes, she did. And she'd be right to do so. But had she? Who could tell?

"It's unfortunate the professor in question acted inappropriately," was my measured response.

Patrik looked shocked. "His career could be ruined. He has a good brain."

"Then he should have used it to think before he acted," I replied, hoping my voice didn't sound as angry as I felt. "Did he fight the allegations? Say the claims were false?"

Again Patrik shrugged. "I think not. Maybe he didn't want to make a fuss."

"Maybe he knew he didn't have a leg to stand on."

"Excuse me?" Patrik seemed confused.

"Sorry, too idiomatic. Maybe he knew the allegations were true," I whispered.

Patrik looked as though I'd lobbed an insult directly at him. He took a moment to finish his coffee. "She's overconfident, that one," he added vehemently, not wanting me to have the last word. "Back in the day she'd have been investigated."

I couldn't help but smile. "'Back in the day?' What a very Canadian expression, Patrik. Have you been researching Canadian sayings you could pop into your conversation to help me feel more at home?" I hoped he'd understand I was joking. He didn't.

Looking shocked he replied, "Don't you know I studied at the university where you work in Canada? I did my postgraduate work at UVan."

I shouldn't have been as surprised as I was; the links between the universities in Vancouver and Budapest are close and have extended for over half a century. "No, Patrik, I didn't know. Under whom did you work?"

"Professor Hollingsworth," he replied, puffing out his chest a little. To be fair, if he'd done his postgrad work under Hollingsworth he had cause to be proud; the man was world-renowned for his breakthrough theories concerning the psychology of group dynamics. In his field he was on a par with Kurt Lewin at MIT. Maybe Patrik had depths I hadn't suspected.

"So you did your master's with him? In group dynamics, or something related?"

Patrik glanced around, vibrating with enthusiasm. "I was there when he was working on his paper. You know, *the* paper—the one that got MIT worried. It was thrilling. Indeed, at the end of the paper he thanked me personally for my contributions to his experimental work. Have you ever been involved with that sort of project? Something that changes all the texts thereafter."

I sighed. My head of department's words—"publish or perish"—rang in my ears. Reminded of my academic responsibilities, I realized I had a long afternoon of work ahead of me. "I really should be going, Patrik. It's been kind of you to bring me here, but I have a good deal of work to do back at the flat."

"Your flat? This is an interesting term, and it relates to your own past, I believe. You are not originally Canadian; you are from Wales. I am correct?"

"My accent is Welsh, and that's where I was born and raised—so I will always be Welsh, and now that I'm a Canadian citizen I'm becoming Canadian. It is the way life goes for those who migrate from one country and culture to another. We never lose our 'old' cultural roots, and no matter how hard we try, the new ones we put down will never have a chance to bury themselves as deep. So, my new growth will be in Canada, but my life-roots will always be in Wales. I believe I share my Celtic background with parts of Hungary."

"Indeed, there is a great deal of activity on the island of Csepel in the Danube because of the discovery of Celtic coins and burials from the time before the Romans crossed our watery border and arrived in this area."

"I understand the Celts were here in prehistory, in the area of the Gellért Hill?"

"This is also true, I believe. You think you Welsh are the true Hungarians?" There was a slight twinkle in his eye.

I smiled. "Not at all, but I never cease to be amazed at the reach and influence of the Celts during prehistoric times. I suppose it allows me to feel connected to a great depth of history in many parts of the world."

"I am still surprised you would prefer to leave the HUB to work at the flat, or apartment. Wouldn't you be happier working at the university? The HUB has such good facilities."

I pictured my ten-by-ten, blank-walled office at the HUB, and my apartment with a large window overlooking the Danube. "The flat's comfier, and I like to wander about while I think," I replied honestly.

"And you can smoke at your apartment too," replied Patrik with a knowing smirk.

I was puzzled. "What makes you think I smoke?" I'd stopped sixteen and a half months earlier.

Patrik leaned in. "You look the type."

"I gave it up."

Patrik shrugged. "Ah. What a pity. The apartment you have is a smoker. A lot of them still are, especially the older ones. I have been there, you know. The HUB keeps it for visiting professors, and some previous tenants have had parties there—inviting colleagues around for a few drinks at the weekend. We've had some good times in it."

I felt irritated. Knowing I could get away with smoking in my temporary home immediately gave me some terribly naughty thoughts about puffing away for a few weeks. Bud would never be any the wiser,

I told myself. I was angry at my own weakness, which this prissy little man was all but throwing in my face. I stood up and gathered my multipurpose hooded raincoat about me. "Thanks for bringing me to such a super lunch place," I squeaked out.

"You're welcome."

"I owe you one," was my flippant departing remark.

"I'll take you up on that," was all I heard as I headed out into the rain, cross with myself, seething at Patrik, and suddenly desperate for a cigarette.

A Personal Conversation

I PUT IN A GOOD day at my desk on Saturday. My head was full of facts and figures connected with the research I was working through; I love the thrill of the chase when you're pulling together the myriad pieces of a puzzle to prove a hypothesis. When it was almost 7:00 PM, which was when Bud and I had agreed to Skype, I guiltily cleared away the ashtray sitting beside my computer, and stuffed the offending pack of Sopiane cigarettes into my pocket. I rationalized it was all Patrik's fault I'd caved into my addiction. I'd bought a couple of packs of the local brand on my way back to the apartment the day before—they weren't too awful, and I'd enjoyed the huge rush the first one had given me when I'd smoked it. Addiction's a dreadful thing.

When I saw Bud's face on my laptop screen it was almost too much to bear—the next weeks were going to feel terribly long. After bringing me up to speed on his mother's progress, Bud changed the topic, eager to tell me what else he'd been up to.

"I visited Marty yesterday after all. He sends licks, woofs, and wags," he began, his face creased with a broad smile. "He loves it out there with his dog buddies. And Sheila says hi, as does Jack. I managed to get an hour or so with just Jack, and we wandered the property with the dogs, in the rain. It was good to be out and about, having been cooped up here for so long. Interesting, too. Turns out he remembers a fair bit about the Seszták case. Even so, we're not much further forward."

I was delighted I'd been right to think Zsófia's query would be a useful distraction for Bud, and returned his excited smile. I sat back in my chair. "Explain, Husband."

Bud leaned forward. "Jack was young, still in his twenties, and just a junior officer at the time. He moved from Burnaby RCMP to the Vancouver Police Department not long after it happened, so he left the case behind, but he never forgot it."

"You cops never do, do you? Forget the unsolved ones. It's the lack of resolution—the injustice of it all. I bet there are a few cases haunting you still, but we'd better not get into that. Tell me what Jack remembered."

Bud relaxed into his seat and said, "Odd thing, for Jack—he mainly remembered the kids, he said. He and Sheila never had any of their own, as you know. Yeah, he's a happy uncle and so forth, but not the most kid-oriented guy I know. In this case, however? Different kettle of fish. Like you said, the dead woman was the mother of a boy and a girl. Not that they were really *kids*. The girl was about twelve or thirteen and took it in her stride—a real resilient type, he said—but the boy, who was nineteen and studying at the university, didn't talk. At all. To anyone. About anything. Clammed up completely for weeks before he would say a word. Initially, some of the higher-ups thought it was because he was hiding something, but it turned out he was a pretty frail type, and he ended up suffering a complete breakdown. He got some treatment, and they finally interviewed him a couple of months after the event. Jack reckoned the shock of losing his mother affected him deeply. The husband . . ."

Bud looked away from the camera and I could tell he was consulting his notes—some habits never die.

"Yes, Husband?" I couldn't resist.

Bud tutted at me. "Jack said he was devastated. They checked him out, of course—always check out the partner or spouse first—but it seems he was clean. Hadn't reported his wife missing because he didn't know she was; she wasn't expected home that night. He was at home all night in charge of the daughter, while the wife was due to stay with a female friend who lived farther down on Burnaby Mountain. She did that sort of thing quite frequently, it seems. They'd get together for an evening and she'd stay over rather than disturb the family by coming home late. Oddly enough, the friend in question lived just a couple of blocks away from where you used to live. Anyway, the friend claimed she wasn't certain Ilona was definitely coming over to stay with her because they had an informal standing arrangement, so she didn't worry when Ilona didn't show. The son? He was old enough to look after himself, though the father confirmed he never left the house that evening or night either. A couple of people saw Ilona near her house, which itself was on campus, around five, then her body was found the next morning. No sexual interference, no apparent theft of valuables from the remains. Purse was found some distance from the body, but the contents were all accounted for."

I gave it all some thought. "Cause of death? Did Jack know any more than was in the newspapers?"

"Nope. Plain old bashed on the head. Bit of a mess, apparently, but face still identifiable. No attempt made to disfigure her after death, or anything of that sort."

"Any idea about the murder weapon?"

Bud perked up. "Now that he did know about, and it's not something they gave to the reporters. Jack recalls the forensic guys were pretty sure she was hit by a rock. Is it rocky on the bike path area? Do you know it, Cait?"

I snorted. "It's a bike path, what do you think? You know very well I can't even ride a bicycle, so, no, I'm not overly familiar with any of the cycling trails at UVan. That said, I know where this one is—and where it runs from and to—because it's signposted on the campus roads. I'd say it's a trail that would be used by energetic riders heading up to the university; it's a shorter route than the road, but much more steep. The other thing I happen to know is that it was officially opened in 1975—there's a plaque that says so on the roadside. These days it's densely wooded on both sides of the path, or at least along the part you can see from the road as you drive past it, so maybe logs or branches would be easier weapons of opportunity rather than a rock. But back then? If it had just been opened, freshly dug into the mountainside, or however they prepared it, then maybe it would have been rockier. Why did they reckon it was that type of object?"

"Irregular shape of the wound, dirt in the wound, but no plant matter or wood residue. One hit only—a seriously heavy whack on the side of her head. The theory at the time was that she might not have seen it coming; they weren't able to determine whether or not she was facing her attacker when she was struck. Apparently a lot would have depended on whether the attacker was right- or left-handed, but they couldn't be sure of which. No real directionality of the blow either. Couldn't say if the assailant was shorter or taller than her."

"And they never found a rock or stone with blood on it?"

"Nope. Maybe that's because of something else Jack mentioned— the rain. Seems it was horrific at that time. Forensic guys couldn't say if blood had been in certain spots and had simply washed away, because the path was almost a river in places."

It made sense; the rain across the whole of the Lower Mainland in BC just doesn't know when to stop sometimes. "Time of death?"

Bud consulted his notes. "Jack couldn't remember exactly, but he seems to think it was the night she disappeared, not the morning she was found."

"It was October, during term time, and on the day of convocation, so you would think if her corpse had been on the bike path all night, someone would have seen it before it was found. I wonder when lectures started back then. We kick off at 8:30 AM nowadays, so cyclists would be on the path hours earlier. Had the body been moved?"

"Yes. It was found just off to one side of the path, rather than lying across it, and Jack said he remembered they were told the body *had* been moved after death. He's pretty certain lividity, and the time of death, suggested that fact, though after all these years he's a bit vague, to be honest."

"And he couldn't recall any firm suspects being in the frame?"

"Every lead they had, they followed to a dead end, he said. It's not much, is it?"

I supported my chin with my hands as I leaned forward. "It's more than nothing, but not a lot. Was Jack involved with interviewing possible suspects?"

Bud cracked a smile. "Too junior. He was tasked with questioning potential witnesses—for days, apparently. Got nothing. In terms of background on the victim, he recalls how everyone said she was great fun, a good wife and mom. She helped and supported her husband, and was a perfect prof's wife. No one had a bad word to say about her."

I sighed. "That takes some doing."

"What does?"

"Living the university life and no one saying nasty things about you."

My face must have given me away because Bud leapt to my defense. "Hey, you're good at what you do. It's not your fault your department head expects you to play at politics."

"It's not that—it's . . . oh never mind. Let's focus on this. Any view as to how we might progress?"

Bud didn't say anything for a moment, as he noisily rustled through the pages of his notebook. "Jack thinks all the files would likely still be with the Burnaby RCMP at their new HQ. He's going to make a few calls. Said he'd let me know how he gets on as soon as he can."

"That's good of him. Say thanks from me?"

"Dare I ask if there's any more news from UVan about your job?"

I rolled my eyes as I replied, "Two emails, both of which mentioned my married status. I don't know why. Gerry Brightwell got married last year, and I bet they aren't citing that as a factor in his suitability for a continuing role there."

Bud sighed heavily. "If they're going to make life difficult for you because you and I are married now, I feel responsible for that. What is it they said, exactly?"

I felt bad for him. "I'm sorry—I didn't mean to make it sound as though any of this is your fault. You know what? Until someone says something concrete, or does something specific I can react to, I'll keep telling myself they can imply all they want—I'll do the best I can with this paper and show them all just how good I can be. I think it's almost done. I had a bit of a brainwave last night, and it seems to be working through all right."

"That's the attitude, Cait. Stick it to them. Tell me about this brainwave? Was it tsunami-sized?"

"Not exactly, but I don't want to talk about that—I'm cogitating on it so I need to think about something else for now. I'd rather talk to you about the Seszták case. Jack will get back to you, you said, and you might be able to track down the files, good. Anything else?"

"Good grief, you're like Marty with a chew toy. Okay then, one interesting thing is that Jack wondered how it all would have affected the kids. Like I said, it surprised me he was so focused on them in his recollections of the case, but it's certainly what he remembers most vividly. The son's breakdown was pretty extreme, but he mentioned the daughter's response was significantly different, and much more like that of her father. He said he only met the father—the dead woman's husband—once, and he seemed like a pleasant enough guy, but a bit fatalistic about the whole thing. Neither he nor the daughter seemed broken by it; they were stoic in the face of the tragedy. Of course, higher ranks would have dealt with the main players on an ongoing basis, but Jack recalls not one of them thought the husband had done it—even if he had been able to sneak away from the kids that night."

"So both children were at home that evening, and asleep in bed that night? They all three agreed on that?" Bud nodded. "Anyone else in the home?"

Bud shook his head. "Jack recalled something about the family having a lodger at some point prior to the killing, but there was no one else either resident at the home or visiting overnight at the time."

"So the father could have left his son and daughter asleep and 'encountered' his wife on the bike path later in the night—maybe as she was, what, returning after some sort of assignation? Any thoughts she might have been having an affair? You know—a lovers' tryst gone wrong? Or something the husband found out about?"

Bud sat forward. "Jack said no, no one thought so at the time, though he said there were a few 'whispers' about her because of her lipstick."

I sat forward too, to be "closer" to my husband. "Her what?"

"I guess maybe back then people thought only a certain type of woman wore bright red lipstick. As I seem to recall—and you have to admit I was just a youngster in those days—the girls favored pastels in the mid-seventies. Mrs. Seszták was apparently well-known for only ever wearing red, which some took to mean she was a woman of a certain sort."

I narrowed my eyes in an attempt to look threatening. "What *exactly* were you up to back in 1976? You were nineteen, so what could you have possibly been doing that would mean you remember girls wearing pastel shades of lip color?"

Bud blushed. "Nothing, sadly. I was your typical pimply youth, and, at nineteen, I had my nose in a book rather than anywhere else; studying for my RCMP entry exams was my sole consideration."

"When I get home I'll let your mum pull out all those old photo albums she's always threatening me with, and I can see just how spotty you really were. But, for now, let's make the most of you having passed those exams. I have to say I don't see how wearing red lipstick—now or then—is a sign of being any particular 'type' of woman, though I suspect it signifies a certain level of self-assurance, or maybe an effort at false bravado. Funnily enough, it's one of the dead woman's granddaughter's trademarks too—red lipstick, dyed red hair to match. However, let's put those rumors about Ilona Seszták to one side for now, unless there's something to substantiate them. Tell, me, did Jack have anything else to add?"

Thousands of miles away, Bud looked resigned as he shrugged and shook his head.

I let my frustration show. "It's all so long ago and, from here, so far away. Without access to the files I can't see how we can progress, unless I can get together with the family at this end."

"Cait, stop it. You promised you wouldn't get involved. You threw me this 'case' as something I could look into to try to stop my brain from falling out of my head with boredom. There's no need for you to do anything."

I smiled sweetly. "I wouldn't be 'getting involved.' Maybe Zsófia could invite me to visit the family home for coffee, or something. I think it would be interesting to meet her mother—even if she doesn't want to discuss the matter at hand, I'd welcome the chance to make an assessment of her. I'll mention it to Zsófia when I see her next."

Bud raked his hand through his hair. "There's nothing I can say to stop you, I know. So just be careful, Cait."

"'Careful' is my middle name," I mugged.

"No it's not, and it never will be. Your middle name's much more likely to be 'catastrophe.'"

When Walls Speak

FOR SOME UNFATHOMABLE REASON I felt wide awake the moment my eyes opened on Sunday morning, which is a rarity for me. Pushing open the windows in my sitting room, I let out the stale air I'd created with my guiltily smoked cigarettes the night before, and allowed the chill of the November morning to further invigorate me. It was the second day of a new month, one when the temperature in Budapest was apparently due to take a turn toward the lower parts of the thermometer. The rain had stopped, and the sky finally had a hint of the palest blue about it—a pleasant relief from the constant gray of the past couple of weeks. The ancient city lay stretched out below me, the Danube a wide, glittering ribbon weaving through the urban landscape.

I enjoyed my coffee, but knew my head wasn't in the right place for me to be able to settle to work on my paper. I'm far from the world's most active person, but I suspected a bit of a walk might do me good. I remembered what Zsófia had said about her weekend job. I checked my watch: it wasn't even nine o'clock, so I had lots of time to get sorted, enjoy my coffee, and get down to the Hotel Gellért by 11:00 AM, which was when Zsófia had mentioned she'd be finishing her shift as a water-aerobics teacher at the spa pool there.

As I left my apartment, I opted for my old but much-loved winter coat with the mock-fur collar and was glad I had. The bus journey was chilly, then it was even colder when I got off; the wind whipping across the Danube was bitter. As I walked beside the river, I seemed to be the only person feeling the cold; the locals were bareheaded, wearing short coats, and smiling at the blue sky peeping between the clouds. I felt like a bit of a wimp.

Scuttling along, I headed for the imposing gray stone hotel, which takes up a whole city block beside the beautiful Liberty Bridge. Walking through the grand entrance I was greeted by a doorman who fulfilled his function without a smile. Inside, the warmth hit me immediately, and I released my grip on my collar. Marble columns soared two floors, supporting a balustraded balcony around the entire space. I spotted the rightly famed stained glass windows that backed the main staircase, and noticed the exquisite floors. I was surprised the tourists taking advantage of the lounge didn't appear better heeled. I got my bearings and tried to work out how to get to the spa part of the hotel, but ended up having to ask at the front desk. I was told, quite abruptly, that I'd have to make my way to the spa by going outside the hotel, because the internal corridor leading there was only for the use of guests.

To be fair, it didn't take me more than a few minutes to find the public entrance to the baths, and I asked the burly woman at the entry desk if I could see Zsófia Takács. A few minutes of conversation resulted in me being directed to a staff room opposite the desk; the woman kept an eye on me as I knocked. Needless to say, my student was surprised to see me when she opened the door. She eagerly offered to show me around the place before we headed out, and I knew it was too good a chance to miss. She tucked my coat into her locker, and I even relinquished my scarf.

As we walked, she whispered to me that she'd prefer not to talk about her grandmother while we were within earshot of members of the public. With Zsófia as my guide I enjoyed my tour of the fabulous spa and baths, created during the height of the Austro-Hungarian Empire's love affair with ornate details. Dazzling blue tiles set with glittering mosaics ran between imposing marble columns; jewel-toned stained-glass windows filtered away the outside world; flamboyantly sculpted spouts sent the thermal waters cascading into the dazzling pool. However, I was glad to move away from the humidity and echoing noise and retire to the little staff room. I thought there we'd finally have a chance to talk properly about her grandmother's tragic end, but Zsófia still seemed convinced we might be overheard. Thus, it wasn't until we were outside that I managed to tell her what Bud had been up to.

As we walked among the Sunday afternoon gaggles of tourists and locals, Zsófia pushed her arm through mine, so our heads were as close together as it's possible for two full-hipped women's heads to be. We stopped talking about the case when we took the metro across the city to the Opera, where we alighted and walked to Zsófia's house. When we arrived, she briefed me.

"Let me take the lead? I'll tell Mama who you are, but not why you're here. I don't want her to think I'm digging this up. Mama never wants to talk about it, which I understand—even though it doesn't help me. She knows I have a visiting professor from Canada, so let's use that as the reason I have invited you. You might not get to meet Uncle Valentin. We'll see how he's doing."

As she spoke, I took in the exterior of the place we were about to enter. I reckoned her family had an apartment in the building, which was massive. As soon as she unlocked the front door I knew I was wrong—this was not an apartment building, it was a home. Someone in Zsófia Takács's family had money—and lots of it.

I made sure I shut my gaping mouth as I took in my surroundings. Marble floors, a curved staircase with gold-leafed ironwork, and a magnificent atrium greeted me—as did a small King Charles spaniel skidding on the tiles as it ran toward us, yapping excitedly.

"*Higadj le*, Szemere! We have a guest." The girl bent to scoop up the dog, which smothered her with frantic licks. I suddenly missed Marty's "kisses" and couldn't help but pet the little creature. His round eyes surveyed me with near-disdain. Depositing him onto the ground,

Zsófia magically produced a tiny treat from her coat pocket. It seemed to be the sign he needed to start wriggling around her ankles as we tried to cross the cavernous entryway.

"SzeSze gets overexcited," explained Zsófia unnecessarily.

"I understand entirely." I told her about Marty as we moved toward a hall closet about half the size of the apartment in which I was staying. Finally rid of my outer layers, I gave in to my awe and said, "This is an impressive place."

Zsófia gestured to an opening that led to a spacious and tastefully appointed sitting room. "It's my uncle's house, and we live here with him. It was his choice. Mama and I are eternal guests. It's been my home for much of my life, and I used to love it when I was younger. But now? Sometimes I feel it is like a gilded cage."

I judged the expression on her face to be one of resignation rather than anger, though I found it hard to reconcile her talking about having once been young when she was still barely twenty.

"You're fortunate to have a family member who's able to own a house like this, and to have you live in it with him."

"I know, I'm *lucky*." She made the word sound like a dreadful curse. With a sigh, she continued, "I expect you're wondering how my uncle made his money." I was. She walked to a bookcase set into the wall and pulled out a fat volume, which she passed to me. It was a signed, first print run, first edition of *Warrior* by VS Örsi. As I read the spines on the bookshelves I noted each volume bore the same author's name, and the multilingual titles told me I was seeing dozens of editions of the same five works. A penny threatened to drop, but my theory didn't make sense.

"Your uncle collects, and trades in, first editions of the works of VS Örsi?"

Zsófia smiled. "No, my uncle *is* VS Örsi."

I was surprised. "Your uncle Valentin? Valentin Seszták?"

"VS is for Valentin Seszták, and Örsi was my grandmother's maiden name."

I digested the news. Zsófia's uncle was the world-renowned, though reputedly hermit-like, author of what, in the past few years, had become a global phenomenon—the Bloodline Saga, a collection of five novels that had outstripped the popularity of Tolkien's and JK Rowling's works combined.

"Do you know his books?" asked the proud niece.

I weighed my response. Telling her I'd avoided them like the plague didn't seem appropriate, but I was there to get to know her family, so I decided on a middle path. "I confess I haven't read them, though I know a little about them, and about the reputation of the author. But maybe you could tell me more?"

Zsófia joined me on the sofa and warmed to her topic. "After the first couple of books appeared—*Warrior* then *Offspring*—a teenager in Idaho developed an online game based on their characters and storylines. Did you hear about how he sold his game to an international company for millions of dollars?" I told her I had. "The books, originally produced in small print runs by a tiny publisher here in Budapest, became immediate bestsellers—almost helped by the fact the publisher couldn't print them fast enough to meet demand, and they weren't available as e-books. It became obvious that gamers might like to play online, but preferred to read hardback books, and the Bloodline Saga's third volume, *Territory*, topped the global bestseller lists for months, the word spreading far beyond the gaming community."

"I understand the books tell a historical-mythological tale, set somewhere in Europe during what might be the Middle Ages. Is that about right?"

Zsófia beamed. "Indeed. Uncle Valentin is so clever. The story is about a multigenerational family steeped in carnage, power, blood, devastation, battles, and more blood." She laughed a little, and I returned her smile. "They are popular among boys and men searching for a complete otherworldly experience where they can—let's be honest—fantasize about violence, pillaging, and debauchery. The books also feature enough strong warrior female characters that even young women turn to them for role models."

"Your uncle seems to be living well off his creations," I said, looking about me.

"Yes, he is, and because of it, we are. By the time the world lined up to buy the fourth book, *Borders*, there was talk of a television series. Movies were rumored when the TV series became required viewing. With book five, *Inheritance*, what started as a cultish phenomenon had become mainstream, and—you are correct—highly lucrative."

"Wow, I had no idea," was my pathetic response to the revelation. Even though I was no fan, I didn't live under a rock, and you couldn't use the Internet on a daily basis without there being some rumor about when the final book in the double-trilogy would see the light of day; millions of people around the world were, it seemed, desperately awaiting what everyone knew would be the last ever book, to find out what would happen to which characters, and how. It, therefore, seemed polite to ask, "Has he finished the sixth book yet?"

I was floored when Zsófia burst into tears at my question. I scrabbled in my handbag in search of a tissue. The only ones I found were all in little balls, so I had to sit there and hope she could find something to wipe her face with. She did, and I allowed her a few minutes to sob quietly. As I made sympathetic shapes with my face, I wondered why she found the mention of book six so upsetting.

Finally composing herself, her voice was thick when she spoke. "I can't be certain he ever will finish it. I hope he will. I have to believe he will. But . . . he's sick. It's Alzheimer's. He's quite old, I suppose—fifty-six. It's hit him hard in the last year. He's up, he's down. It's awful for him. For us, too."

My heart went out to her even as I marveled at the view of what constituted "old" from the vantage point of a young person. *Fifty-six? The same age as Bud.* "That's pretty young for that disease," I said. "I'm sorry to hear it. Not because of the books, but for him, and for you and your mum too, of course," I added quickly.

Zsófia managed a smile. "Thank you. And don't mention this at the HUB, please. Absolutely no one knows about my uncle, and if anyone there knows about the murder of my grandmother, they've certainly never mentioned it. I would prefer to keep it like that."

I could imagine she would. The attention either piece of information might draw to her would be both unpleasant and overwhelming. I wasn't at all sure about how to continue our conversation—we'd been focused on her grandmother's murder before we'd arrived at the house, and now we were swimming in even more challenging waters. I decided to give her a chance to backpedal.

"Are you sure you want me to meet your mum today? Are you feeling up to it? We could do it another time."

Smiling weakly the girl wiped off what was left of her eyeliner as she replied, "There are tears here every day, for all of us. It's not a happy house. Today. Tomorrow. It will make no difference. When Uncle Valentin is having a good day, we try to smile for him. When it's not such a good day, or hour, we try to be strong for him. So we hold in our tears until we are not with him, then let them out with each other. He was still asleep when I left for my shift at the Gellért this morning; let's at least see how he's doing. We have nurses to help out, and there's always someone available when he needs them. It's best that way. Mama can't do it all. Come on—we'll see Mama first."

I agreed, recognizing her resilient response as something I understood, and followed her up the staircase that curved from the entryway to the first floor, where she told me the sitting room was located. When we got there I realized that "sitting room" wasn't an adequate name for the elegant salon, which offered views through large windows to the impressive, tree-lined boulevard outside. I imagined the summer greenery would be a magnificent sight, but the bare, black winter branches were also impressive, in a slightly menacing way.

An ornate, gold-framed sofa—at least ten feet in length and almost entirely covered with newspapers—sat beneath a window. Upon it lounged a woman with long dark hair, snuggled in a comfy sweater and leggings. She was wearing large wireless headphones, had a bottle of wine on the floor beside her, and was conducting an invisible orchestra with a wineglass that was all but empty. Oblivious to her surroundings, she was surprised when her daughter entered her line of sight. She leapt to her feet, spilling the last drops of wine on her sweater.

"Zsófia—we have a guest?" she asked in Hungarian, pulling the headphones off her ears.

"Yes, Mama," said Zsófia in English, "this is Professor Morgan, from the University of Vancouver. I told you about her. I invited her for coffee. She visited the Gellért this morning, so I took the chance."

"Professor Morgan," said Alexa Takács with a smile I judged to be forced, "you're welcome in our home. Zsófia's has told me a great deal about you." Her accent was Canadian; a couple of decades of life in Hungary had given it the twang of a more European cadence, but she was able to switch from English to Hungarian the same way Canadians can from English to French. "I'll get some coffee organized. We won't have our meal for a couple of hours yet, so I hope coffee and cake will work for you, Professor? Or would you like something stronger?" She picked up the bottle from the floor and waggled it at me.

"Please, it's Cait—while we're here," I winked at Zsófia, "and I'd enjoy some cake with coffee, thanks; it's chilly outside."

Alexa peered through the window at the skeletal trees. "Not as cold as it'll get," she said bleakly. She stubbed her feet into a pair of slippers and gathered up the newspaper, dumping it onto the parquet floor. "Here, come, sit down, and make yourself at home. Just give me ten minutes."

Passing her daughter, I heard her hiss in Hungarian, "You might have phoned," then she was gone.

Zsófia and I simultaneously pulled a face at each other, then grinned. "Mama will forgive me," said the girl quietly.

Deciding to take my chance to find out what I could before our reluctant hostess reappeared I asked, "So you were born here in Budapest, but your mother was born and raised in Canada?" I knew what Bud had told me, but it never hurts to have "facts" supported by more than one source.

Zsófia indicated I should sit as she replied, "Yes, she grew up in the family home on the campus of your university. Uncle Valentin was six years old when she was born, and then her parents had what she says they always referred to as 'the perfect family.' Mama was just thirteen when her mother was killed. Uncle Valentin was nineteen. Grandfather continued to teach until the fall of the Communist regime here, then he brought Mama and Uncle Valentin to Hungary—to Budapest. By then he was seventy-two years old, and decided it was time to remove himself from his position as a professor emeritus. He wanted to spend some time, he told my mother, with the people still living here that he had lost when he escaped to the West in 1957. His brother-in-law didn't manage to get out, you see, so Grandfather hadn't seen him in almost forty years. They had been close when he and my grandmother married. He had no family of his own—they were all killed in the war—so Tamás and Klara Örsi were like his own brother and sister. You saw Klara at the New York Café; she is the wife of my grandmother's brother, Tamás Örsi."

"It must have been quite the reunion," I said, unable to imagine how it must have felt for her grandfather to be able to return to his homeland after such an absence.

Zsófia stood and wandered to the window. Her back was toward me so I couldn't see her facial expression, but her voice sounded distant. "I don't know; I suppose it must have been. It's difficult for me to imagine, to be honest. It's like a story, not reality. Grandfather died the year I was born. Mama and Papa often told me when I was young about how they were fortunate to meet when they did, because Grandfather was not a well man. They married quickly so he could be at their wedding before he died. Then, when I was only six, my father became ill. He died when I was ten. Cancer. Mama has lost a lot of people. She never talks about Grandmother, or Grandfather," she turned and smiled, "but she will tell you, if you give her the chance, how it was love at first sight for her and my father. She prefers to tell happy stories, not sad ones." She rolled her eyes. "It's a positive way to look at life, but the stories about her and my father are all very . . . slushy."

I wagged my finger at her playfully. "Hey, you're talking to a woman who is still in the first year of her marriage. Be careful how you make fun of love."

"Really? You didn't marry until now?" Zsófia looked shocked.

I wondered how old she thought I was. "Do you have plans to marry young? I dare say there are one or two men at the HUB who'd be happy to know that."

Zsófia rejoined me on the sofa. "You mean Laszlo, who follows me about everywhere?" I agreed. "Or maybe you mean Professor Matyas? He never seems to be more than a few feet from me wherever I go."

Given the way Patrik had spoken so spitefully about Zsófia, I was puzzled about why he'd want to be anywhere near her at all. "Do you mean he's stalking you?" I was concerned maybe a line was being crossed by a colleague.

Zsófia waved an arm, replying, "No, not stalking. I do not mean this. He's just—always *there*. Smiling. Do you know what I mean?"

Why are young people always so vague about everything? "What do you mean, *specifically*?"

Sighing, the girl spoke reluctantly. "I walk to a class, and I pass him in the corridor. I leave a class, and he's outside the room I am leaving or need to enter. He wanders past me in the library or study rooms. Or he's right behind me getting coffee or a snack. Just *there*. Always. With that smile. And those ties."

At least I knew what she meant about those aspects of the man. His choice in ties was atrocious, as was his worrying grinning. "Is it only at the HUB that you see him all the time? Not outside—you know, when you're out on the town, or whatever you get up to when you're not studying."

Zsófia's face fell. "I'm either at school, studying here, practicing my singing, or performing. Of course there's my job at the spa, but that's because I really want to earn a little money that's my own. Mama and I live here for free, and Uncle pays all the bills, but I like to have a little cash of my own, without having to always owe my family everything. I've seen Professor Matyas at a few of my performances, but I don't mind that so much—he applauds with great enthusiasm, then others join in." She finally grinned.

As her mother pushed a wheeled trolley into the salon, Zsófia leapt up to help with serving coffee.

"How's Uncle today?" asked Zsófia.

"Pretty good," replied her mother with an apprehensive glance toward me.

"I told her about Uncle's condition, and about his writing," said Zsófia. Alexa looked uncomfortable. "It's for the best, Mama," her daughter reassured her. "Besides, I am sure there's some sort of student-professor privilege, isn't there, Professor?" She mugged a goofy smile.

I smiled but shook my head. "Not to my knowledge, Zsófia, but you and you mother can rest assured I'll respect your wishes for confidentiality."

It was clear Zsófia had inherited her mother's limpid brown eyes, as both women gazed at me sadly. "It is a terrible disease," said Alexa quietly. "Sometimes he's like the old Valentin, other times he's gone. Completely gone. It breaks my heart." Her eyes filled. "He's my big brother, and I always looked up to him, tried to look after him when he needed it, even though he was—a little different. His mind was so sharp, so inventive. But now? It's a tragedy."

I allowed a moment of silence to pass before venturing, "Has this been a recent development?"

Alexa shifted in her chair. Her microexpressions told me she'd made the decision to confide in me. "Valentin always marched to his own drum. Back in the day, he'd sometimes stay in his room for a week, then come out ready to take on the world, until something didn't go his way, then he'd retreat into his shell again. And that was even before . . . well, while he was still a teenager. Because his lifestyle was so unusual, I didn't think anything of his oddities. It wasn't until a couple of years ago that I began to realize maybe what we had come to think of as normal behavior was anything but. That's when I managed to get him to agree to some tests, and he was diagnosed."

"It's such a shame he's not able to really understand how much pleasure his work has given so many people," said Zsófia gently.

Alexa replied, "That's not because of his disease, my darling. He never really cared about what others thought of his work anyway." Looking directly at me, as though seeking my understanding, she added, "That's the thing, Cait. He never sought out wealth, and always shied away from fame; Valentin just wanted to tell his stories. He was happy when people paid him huge amounts of money to do so, but he'd have written the books anyway, whether they were published or not. The saddest thing is, I don't think he'll ever finish his saga, now."

"He might, Mama. I'm doing everything I can to help him get to the end," said the woman's daughter.

Alexa looked at Zsófia with round, warning eyes. "Shh now, child."

Zsófia blushed. I wondered what secret the women were sharing, and was on the point of asking when Zsófia said, "I am comfortable with Cait knowing I am helping Uncle with his book."

"Helping?" I had to know.

"She doesn't mean anything," snapped Alexa.

"Mama, I believe we can trust Cait to know the truth," said Zsófia gently.

I was beginning to feel rather uncomfortable with the number of secrets I was becoming privy to, and wondered how many more this odd family harbored.

The young girl leaned in and continued, "Uncle Valentin writes often, but the story he's telling gets muddled sometimes. It started to happen toward the end of book five, so I helped tidy it all up and even typed it all up on his old typewriter before we sent the manuscript to his publishing house. They didn't seem to notice anything was amiss, so I've been doing it for this book too. Unfortunately, his grasp on the storyline is slipping more and more. I try to sort it all out, but I just hope I end up getting it the way he meant it to be. Sometimes he doesn't finish sentences, other times a chapter seems completely out of place—if he manages to finish a chapter at all."

"You're such a good girl," cooed Alexa, beaming at her daughter. Turning to me she added, "Looks and brains, and a heart of gold, this one. She's my little princess."

I smiled politely at the proud mother, who I noticed wasn't having coffee, but rather another glass of wine.

Zsófia tried to fob off her mother's indulgent compliments with, "I don't mind doing it, Mama. You know I'm happy to be able to help him. I love his books, and the characters are all like family to me. They've been a part of my entire adult life, you see, Cait, and I'm not what anyone would call a 'big mixer,' so they sometimes seem more real to me than living human beings."

"Do you feel upset when he kills off characters you've grown to love?" I asked. "Although I haven't read them, I understand that's one of the features of his work—that he'll kill off prominent characters."

Zsófia shrugged. "I'm not sure any of them are truly 'loveable.' They're all utterly self-obsessed and prepared to do anything to survive, or so their part of the family can retain power. Driven and bloodthirsty, yes, but loveable, no. I enjoy reading his battle scenes, but my favorite parts are those where he emphasizes the intrigue and behind-the-scenes power plays. All those informers whispering behind the tapestries and handing out poisoned chalices—wonderful."

Alexa tutted. "Maybe you should look less gleeful about that sort of activity. This family has suffered because of it."

I was on full alert. "How so?" I asked as innocently as possible, while taking my last mouthful of moist cake. I hoped for a seamless segue into the tragedy in Canada, but was surprised by Alexa's sharp response.

"Answering that sort of question can have serious consequences. There might not be an AVO anymore, but now there's the TEK."

I was nonplussed. Alexa had acknowledged that the infamous Hungarian secret police of the 1940s and '50s, the AVO, no longer existed, but had suggested the anti-terrorist force known as the TEK had replaced it. Maybe I was barking up the wrong tree, but I had to try to understand what she meant. "You think of the TEK as the new secret police in Hungary?"

Alexa stood, her eyes blazing. "You must not speak of such things. You never know who might be listening."

I looked around the vast room, then at Alexa and Zsófia, not understanding what the woman meant.

"Mama's right," said my student. She nibbled at her lip.

I wondered if both women shared some sort of paranoid delusion, but told myself off and began to give serious thought to what Alexa had said. It made me consider some of Zsófia's comments about "not being overheard" in a fresh light.

I whispered, "Do you think Valentin's publishers might be concerned Zsófia is helping with his manuscript, and you think the TEK is involved?" It seemed far-fetched, but I couldn't imagine another reason for Alexa mentioning the institution as a potential eavesdropper.

Alexa was pacing the room. She stopped, turned, and mouthed, "You never know." She marched to a discreet audio system in a corner and seconds later we were overwhelmed by the third movement of Bartok's *Cantata Profana*.

With the loud music providing "cover" Alexa sat close beside me and began in hushed tones, "We do not know who is listening to us, but we know someone is. At first we believed Valentin was imagining he was being followed when he left this house, but, even before he was diagnosed, we discovered this was the truth. I, too, have been followed. Please do not laugh when I tell you that to see a man in a dark overcoat standing outside your home, in the heat of summer, can give a person a terrible sense of foreboding."

"It wasn't just a fan of Valentin's work?" It seemed like an obvious question to me.

"No, it was not. Valentin's identity as VS Örsi is not known. Not even his publisher has met him face to face. They communicate only through emails."

I wondered if that was a normal way for a publisher and a bestselling author to communicate, but realized it was a relationship beyond my experience, so accepted Alexa's version of events as truthful.

"I have been most careful to not tell anyone, at all, about him," added Zsófia. "And I trust you to keep our secret."

I signaled my promise of discretion with a smile, and used its cover to try to find out something more. "You said earlier your family has been affected by the activities of informers in the past. How?"

Alexa took a deep swig from her glass and spoke quickly. "My uncle Tamás—that is, my mother's brother—was an informer for the AVO during the years when the Communists held sway over Hungary. His cover was intact right up until 1992. But when his role was discovered? Let's just say he is dead to many people. My late father didn't know what his brother-in-law had done until they met again here, in Budapest. It was a terrible shock to him. To us all. Tamás acted in an unforgiveable way, informing on his friends and neighbors. We have cut ourselves off from him and his wife since my father discovered the truth. No one in our family will ever speak to them again."

Keenly aware that either Alexa was lying about that last fact or she didn't know Zsófia had spent enough time with the renegade Klara to have learned a host of traditional songs, I felt I was being pulled into a nightmarish world awash with the ramifications of Cold War politics both inside, and beyond, the Takács family. And I still couldn't make the connection between what Alexa was telling me and the initial reason Zsófia had brought me to the house—the death of her grandmother. If, indeed, there was any.

"What's that noise? You know I hate Bartok!"

We all turned to see a man standing just inside the room dressed in an original Vancouver Canucks stick-in-rink jersey and pajama bottoms. He was bald, with a long, straggly gray goatee, and was waving a hockey stick. He ran, barefoot, across the room, and switched off the music system. "It's just noise," he bellowed. "You know I can't stand it. What are you doing?"

"Valentin, it's all right, please calm down. We were just entertaining our guest," said Alexa, looking anything but calm herself. "She's the one I told you about when I came upstairs earlier."

Valentin Seszták held the hockey stick above his head and shouted, "I know. From Vancouver. You told me. I remember. It was, like, five minutes ago! See? See? I kept my old jersey." I smiled as I acknowledged what was clearly an old favorite. "Had it since their first NHL season, 1970. Still fits, eh?"

Valentin's appearance, while odd, was a thoughtful recognition of our shared background. I'd envisaged a man of Bud's age, but what I saw was a more wizened person than I'd expected. His Canadian accent was something I almost didn't notice—it was exactly what surrounded me every day back home, so was only remarkable in that I was hearing it here, in the heart of Hungary. I suspected the fact that he didn't mix with many people meant Valentin's Canadian twang had remained unaffected by his time in Budapest, unlike his sister, who presumably spoke Hungarian when going about her daily life outside the home.

As Valentin twirled, so I could better admire his shirt, a flushed-faced man I assumed to be Valentin's nurse joined us.

"There you are," he said with a relieved sigh. "I lost you for a moment, Valentin."

"Here I am, Martin," giggled Valentin. "Safe and sound. All that time you spend at the gym, but you're still not as quick on your feet as me, eh?" He winked at me, and an impish grin creased his face. "She loves it, I can tell," he added, pulling at the jersey. "Kurtenbach was the Vancouver Canucks' first captain," he told Zsófia, proudly displaying the shirt's "C." "Know anything about the guy?" he asked me brightly.

I decided to try to make a friend. "He was from Saskatchewan and was with the pre-Canucks version of the team in the Western Hockey League. He played 639 NHL games over ten seasons, scoring 119 goals and 213 assists, for a career total of 332 points. Retired from the Canucks with a knee problem in 1974, coached their farm team for a few seasons, then the Canucks themselves. First guy to be inducted into the Canucks' Ring of Honour, on October 26, 2010. He dropped the puck at the game against the Avalanche that night. I was there."

Valentin's mouth made a little *o*, then he flung his arms around me and said, "At last, someone who loves hockey as much as me. Come on, come on, let me show you my memorabilia."

He released his bear hug, then wrapped his skinny arm around my shoulder, looked down at me from his six feet, and laughed heartily. "Play that Bartok as loud as you want, Alexa. We'll be back. Eventually."

All I could do was turn toward Zsófia and Alexa and throw them a resigned shrug. They wore matching expressions of horror, but remained stock-still. I had no idea where I was being taken, but suspected I'd be required to call upon my eidetic memory, and the fact I'd once decided to read up on all the old Canucks' statistics to confound a particularly irritating student.

Words from the Past

VALENTIN SESZTÁK'S HOCKEY JERSEY SMELLED of feet. I didn't know why—didn't want to think why—but it did. I pulled away from his embrace as elegantly as I could, and he seemed happy enough to take the lead as we mounted the staircase for two more floors. We finally entered a door directly above that to the salon we'd just left.

"We don't need you in here with us," called Valentin to the nurse who'd followed us up the stairs, "but feel free to brood and hover, just like you always do."

I expected another room of the same proportions as the one below, but what we entered wasn't so much a room as a world. The space was L-shaped, twice as big as the salon downstairs, and filled with a regimented collection of the deadliest weapons I'd ever seen. Many of them, alarmingly, seemed to be covered with blood. The walls were bedecked with papers upon which were scrawled names, dates, and events with pieces of string pinned between them like a web. It looked for all the world like one of those rooms every obsessed detective is supposed to have behind closed doors, where they plan how to track their nemesis.

Glancing around, I couldn't see anything resembling hockey memorabilia, unless you counted a hockey stick with its blade sharpened to a bloodied point, so opened with, "This is an incredible collection of . . . um . . ."

"Weaponry, woman. It's weaponry. All personally selected by me as the deadliest, and most effective, form of tool with which to achieve a specific end result." Valentin gleefully snatched up a mace and chain. "This, you see, has just the correct length of chain and weight of spiked ball to allow a person to wield it above their head and smash it into the shield of an oncoming warrior *if* the person wielding it is on foot, rather than on horseback." He began to swing the mace in a circle above his head, and the sight was not only terrifying but also bizarrely heroic—despite the hockey shirt and pajamas. I was relieved when he allowed the ball to stop spinning and placed the vicious-looking thing on the floor.

"And this is all research for your books?" I couldn't imagine there'd be any other reason.

"Sure is. I like to explain how it feels for a character to kill someone in a particular way. This helps."

I was apprehensive as I asked, "And the blood?"

Valentin kept a straight face as he replied, "I have to practice on people my sister drags in from the street," then he bellowed with laughter.

"I bet your books are fun," I said.

"They are," said the author with a smile. "Some people get the humor, others don't. Okay, I guess most don't, but it's there if you can see it. The only way families get along is by finding the balance between fighting and laughing. That's what I write about. So, what are you more interested in—hockey or my books?"

I weighed my response. "I'm more interested in you than either."

Valentin pushed a couple of broadswords off a chair and sat down, his pale, skinny legs poking out from the bottom of his pajamas. His feet were filthy and so leathery I judged he didn't wear shoes as a rule.

"Did Zsófia tell you I was mad and needed a shrink? That's what you are, right? I've met a few in my time, so I can spot them a mile off."

I decided to give as good as I was getting. "No, I'm not a psychiatrist, I'm a psychologist. And I won't be doing any work with you. Zsófia invited me here because I'm visiting from the University of Vancouver and she thought your sister might enjoy meeting someone who knew the place where she grew up. You too, of course, but she wasn't sure if—"

"I know, I know. She didn't know if I'd be having a good day or a bad day."

"Exactly." I didn't see any point in disagreeing with the man, who I could only assume was having a good day.

Valentin picked up one of the swords lying at at his feet, and began to swat it about in front of himself. "I don't know the difference between the two; they tell me when I've had a bad day, but I don't remember it. So I guess that's all right. Then there are days like today, when I look out at the sunshine and the world's a great place to be in, and all I want to do is write and write and write, and get to the end of my story. Sometimes it feels like it's getting farther away all the time—like one of those dreams where the corridor keeps getting longer no matter how fast you run." He replaced the sword gently on the floor.

Looking down at me, he said quietly, "So you're from UVan, eh? What's it like there these days? Changed much since my time?"

Although I reckoned I knew the answer I asked, "When were you there last?"

"Ninety-two. Kristóf brought me and Alexa here that year. Haven't been back since."

I found it interesting that he used his father's given name, rather than his parental title.

"In that case you'd notice the difference. The school does a roaring business in the overseas student market now, so they have the money to rapidly construct many new buildings. I'd say the place has almost doubled in size since you left; largely in the past decade."

Valentin looked thoughtful. "Shame. It was just about right. I was a student there; did you know that?"

"No," I lied. "What did you study?"

Valentin's face creased into a rueful smile. It was odd to see a man with a beard but no mustache, but at least it allowed me to see more of his facial expressions. "Psychology, of course. Kristóf wouldn't have had it any other way. Kind of the family business. Kristóf, me, and Alexa. All of us. Alexa only at evening classes. She didn't attend university."

"I didn't know your sister studied psychology too," I said, hoping to discover something.

A glint in Valentin's eye as he said, "So you knew I did," made me realize I was talking to a perceptive, intelligent man.

I made a split-second decision. I was in the company of a man who was quick on the uptake, but succumbing to a disease that meant he might lapse at any time; I felt I had to grab my chance to find out whatever I could from him, to be able to help his niece.

"I'm going to come clean," I half lied.

"Good, it'll save time."

I felt a bit exposed, standing in front of him surrounded by lethal weapons, so I pulled a stool from beneath a desk and sat down, just feet away. The broadswords bisected the space between us. It was a dramatic setting for what might be a difficult conversation.

"As you know, I teach at the university in Canada where your mother was murdered. The case is well-known by everyone at UVan."

"I guess an unsolved murder will always be talked about," replied Valentin, not looking terribly upset by the idea.

"Quite right. And with me being a professor of criminal psychology, and someone who specializes in victim profiling, it's the sort of case that interests me. I hope you don't mind me speaking about your mother's death that way? I am acutely aware I'm talking about a real person, and to a family member who was deeply impacted by her death."

Valentin pushed at the broadswords with his toes. "It all happened a very long time ago. Wounds heal."

I wondered if the man who'd had a breakdown following his mother's murder had truly reconciled himself to the brutality of the crime that had taken place. "The thing is, Valentin, with me being here, and becoming more acutely aware of your mother's death, I've been talking things through with my husband—who's a retired homicide cop. He's back in BC right now and he's been able to get in touch with some of his old contacts to see what he can unearth. So far I've been able to gain some insights from a junior officer who worked the case, but I know very little. I understand you found it challenging to cope with your mother's murder at the time, but I suspect there's a good deal you could tell me, if you chose to, now. Would you be prepared to do that? It might help the whole family."

Valentin stared into my eyes as though he was trying to see my soul. I returned his gaze. I knew in that moment I needed to read the books he'd written.

After a few moments of silence, he closed his eyes. Tears rolled down his prematurely lined cheeks. He whispered, "Kristóf made me go see her. She was on a metal gurney. They'd cleaned her up, but she was still a mess. A weird consistency to her flesh; almost translucent. Waxy. I'd never seen a corpse before, and I thought she'd be pale, but she wasn't. Her face was all red, mottled. She looked flushed. The side of her head had been shaved. There was a big star-shaped crack in it. Kristóf made me look at that, too. Alexa was with me. She held onto me, tight, then he ripped our hands apart and made us both feel the wound on the skull. He said it would be good for us. He was wrong." His clenched fists relaxed, and he opened his eyes. "It was a cruel thing to do, but he was a cruel man. He made my mother suffer terribly. Me too."

I felt my heart thump in my chest, the recollection of my dead ex-boyfriend Angus's angry fists making me feel immediately sick. "Do you mean he was physically violent?" I managed to say.

Valentin sat back in his chair and waved skinny arms inside his oversized hockey shirt. "No. That would have been beneath him.

He did it all with his words." He spat out the final syllable like a rifle shot. "The man who led more than a hundred souls away from the tyrannical boot of the Communists, and harried governments into granting them safe passage to Canada, was also well-versed in psychological torture. The iron will he needed to do good, he turned upon us, his family, in spite. I hated him. My mom was the only light in my life, and she was snuffed out. She loved to laugh, and Kristóf didn't like the sound of laughter, not unless it was because he'd said something he thought was amusing. Then? You'd better laugh, and loudly, if you knew what was good for you."

I waited a beat. "Do you think your father might have killed your mother?"

Valentin leapt from his seat, grabbing up a broadsword as he did so. Holding it in two hands above his head, ready to strike down, he bellowed, "Did my father kill my mother?" He howled like a wild animal and swirled the sword. "Who are you, whore? From whence have you appeared? I know thee not!"

The person I'd been connecting with had disappeared, and I was immediately on my guard. When people talk about "fight or flight" they're referring to a physical response to a frightening stimulus, which means the body produces adrenaline that will allow a person to either flee the danger more quickly than they normally could or to fight with more power than they'd usually possess. At that moment I knew flight was the better response to my situation, so I didn't stop to think. I jumped from my stool and ran toward the door through which I'd entered. As I pulled it open, Martin, the nurse, bumped into me.

"What is it? I heard him howling again. That is never good," he said, an urgency in his voice.

I got out and pulled the door closed behind me, panting. "He's got a broadsword in his hands, and seems to think I mean him harm. He's having a violent episode. Is that normal for him?"

Martin sagged, then pressed a button on the end of a pendant he was wearing around his neck. "I will handle this. I've called my colleague," he said with resignation. "It takes two of us when he is this way." A tall man in his thirties who was more than passingly familiar with a gym came rushing up the stairs, two at a time.

"You go now, please," Martin said to me. "We will take care of this."

The worried faces of Zsófia and Alexa looked up at me as I descended the stairs. "Are you okay?" asked my student.

"I'm fine. It seems I can move across a room quite quickly when I need to."

As I reached the two women they each put a hand on one of my shoulders. "It's a skill we all have developed," said Zsófia. "Uncle shouldn't have all those weapons up there."

"I think that's a valid observation," I said, my heart still thumping. "They're pretty dangerous. Won't he give them up?"

"They are almost all gone. What you see there now is just a fraction of what he used to have," said the sick man's sister, "besides, they're just props really. They wouldn't do anyone much harm. Made of polystyrene, rubber, and plastic, for the most part."

I pictured the weapons in my mind's eye. They'd looked real enough to me, and I said so.

"I understand what you mean," said Alexa, "but, honestly, they're just fakes. You needn't have worried. While he sleeps, we'll take a few more away. We do it this way so he won't notice. It's not that they are dangerous, you see, I just don't think the atmosphere they create is healthy—even though he says he needs them for his research."

Struggling to reassess the amount of danger I'd truly faced, I felt embarrassed at running off.

"He always notices when we take things—if he's having a lucid period, that is," said Zsófia, seeming to not realize my consternation. "His collection is extremely well organized. He's that way about everything. A place for everything, and everything in its place."

We were back in the salon when Alexa offered me another piece of cake. "The coffee's cold now," she said. "But there's still wine." She held up a half-empty bottle; I wondered if it was her second of the day. If it was, and she was still appearing to be only a little tipsy, I reckoned she must drink a great deal on a pretty regular basis. It had been that way with Angus; an alcoholic can function when they've glugged their way through enough booze to leave most non-alcoholics utterly incapacitated. I knew why Angus had drunk—to bury the feelings of loss he had about his own childhood, he always said. I wondered what it was that Alexa was using alcohol to wipe from her mind. Jack White's recollections of her as a resilient young girl were from decades earlier.

Finally, seated, though still shaking, I accepted the cake, hoping it would steady my nerves. I dragged my mind away from my concerns about Alexa, and decided the best thing I could do was try to comfort her. Despite the glass of wine in her hand, she looked genuinely concerned about my state. "Valentin was fine for most of the time, and he's fiercely intelligent, highly perceptive. I don't think it's a bad idea to thin out his collection of deadly weapons a little—though I expect it causes a different sort of problem for you when he notices they've gone."

"You're right," replied Alexa. "He notices everything, when he is himself. But his periods of lucidity are now broken by longer periods when he's not himself. He's not always violent, of course. Just confused usually. And he tires so quickly these days, which means his good times are shorter and shorter." She took a deep swig from her glass, almost without noticing, it seemed to me. "He wanders now, so we have to lock his rooms at night, otherwise he might do something bad."

I noticed her hand had begun to tremble. She placed the glass on a table and pulled a handkerchief from her pocket. As she wiped at her tears, she and her daughter grasped each other's hands.

"Uncle's such a worry for Mama," said Zsófia. Her eyes were glassy with pain and tears.

"I can understand that," I replied. Stuck in the presence of two weeping women, with a half-eaten piece of cake in my hand, I did the only thing I could think of—I stuffed it into my mouth and chewed as fast as I could. I was beginning to get a grip on my own emotions, and felt ready to take the conversation forward when they were able.

I had to wait a few moments until I sensed the time was right, then I took my chance. "While we were chatting about this and that, Valentin said a few things about the death of your mother, Alexa," I lied. The woman looked shocked. "Coming from UVan as I do, the tragedy of your mother's death is well known to me. Is it something you and your brother ever talk about?"

Alexa stared, open-mouthed, at me, and I could tell Zsófia was pretending to be surprised.

"My brother spoke to you about our mother's murder?" asked Alexa finally. Every syllable dripped with disbelief.

"He did."

"I'm amazed," she said, looking it. "He's never, ever talked to me about it. I'm his sister. Why on earth would he say anything to you—a complete stranger?"

I felt I had to tread carefully, and I didn't want to reveal Zsófia's private request. "Maybe because I'm a psychologist and he felt I could help him work through something?" I ventured.

Alexa drained her glass. "Like what?" she snapped. I noticed her daughter wasn't making eye contact with either of us.

"Alexa, I don't know the extent to which your brother was speaking about real facts or something he's maybe imagined, so do you mind if I ask you some direct questions? They might be difficult for you to tackle, though."

Alexa plonked her empty glass on the table and flung back her head, her tearful eyes glittering. "Ask away," she said as though throwing down a gauntlet.

"Did your father take you and your brother to see your mother's remains in the morgue?"

Zsófia's sharp intake of breath drew a sideways glance from her mother. Nostrils flaring, head still held high, Alexa said, "He did."

"Oh, Mama, that's terrible. I couldn't look at you—like that. Why did Grandfather make you do that?"

I could see a vein in Alexa's neck throb as she replied, "It was good for us, Zsófia. We needed to understand our mother was gone, and the best way for us to realize that was to see her dead. A coffin is nothing. It's just a box. To know a person is gone you have to see them, feel that the life has left their body. Even an open casket, with a body primped and prepared so it looks like the person is just sleeping, doesn't help. You have to touch their wounds. You have to feel the death."

As the grown woman in front of me spoke I knew she wasn't the one forming the words; her father had given them to her when she was no more than a child, and she was passing them on to us.

I ventured, "With your father being a renowned psychologist, and understanding the psychological role of closure, I still have to say you were very young at the time, Alexa. Maybe seeing your mother that way was a little harsh." I had decided to understate my own reaction in order to try to find out how the experience had made Alexa, and Valentin, feel. "As Valentin was speaking to me about this event, I noticed he clenched his fists, which suggests to me he was holding tight to the memory and the anger it made him feel. He told me you and he were holding each other's hands, but your father pulled you apart. As I said, I realize you were just a young girl at the time, but could you maybe try to explain to me how that event made you feel? I didn't have the chance to ask your brother."

63

Alexa studied the ceiling as she appeared to think about my question. Her fingers moved as though she was trying to grasp memories in the air. "I don't remember holding Valentin's hand. What I remember is Kristóf placing my fingers almost inside the wound on Ilona's head, telling me to feel the edges of the cracks in her skull. That was how I would know her life had gone, he said."

Pushing aside the horror I felt at imagining poor little Alexa being made to perform such a cruel and nauseating act, I noticed she, as well as Valentin, used her parents' given names rather than their parental titles. It was puzzling, so I took my chance to ask why.

Alexa's tone suggested she felt she was on firmer ground when she answered, "When I was little, Valentin always called them Kristóf and Ilona—so I did too. They never said I should call them anything else." It seemed to be completely natural for her, so I told myself maybe there was no deeply suggestive reason for it, after all. "Names are just words. What does 'father' or 'mother' mean?"

Fat tears rolled down Zsófia's youthful cheeks as she looked at her mother's impassive expression. "Oh, Mama," was all she could manage. Then, "I didn't know Grandfather made you touch Grandmother's corpse. How horrible for you."

Alexa tossed her head and screwed up her face. "I got it. Of course I got it that Ilona—my *mother*—was dead. Gone forever. Kristóf told me I would be the woman of the household from then on, and that's what I became. I looked after him—and Valentin, of course. I ran the house. They didn't help much. I grew up that day."

"But Valentin didn't, did he?" I said.

Alexa's chin fell, and she pinched her bottom lip between her fingers. "No, he didn't. You're right. I grew up, but he became like a little boy again." She looked at me as though begging for my understanding. "I'd always thought of him as grown-up, you see. My big brother, Valentin. But after that? He changed so much." She reached for her daughter's hand, not making eye contact. "Kristóf didn't see it. He seemed to think Valentin had been 'cured' when he came out of hospital that first time, but I knew he was still horribly unhappy. Kristóf didn't even spot that my brother was taking drugs; I had to tell him."

"Uncle Valentin did drugs?" Zsófia sounded surprised. Turning to me she added, "He always says he hates taking any medications because they make him feel not like himself."

"That's exactly why he took the stuff back then," said Alexa, a wry chuckle coloring her tone. "Of course, I was just a kid, but I knew generally what was going on. Guys would turn up at our house to sell him whatever it was he was taking. All times of the day, but always when Valentin and I were alone. I didn't know what he was taking; I just knew it wasn't right. So I told Kristóf." Alexa paused and looked at her daughter with great affection. "I tried to be a good girl for my father, as you always were for yours, my darling child. You were your father's princess, as I was for mine. Kristóf went nuts, of course. I'd never seen him so angry. Ever. Valentin hadn't left the house much for about a year after Ilona's death, but when Kristóf screamed at him that he couldn't go out at all for a month—that he was grounded—Valentin took it as more of a punishment than I'd expected he would. That's when his tantrums began."

"Might your brother have been going through withdrawal?" I asked gently.

Alexa furrowed her brow, poured the final drops from the bottle of wine into her glass, and sipped. "I guess, but young as I was, how would I have known? Kristóf locked him in his room for weeks. There was a lot of anger in our home, even more than there had been before Ilona died. There was screaming, and begging. Maybe you're right, Cait. Perhaps that's what it was—withdrawal. But withdrawal from what, I don't know."

"What about afterward, Mama?" asked the woman's daughter gently.

Alexa smiled, dangling her glass between her fingers with an ease borne of great experience. "For a while it was okay again. Kristóf and Valentin would go for long walks and come back full of fun and stories about what they'd seen on the trails. I was keeping house at the time, the best way a teen could, so I recall we had a lot of easy-to-cook meals. I'd make up lists and Kristóf would do the shopping; we'd all share the cleaning. Well, I guess we didn't do much cleaning really, because Kristóf and I were out all day—I kept up my grades throughout school you know," she looked proud for a brief moment, "and Valentin didn't care about that sort of thing." She paused, and her face fell. "Then it changed again. The winter came and Kristóf got busy at school, I guess. That was when Valentin first got into trouble with the police. I remember they brought him home one night in a cop car. Kristóf went berserk, locked him in his room, and we repeated the pattern all over again. I don't know how often all that happened. Lots of times."

"Poor Mama," said Zsófia, touching her mother gently on the leg.

"It must have been tough for you," I said.

Looking haggard, Alexa replied weakly, "I guess. I don't think I really had a childhood after Ilona was killed. I was done with being a kid, and I've been Valentin's guardian ever since." For the first time I noticed she was slurring a little.

I felt it was time to leave, and said so, but had a final request to add. "I wonder if I could beg a set of Valentin's books, so I can read up on his work? I'll take good care of them, but maybe you have some here that aren't first editions?"

"Sure," said Alexa heavily, looking at her daughter. "You can bring them back when you come for your next visit."

"Let me get that sorted for you, Cait," said Zsófia, rising. "We'll pick them up as you leave."

All finally standing, I was hugged by Alexa, who swayed a little as I held her, and I promised to return, as she'd asked.

I pulled on my coat beside the front door as Zsófia packed a set of five fat books in two bags. "I'll read these, and I'll pass on what I've learned today to my husband in Canada, okay?" I checked.

"Please," replied Zsófia, her eyes pink and raw. "Thanks for not mentioning that I asked you to do all this. But I think now you can see it's not just me who needs help. We all do." She hugged me, and then I left.

As I made my way to the metro station, I couldn't help but feel the weight of the sadness in the home I'd just left. I knew a fair bit about alcoholism—living with Angus for years had taught me some harsh lessons. It sounded as though Valentin had reacted to his mother's murder almost instantly, with a state of nervous collapse followed by drug use. Maybe alcohol was Alexa's way of "managing" the grief she felt over the loss of not only her mother decades ago but also her seemingly beloved father, her husband, and now her brother who, though still physically present, was no longer the person he once had been. I was pretty impressed by how Zsófia had managed to handle her home life and still be the bright, optimistic, hardworking young thing she was. Good for her.

Conversations Afloat

THE WORKWEEK FLEW BY WITH little passing between Bud and myself that wasn't a health update on his mother, or a rant about all of the poisonous emails flying around my department back at UVan. There really wasn't much either of us could do about the Ilona Seszták case, because he was waiting on developments regarding access to old files, and I had grading to get through and my research paper to keep on top of.

By Friday night I was feeling the strain, but was finally clear of my purely academic commitments for a couple of days, and I knew I had reached a vital "stewing" point in my paper; sometimes I have to let things sit in my brain for a while before they finally crystallize and deign to come out of my fingertips onto the keyboard. A break was in order, and I wanted to plow through the five volumes of the Bloodline Saga before Sunday, when I'd been invited to return to the Seszták/Takács household. By the time I was munching my way through a platter of cheese and crusty, fresh bread for lunch on Saturday, I was so familiar with the world Valentin had created within his books I felt as though the view beyond my window was the dream and the violent realm he described so vividly was reality.

It had been a long time since I'd read such a large dose of fiction, and I was quite enjoying it—despite the blood and gore—so the last thing I felt like doing was spending a Saturday evening on a riverboat with my students, but that was what had been planned for me. Being an ambassador for UVan at the HUB had its responsibilities, whatever might be going on back at my department.

Like everyone who's ever visited Budapest, I'd seen the dinner boats tied up along the Pest side of the river between the iconic Széchenyi Chain Bridge and the Elizabeth Bridge. All I had to go on was a sailing time and a dock number, so I splurged on a taxi to take me from my apartment to the right spot, because I really didn't fancy tottering along the edge of the Danube looking for the right boat to board on what was turning out to be a bitterly cold late afternoon.

My heart sank when I saw the vessel in question; the oldest of the lot, it had open balconies atop, and lower decks with windows someone had seen fit to open halfway. I walked the rickety gangplank with apprehension, and entered the main body hoping the only thing that would sink that night would be my heart. Once inside I could see why someone had opened the windows; I'd cut my arrival close to sailing time, and a hundred or more warm bodies had already created a good deal of humidity in the gloomy dark-wood interior.

Just when I thought the prospect of the evening's festivities couldn't get any worse, I felt a hand grab my elbow and I spun around to find myself facing Patrik Matyas.

"Cait! How wonderful, you came. I told the doubters you would. Good for you. The cloakroom is at the stern, near the WC, and the bar's at the other end. Why don't you drop off your coat while I get you a drink?" He sported a particularly flamboyant, floppy bowtie with scarlet and yellow stripes, and was almost vibrating with excitement.

I tried to not sigh while accepting his offer as graciously as possible, and asked for a Soproni. As I lined up to hand off my heavy outerwear, exchanging pleasantries with the few students, staff, and faculty I recognized, I began to hope the beer would be cold, because the boat was stifling, despite the open windows. I also wondered why that odious, grinning little man had said some people thought I wouldn't show up. Why on earth would anyone think that? I'd been working really hard at being the most affable version of myself whenever I talked to anyone at the HUB. Was I really that transparent? Did I come over as standoffish? I felt quite unsettled.

The boat was underway by the time I reconnected with Patrik. I was at least relieved to see my beer bottle was dripping with condensation and promised immediate refreshment. I made sure I didn't grab when I took it from the man's damp hand and held it toward him saying, "*Egészségedre*," which I made sound like "eggy sheggy drey." I might have an eidetic memory that allows me to learn most of what I need of a new language pretty quickly, but my pronunciation is often mangled by my Welsh accent, so I was hoping for at least a smile at my attempt, but Patrik glared at me. I added, "Was I that hopeless at saying 'Cheers' in Hungarian?"

My fellow professor's face was a picture of prudish disdain as he whined, "Since 1848, when the Austrians clinked their bottles and glasses and shouted 'Cheers' to each other in celebration of defeating our brave national heroes, no self-respecting Hungarian has done this. It is not what true Hungarians do."

I couldn't help but notice pretty much every other Hungarian on the boat was proving him wrong, but I let it pass with no more than a mumbled apology, and glugged my beer. He did likewise, and we fell into an awkward silence for at least two minutes. I found I'd all but finished my beer already, and I spotted an escape route. "I was rather thirsty, Patrik, and it's quite warm in here. How about I get us another?"

He looked surprised as he raised his almost-full bottle of Borsodi. "I don't seem to be able to keep up with you." Even though he giggled like a naughty schoolboy, he made me feel as though I was being judged. His prissy, "I will take my time, thank you," made me want to pull one end of his bow tie and flounce off.

Instead, I managed a polite, "If you don't mind, I'll pop to get another for myself then, Patrik. I'll see you later, maybe." I didn't hang about.

I wriggled my way toward the busy end of the boat. Milling about within the throng I felt uplifted by the snippets of conversation I overheard between staff and faculty, and within student huddles, though I noticed the lines between the different age groups were pretty sharply drawn and the cliques weren't mixing much. The fee I'd paid for the trip included a buffet dinner, and I'd opted for what they referred to as the "optional beverage package," which I discovered meant I could have as many soft drinks and beers, or glasses of a few nominated wines, as I liked. As I sucked on my second beer I suspected a slippery slope was ahead of me unless I switched to something non-alcoholic, and promised myself I'd do just that after the second bottle.

I was a little apprehensive when Zsófia, with the inevitable Laszlo in tow, approached me. I knew she wouldn't want to talk about her family while we were in the company of others, but everything I'd discovered about her circumstances weighed heavily on my already overloaded shoulders.

"It is good to see you, Professor Morgan," said Laszlo loud enough to be heard above the babble. "This is a good night, is it not? I see you have a beer. May I bring you another?"

"Thanks, I just started it," I said, holding my half-empty bottle toward him.

"Cheers!" he said in English, clinking the neck of his bottle against mine.

I returned the action and repeated it with Zsófia, then noted, "I was told earlier this isn't something Hungarians do. Indeed, it was suggested to me they haven't done it since 1848."

The two youngsters exchanged a significant look and giggled. "Was it Professor Matyas who told you this?" asked Laszlo, grinning.

I shrugged, knowing they'd both understand.

"Ignore him," said Zsófia, bending toward my ear. "He's a funny little man who thinks himself a nationalist. He has no idea everyone thinks he's hilarious."

"He's not funny, he's dangerous, Zsófia," said Laszlo in a lower voice. "I keep telling you this. He's not the sort of man you laugh at. He looks at people as though he knows all their secrets. And he's so sly, I bet he does."

"Come off it," guffawed the girl. "He's creepy, yes, but he's a buffoon, and we all know it. But he must be respected because he is a professor, so we all keep quiet and pay attention in his classes, and listen to him drone on and on about *the* paper he was involved with a hundred years ago. I don't think he's published anything much himself; he's only ever co-authored."

"No originality," observed Laszlo sagely.

The young can be so earnest, even while being illogically idealistic and judgmental. I decided not to comment. It was more fun to watch the scene play out.

"The one thing you can be certain about is, if he were a part of a group, he'd be the least dynamic person in it," said Laszlo, nudging Zsófia's arm.

The girl played along, acknowledging the boy's joke about Patrik's area of specialism, and I gave him a weak smile in response to his little dig at the man who was, after all, my co-worker—even if only for a little while. "He worked with Hollingsworth, in Vancouver," I said, trying to give my colleague the benefit of the doubt.

"Don't we know it," replied Laszlo, rolling his eyes.

Zsófia agreed, "He mentions it in every class, without fail. It was his shining hour, he tells us. It seems he peaked early." She caught the slight rebuke in my eyes and changed the subject. "But enough about him, what shall we do tonight, professor? Would you like to see the sights as we cruise? You should; it's the best way to see the city, from the river. Will you be a tourist tonight?"

Suddenly the idea of huddling into my coat on a cool—okay, extremely chilly, but at least less noisy—outer deck seemed appealing.

"I might do just that. We seem to have stopped turning, so I suppose we'll head off now."

"We'll come with you," said Zsófia with enthusiasm. A few minutes later I was wrapped in my coat and scarf, the icy breeze chilling my nose. The three of us found a spot out of the worst of the wind to take in the sights gliding past us. The sky was black; no stars or moon showed through the clouds, which was the perfect backdrop for the floodlit beauties of Budapest. I enjoyed the maniacally Gothic parliament building, the graceful swags of the suspension bridges, the stark white of the Fisherman's Bastion and Royal Palace, and the glistening reflections of it all on the inky waters of the Danube. I struggled to stop the "Blue Danube Waltz" from playing in my head, but failed miserably, as I suspected every tourist did. Zsófia and Laszlo threw me titbits of history as we moved along at a stately pace, but eventually it got too cold for us all, so we moved back into the warmth of the interior areas.

"Let's go here before they open the buffet," said Zsófia, steering me toward the WC. Once inside the tiny compartment she whispered, "Are we on for lunch tomorrow?"

"Yes, I'll arrive around two, as you asked. I should have finished reading your uncle's books by then, and Bud has said he'll send me any updates he gets by email, though I don't have much fresh news for you."

"Anything at all?" pleaded the girl, whose face, like mine, was pink with cold.

We both used toilet tissue to tackle our suddenly runny noses. "I know you're intimately familiar with your uncle's books, but have you ever considered why he writes them? I mean, why those tales were inside him, needing to be told?"

Zsófia stopped tidying her windswept hair and stared at me, the light of an epiphany in her eyes. "You've been reading them as a psychologist, haven't you? I should have done that," she snapped, clenching her little fists with annoyance. "I never thought of them that way before. I've only ever considered them as something he's made up. As pure fiction."

"I understand why you would do that, but you're right, I've been reading them in a different way, and I have a few questions for your mother. Do you think she'd be open to that?"

The girl clutched my arms. "Cait, there's been such a change in Mama. It's as though a dam has burst. She's spoken to me about her young life in Canada more in the past week than for the whole of my life. I've even learned she used to play the piano and enjoyed singing when she was a girl—though she hasn't done any of that since Ilona's death, it seems." Zsófia added, "I know she drinks too much sometimes. She's been that way ever since Uncle Valentin was diagnosed. She wasn't like it before, and she's been a little better this week. It's like having my old mama back—but even better. I know this is difficult for her, but I think maybe we're doing the right thing." She locked herself in the cubicle and shouted, "Not a word out there, okay?"

"Okay," I replied, then a woman I vaguely recognized, who worked in the payroll office, squeezed into the waiting area, and I chatted with her as loudly as I could, so Zsófia knew we had company.

The buffet was plentiful, varied, and welcome. I'd only had cheese and bread for lunch, so engrossed in Valentin's otherworld of warriors and bloodshed had I become. To be frank, the amount of carnage in his work didn't exactly stimulate the appetite.

I didn't really need Laszlo's kind explanations of the dishes on offer; due to my many visits to various butcher shops over the past weeks they were all pretty familiar. The obligatory steaming goulash, crisply roasted chicken dusted with paprika, glistening mounds of soft polenta, and perfectly spiced cabbage rolls all found their way into my rumbling tummy, and I even managed to squeeze in a couple mouthfuls of apple strudel with whipped cream. I thanked my stars I'd worn an elasticated waistband.

As we ate and drank our fill—I was glad I'd made the change from beer to iced tea, because I'd have exploded otherwise—I couldn't help but wonder about Zsófia's own relationship with alcohol and drugs. If her mother had been drinking heavily for a year or so maybe Zsófia had become accustomed to someone she loved downing a bottle or two of wine each day; I noticed she, like her mother, glugged her drinks rather than sipping them. It made me recall the time my now-late grandmother told me to look after myself when I started dating Angus: "It's not what he drinks, it's how he drinks it," she'd said, rather enigmatically. As time passed I realized she was right; having grown up the daughter of a pub landlord, I guessed she'd seen her fair share of people who drank in many different ways and, in Angus's case, she'd nailed it. Was I seeing the evidence that maybe Alexa's love of booze was something her daughter had inherited? Or was I merely witnessing a young girl blowing off some steam at an event that had been organized with the sole purpose of encouraging conviviality? I hoped it was the latter.

As the gypsy violinist who'd been playing throughout dinner rounded the end of our table I saw a light of recognition fill his eyes. Zsófia mouthed a warning at him, placing her hands in a praying position. He smiled almost imperceptibly. He didn't stay at our table for more than two minutes and, despite his skills, I was grateful, because I'd just about reached my fill of dramatic, tragic violin for the night. My watch, and the familiar sights gliding past the windows for the second time, told me it wouldn't be long before the boat docked at its berth.

"I must leave you ladies for a moment," said Laszlo, and we both allowed him to kiss our hands elaborately as he disappeared between the tables.

"You know the violinist?" I asked Zsófia.

"He's a friend of my great-aunt Klara. In fact, I think he might even be related to her. He's Zoltán, and he's been doing this forever. He's won medals. He's got real Roma blood in him, like Klara."

I jumped in. "Your mother said when your grandmother Ilona escaped from Hungary in 1956, her brother Tamás was left behind and that he became an informant during the Communist era. Do you think he would have escaped too if he could, or was he a true believer in the socialist ways?"

With her face glowing in the warm, humid atmosphere, and her perfectly applied red lipstick almost removed by her food, Zsófia Takács looked younger than her twenty years at that moment. She looked terribly vulnerable, despite her coiffed updo and retro-glam dinner dress.

"I don't know," she answered gloomily. "Until last weekend, I thought I knew everything about my family, but it seems I don't know much at all. No one had ever said anything to me about what Tamás did before then. When Mama told you, that was the first time she'd mentioned it. Ever. I never knew why I wasn't supposed to see them. It was just a rule Mama never explained. He and Klara haven't said anything about it either. Mama and Uncle keep everything bottled up. I thought that was normal and didn't question it. I thought it was all because of Grandmother's murder. But I'm beginning to realize that Tamás and Klara have their own secrets too. Maybe no one ever talked to me about anything because there are so many secrets in our family." She cupped her chin in her hands and leaned toward me across the table. "Secrets are horrible. They are so foolish, too. No one was ever helped by keeping a secret."

"You've asked me to keep quite a few," I reminded her.

"Yes, but they are important secrets."

"I suppose it all depends on perspective," I replied. I spotted Laszlo making his way back to our table. "Come on, we'll have time enough to discuss this tomorrow, at your home, over lunch. I'll see you there, right?" I stood.

Flashing a brief smile at me, Zsófia also stood, then she tilted her head coquettishly at the returning Laszlo, saying, "You said you'd walk me home?"

Laszlo became three inches taller and glowed. "But of course. It would be my honor."

They departed toward the cloakroom, and I was left alone. Irritatingly, this made me an easy target for the dawdling Patrik Matyas, who made a beeline for me, his eyes glittering conspiratorially. I was trapped—I couldn't leave without my coat, and the line wasn't getting any shorter, it seemed. I cursed my lack of forward planning, and decided to endure the man's presence with as much good grace as I could summon.

I joined the line, and he joined me. We exchanged pleasantries about the food, the sights, the violinist's talents. He was being obsequious, but I could cope with that. I didn't even gag when he began to wring his bony hands, Uriah Heep-like, as he described the delightful conversations he'd had with the dean. I made all the right noises in all the right places in our fairly one-sided chat. Then he crossed a line.

"I see you're becoming quite friendly with the Takács girl," he said smarmily. "You should be careful. I've told you about her—she's dangerous to know."

The man seemed to flutter with delight at the merest hint of scandal. I didn't want to betray Zsófia, or her family, but I felt the right thing to do would be to press him on the matter. I believed I would have done it even if I hadn't known the girl as well as I did.

"You say Zsófia's made accusations that have ruined a man's career, Patrik. I must say I feel it's highly unprofessional to gossip with colleagues about students. If that's normal practice here at the HUB, I have to say I don't care for it."

"It must be the same at your university," replied the man, sounding surprised I'd spoken so abruptly. Avid gossipers never seem to think what they do is wrong, I have found.

"No, it's not. At least, it's not in the circles with which I am familiar. A person's reputation is a delicate thing. It's not to be smeared in the public arena when you have no facts to back up your accusations. Unguarded words can damage a person's entire life. You told me you weren't even sure she was the student involved, yet you continue to press the matter. Why is that, Patrik? Surely, as a psychologist, you would expect me to question whether that says more about you and your personality than that of the person about whom you are speaking?"

I reached the front of the line then, and handed my ticket and a tip to the small, round woman who'd spent the past few hours behind the wooden counter of the tiny cloakroom. Patrik didn't respond with words; instead he looked at me with a mixture of shock and pity. Grabbing my coat, I pulled it on with a swift motion and moved aside to allow the person behind me to step forward.

"Forgive me, Patrik, I need to get back to my apartment as quickly as I can. I have a date with my husband to connect via Skype in—" I glanced at my watch, "less than an hour. I need to get myself a cab and get home. I expect I'll run into you at the HUB next week. Good night."

I escaped as quickly as I could, feeling I needed shower.

Official Reports

I CHANGED INTO MY SNUGGLY, chocolate-brown wrap before curling up on the sofa to talk to Bud. I couldn't get warm, and wondered if I was coming down with something; maybe all of the freeze-sweat cycles of the evening, and mixing with a hundred souls, some of whom were nursing winter colds, was about to take its toll. I hoped not. I didn't have time to be sick.

When Bud's face popped up on my screen I could tell he was way ahead of me; red-rimmed eyes, an already pink-tipped nose, and a general pallor announced his sorry, infected state before his croaky, nasal tones confirmed it. We commiserated with each other, and both agreed on having just a quick chat. Having established the state of his parents, I asked, "Any news about the Seszták case?" Bud visibly bucked up a little.

"I have to admit I haven't gotten around to doing much about it, what with Mom and all, but Jack White's at it like a terrier. He's great, Cait. I couldn't have a had a better mentor, or friend and colleague, and now he's pulled through for us again, just like he did when we were mixed up with all that business in Mexico. To be honest, I don't think he needed much of a push to revisit the case, and he seems to be—well, I guess 'enjoying it' isn't the right thing to say, but you know what I mean. He called me last night, before this bug thing knocked me sideways, so I was able to take down some good notes. But I haven't had the time or energy to type them up, so how about I read them to you now?"

"If you're up to it, and you've got time."

"Yeah, now's as good a time as any. Mom and Dad are having lunch.

Ready? Okay, here we go. Most of the senior guys who worked the case with Jack are dead now, so he's only managed to track down one fellow junior officer of the time. They've compared their recollections, which won't be as detailed as the sort of thing you could come up with, but I think it's worth getting the extra point of view. Everything we have so far is accurate, as far as they can tell, and they agreed the only key fact not released to the press was the belief that a rock was used to kill Ilona Seszták. After Jack joined the Vancouver PD, this other guy stayed on, and he confirmed the case was never closed, but they kept following tips, especially a year later, when they did a reconstruction of the known events. They even had a woman dress up like the victim and mix with the crowds at the next convocation, hoping she might jog someone's memory. Jack's old colleague said it was quite a getup, by the way. Reckoned Ilona modeled her look on Zsa Zsa Gabor. Seems a few students came forward with recollections of possible sightings on the day of the crime, but that was it. All dead ends. Of course, a lot of people who were there a year earlier wouldn't have been there for the reconstruction, but they thought it was worth a try. The husband did an appeal for information, and they used some pretty new-for-the-day techniques, but this is 1976 we're talking about, so no social media to use, or anything like it, of course."

Bud paused to wipe his nose so I took the chance to observe, "It's a shame. This is just the sort of case, where young people might have been witnesses, when social media could have made a difference. At the party tonight you've no idea how many of the students were sitting next to each other, all the while texting or taking photos to post to their accounts. It's a different world now, isn't it? Imagine the wealth of information an investigation like this could have garnered if everyone had been using their cameras and maybe snapping shots of Ilona Seszták on the day of her death. Oh—now that's an idea! I'll get in touch with the folks at UVan to find out if there was an official photographer on the day who might have got some candid shots of the proceedings."

My poor husband didn't look at all well, so I waited while he finished attending to his nose, then I allowed him to continue. "Don't bother, the RCMP thought of that, and they worked through everything they could get their hands on. Jack and his mate think the shots might still be in the file, but he recalls they put a special team to work on just the photos—working out who everyone was, and discounting most of the people in them."

"Ah well, it was worth mentioning."

"It was. Moving on—my information is that no other crime similar to this took place in the immediate vicinity within the ten years surrounding 1976, so there was no suspicion of any connection with any other cases. Apparently we were right to think they gave the husband a long, hard look, but they couldn't place him outside the family home during the hours in question. Same thing for the son and daughter, despite the fact the son popped up on their radar some time later."

"Would those be the times his sister Alexa mentioned to me?"

"Seems that way. Jack's going to follow up on that front. Sounds like petty theft, no violence, but possession too. This was before the days when BC bud was the province's biggest illegal cash crop, and almost a gang commodity. Way before people started to come here to do 'Vansterdam' tours of the cannabis scene. The first pot-festival was held in Edmonton back in 1977, and I know it was something many of us spent a lot of time and effort tackling in our daily routines here. But your Valentin Seszták never served time."

"How did you manage to find that out? You don't still have access to police records, surely?"

Bud managed a smile. "I don't, but I know quite a few people who do."

"Rule bending by my law-abiding, justice-serving husband?"

"All for a good cause, Cait. All for a good cause."

"Granted. I am guessing the father and son alibi each other on the night in question, the daughter too, right?"

Bud looked surprised. "The kid sister? Both ex-cops agreed she was never seriously considered. The strength it would have taken to lift a heavy rock then bash in the woman's skull precludes a thirteen-year-old female. Indeed, Jack said the son was so weedy they didn't think even he'd have had the strength required to deliver the wound the mother had."

I visualized Valentin's wasted body. "He's rail-thin, even now, though he looks like he might have been wiry when he was young. Both he and his sister are tall, but you're right, they don't look strong. Anything more?"

"Not yet. We're not going to know more until Tuesday at the earliest, because Monday's November 11, so it's a day off here—though not for a caregiver like me, of course, or for serving cops, but it's not the time to bother folks with stuff like this. Do you get a day off there?"

"No, it's not a day off, but I will be going out for dinner on Monday."

"Again?" Bud sounded surprised.

"Yes. I'm off to Vajdahunyad Castle for an evening of goose and wine. It's St. Martin's Day, which is a big deal here, and the HUB is marking the day as part of its year of celebration for its anniversary."

"Enjoy," said Bud halfheartedly. "The thought of either right now makes me want to heave," he added feebly, and we said our goodbyes quickly.

When I was alone again, I realized I'd better get some pills into my system if I had any hope of staving off the lurgies, and get as good a night's sleep as I could. I wanted to be up and reading as early as possible, so I had some milk, took some tablets, and wore my wrap to bed. Socks too.

A few hours later I was wide awake, propped up on my pillows, and halfway through the fifth book of the Bloodline Saga; sleep had eluded me, and I'd become so annoyed with all my tossing and turning that I'd decided it was better to give in and get on with my reading. By 4:15 AM I was done, in more ways than one; I'd reached the end of the book, though not the end of Valentin's tales, and I was absolutely exhausted. I finally understood why it seemed half the world was awaiting the final book with rabid anticipation—VS Örsi had provided some wicked cliffhangers at the end of book five. I napped, off and on, until around nine, then dragged myself to the bath and soaked for an hour in the small tub. It helped a little, but there's no substitute for sleeping soundly, so I found myself in a state of torpor as I left the apartment, and not really looking forward to my lunch date at all.

I knew it would take me almost an hour to get to Zsófia's home, so allowed myself time to make the journey with ease, and I was glad I'd already bought some wine and flowers to take with me, because I just wasn't in the mood for shopping. The wine had cost about a third of the price of the flowers, which I'd left resting in the fridge overnight so they'd look fresh when I presented them to my hostess. What I hadn't planned on was the torrential, icy rain, and the crush on the metro, so I arrived at the Andrassy Avenue house soaked, the flowers looking almost as bedraggled as me, wanting to knock back the entire bottle of wine. I pulled the handle that made a bell sound inside the imposing building and waited. And waited. I rang again. Nothing. Then I heard a gut-wrenching scream from above me.

Saying Something Different

AS I PEERED TOWARD THE upper stories of the building from where the scream had emanated, I saw Valentin hanging out of a window, flailing his arms. Alexa was leaning out of a window below him, shouting up at her brother.

"What will people think, Val? Get back inside, right now. You'll catch your death of cold." Alexa looked down at me. "Cait? Nice to see you. I'll be down in a minute."

Both she and her brother disappeared, and I waited at the front door. One of the oddest aspects of the entire incident was that Alexa hadn't acted as though anything out of the ordinary had happened. Maybe Valentin regularly screamed like a banshee from his rooms? I wondered how that went down with the neighbors.

By the time Alexa opened the door and I made my way into the entry hall, I'd managed to compose myself, and I handed her the hostess gifts I'd brought without mentioning Valentin at all. Inwardly, I was delighted when Alexa explained that Valentin had been determined to discover if a person's head would be sufficiently protected in a battle by a certain sort of helmet and had been thrashing a mannequin about in his rooms, screaming with bloodlust as he did so. As she spoke, we made our way to the salon upstairs, and I wondered if her reaction to the whole situation was so calm because she was used to her brother's little "experiments."

Having expected my arrival, Alexa was able to offer a wide array of alcoholic beverages when I was seated. I went with a gin and tonic. She did likewise. I hadn't expected to be alone with Alexa, and her manner and topics of discussion signaled she didn't want to begin our conversation where we had left off a week earlier. Instead she asked me to tell her about the previous night's riverboat trip, which I did in as entertaining a manner as possible, and without mentioning anything about her family.

When Zsófia finally joined us—she'd been delayed at the Gellért Spa—she listened impassively as the tale of Valentin's play-battle was retold by her slightly irritated mother. This allowed me to be more certain my original judgment was correct—what they saw as normal behavior was way beyond what anyone not related to Valentin Seszták might consider usual. I realized I'd have to take that onboard as I made my assessment of the man as a suspect in his mother's murder.

With his experiment having tired him, Valentin would eat in his rooms with Martin, I was told, so we three women made our way to a dining room that adjoined the salon where we'd been sitting.

The setting was grand, to say the least; opulent draperies at tall windows, inlaid wood floors, mirrors along the interior walls, and a highly polished table of massive proportions with three places set at one end. The elaborate table-settings, floral decorations, and ravishing display of fruits as a centerpiece made me suspect Alexa had some help about the place other than Valentin's nurses. I was proved right when a young woman arrived bearing food on a large tray, which she deposited on a long, inlaid sideboard with gold ormolu trim. Alexa thanked her, then rose. Zsófia and I followed her to the food and helped ourselves, buffet-style, to roasted goose and root vegetables.

With a mounded plate in front of each of us, the conversation resembled what I'd expect in any polite company, for about ten minutes. Then Alexa dropped something of a bombshell.

"Cait, there's no question your visit here last week has opened old wounds, for both my brother and myself. I decided not to ignore what happened, so I've been speaking to Valentin about our mother's death, when that's been possible." She paused, and looked first at her daughter, then me. "Zsófia has also confessed to me she begged you to look into this matter, Cait. Is that correct?"

So, the cat was out of the bag and running around the dining room. "She did," I replied calmly.

Alexa reached for her glass of wine and swigged. "I love my darling daughter very much, but, on this occasion, I have had to tell her I think she acted improperly. It wasn't a good idea to go behind my back. Maybe I am to blame for Zsófia feeling she had to ask an outsider to get involved. I haven't been very open about her grandmother and grandfather. Discussing the matter makes me very unhappy."

"That's perfectly understandable," I dared.

Alexa's glare didn't suggest she welcomed my opinion. "Understandable or not, I can see why knowing nothing would make Zsófia want to know everything. But it is still a tragedy, and it still cuts deep—for me and Valentin. As such, and upon sober reflection, I believe the family would now prefer it if you would step down, Cait, and put the matter to one side. We're all going to move on and not allow it to blight our lives any more than it already has."

Zsófia and I both paused, each of us with a forkful of food poised in midair. I especially wondered how "sober" the reflection had been on Alexa's part; the fact she'd already polished off half the bottle of wine at her elbow, whereas Zsófia and I had barely touched our glasses, spoke volumes.

"Mama, you cannot be serious," said Alexa's daughter impatiently, placing her cutlery onto her plate with a clatter. "When we discussed this last night, you said you didn't care if I looked into my grandmother's death. Those were your very words. You 'didn't care' what I did."

Having lived with a person whose memory was often ravaged by too much liquor, I recognized the expression that flashed across Alexa's face; she couldn't recall exactly what she'd said to her daughter the night before, and experience was telling her she'd never be able to retrieve the lost words from the black hole where they'd sunk without trace.

Zsófia wasn't letting up. "How can you have changed your mind about something so important, so quickly? It's not possible. What's happened since last night that makes you say this, now?"

I wanted to take Zsófia to one side and try to get her to understand the vagaries of alcoholism; the mood swings, the mind-boggling shifts in opinion, the forgetfulness, the desperate desire to be understood and loved . . . the passion that tips over into violence in a millisecond. It seemed at least that Alexa wasn't given to violent outbursts—though who knew what had gone on over the years. I judged that if last night's version of Alexa hadn't cared, and today's did, it was the woman who'd been drinking all day who was dismissive, and the one who was still in the early stages of her daily intake who was worried. Which was interesting. Unusually for me, I kept my thoughts to myself. The dreadful tension between mother and daughter wasn't going to be broken by a pithy quip.

Zsófia snapped, "Cait and her husband have already put a great deal of effort into this for us. And anyway—why *wouldn't* you want to know who killed your mother? I'd want to know who did it if someone killed you."

Alexa placed her knife and fork down silently, and glared at her daughter. "I've thought about it at length, and I have discussed it with Valentin. We both agree this is not something we want to revisit. This is *my* mother we're talking about, Zsófia; you really know nothing of her other than seeing some old family photos. You only know what I've chosen to tell you about her. You're my daughter, Zsófia, and I will speak to you about your grandmother more when the time is right. But for now, thank you, Cait, for all you've done, but I'd like you to just stop." She emptied her glass.

As both women's eyes turned to me I said, "I don't think I can do that."

Alexa roughly wiped her mouth with her napkin. "I would prefer it if you did." His tone was fake polite.

"I don't mean I *won't*, I mean I *can't*," I said. "You see, Alexa, my husband's already been briefed by two retired police officers who worked the original case and it really is true that cops who fail to catch a killer are rather like terriers who've failed to catch a rat. They're off down that hole again now, and I don't think they'll reemerge without their quarry."

"I wish my daughter had never asked you to get involved," said Alexa, fuming. "Zsófia, you shouldn't have done what you did. Now how will we stop all this?" Her voice was rough with anger.

"We can't, Mama," said Zsófia. I noted a hint of satisfaction in her voice. "If we support Cait in what she's doing for us, we could all finally understand why Grandmother was killed, and who killed her."

Alexa stood, the feet of her chair sliding silently across the beautifully inlaid wood floor. She gripped the edge of the table. I wondered if she needed to steady herself. Her eyes were darting, and she looked flushed. It frightened me because Angus used to look much the same before he showed me the part of his personality that was most vicious. I instinctively looked around for possible missiles—sadly, there were too many; crystal-ware, cutlery, even dishes and plates might be about to fly. Had it been Angus standing there, drunk and seething, that would have been my assumption. I wondered how it would go with Alexa.

My heart stopped thumping when the woman gathered herself and retook her seat, looking tired. "Oh my darling child, you don't know what you're saying. Isn't it bad enough your grandmother was murdered? Isn't that enough to hide from the world, let alone the truth about who killed her? Knowing who did it, or why they did it, will not bring her back."

I found Alexa's words fascinating. Zsófia looked puzzled, and a silence ensued.

After a few moments, Zsófia's question, "How's your goose, Cait?" surprised me.

"Delicious, thank you," I replied, returning my attention to the meal on my plate. Taking my chance to move away from the subject of a reinvestigation I didn't think I could stop, I dared, "Are you the cook here, Alexa? This meal is wonderful."

Alexa's voice sounded distant, "No, we have an adequate woman who keeps us well-fed. Keeps Zsófia well-fed in any case, as you can plainly see. I eat more moderately than she does."

Zsófia glared at her plate and shoved a forkful of roasted carrot into her mouth. I felt embarrassed for the poor girl. She wasn't out of shape, just well-covered. And if Alexa thought her daughter overweight, I wondered how she judged me, because I had a good thirty pounds on the girl. I took the barb personally, but decided to try to defuse the situation by saying, "I'll be having goose again tomorrow night at the St. Martin's Day celebrations at Vajdahunyad Castle. Is today your celebration of that feast?"

"Yes. Ana, our cook, insists we do it every year," grumbled Alexa. She pushed her half-eaten meal away and refilled her empty glass, hugging the bottle after she'd poured. "I don't know why I let her do it. I don't like goose at all. She's very religious, so we do it for her."

The Alexa with whom I was sharing a tense luncheon seemed to be a totally different person than the one I'd met a week earlier, and I dwelt on why her attitude toward me had changed so markedly. It couldn't have been anything to do with me specifically, I reasoned, because I hadn't told her about the slight progress in the investigation back in Canada. So it had to be the simple fact that someone, anyone, was rooting about in her family's background. As she'd said, of course it would be something about which she'd be sensitive, but Zsófia had hit the nail on the head when she'd asked her mother why she wouldn't want to find out what had really happened that night back in 1976.

We all ate in silence—well, I did. Alexa folded her arms and stared at the glass and bottle on the table in front of her, and Zsófia pushed her food around her plate. I felt I was the only one not acting like a sulky teenager, and was wondering distractedly about how my visit would progress, when the door to the room was flung open by Martin, the nurse.

"Mr. Valentin wants to join you all for lunch. I have told him no, as you said, and have locked his door. He is throwing furniture against it and says he is being starved. Would you like me to sedate him now?"

The two Takács women looked at the man as though he was asking a question they'd heard many times before. For all I knew, they had. Confusion when faced with familiar places or tasks, forgetting to eat, or forgetting one has eaten, and the sad inability to recognize those who love you—and sometimes becoming angry with them because one believes them to be strangers—are just some of the challenging symptoms that can accompany the development of several forms of dementia, Alzheimer's included. I wondered how my hostess would react.

"How does he seem, otherwise?" asked Alexa. "Has he already eaten?"

"As usual, and no," replied the nurse, all business.

"Would you mind if Valentin joined us, Cait?" asked Alexa.

"Of course not." *So long as he doesn't hurl stuff at me.*

"Very well then, tell him to come. And bring him yourself. I don't want him getting lost again, like last evening."

I steeled myself for what might turn out to be an even more difficult luncheon than it already was.

A few minutes later Valentin joined us. He was wearing a dark suit, white shirt, navy tie, and had bare feet. He arrived in a happy mood, helped himself to the food, and joined us at the table, where Alexa ceded her place to him and moved to sit in one of the dozen empty seats beside her daughter.

Eating his goose with gusto, Valentin looked across the table at me and said, "Hi, I'm Valentin. Who are you? Friend of hers?" He stabbed his fork toward his niece, who answered on my behalf.

"This is Professor Cait Morgan, Uncle. She teaches at the University of Vancouver usually, but she's visiting Budapest for a while. She was here last week. Do you remember?"

Valentin paused, stared at me, then returned to his meal. "No. I don't. Sorry. I forget things. It's expected. But Vancouver? I remember that place. Great weed. Too many cops. And . . ." He dropped his fork onto his plate and pulled a pack of cigarettes from his jacket pocket. "Got a light, anyone?"

"You don't smoke, Valentin. Where did you get those?" Alexa sounded tired.

"I do smoke. I must. I've always smoked. You've always smoked, too. They were in my pocket. Did I give up?"

"You did, dear. They must be years old. Give them to me and I'll see to them." Alexa seemed to be operating on autopilot.

He handed the pack to his sister, who stuffed them into her own pocket. Looking directly at me, she said, "He forgets that he gave up years ago."

The man stared at his cutlery as though he wasn't sure what to do with it, then picked up his knife and fork and began to mash his food together on his plate—not the easiest thing to do with roast goose. "It was in the autumn, I recall," said Valentin between mouthfuls of mushed-up vegetables. "She went out. It was raining a lot."

"Who, dear?" Alexa was trying to sound patient.

"Ilona. Kristóf was at home, he was sick. Had a terrible cold. He blamed the students for passing germs to him. She went out to meet a man, and never came home again. That was in Vancouver. At the university. Where you're from." He stabbed his fork in my direction. "I know I'm right. I haven't forgotten that."

"Who did Ilona go to see?" asked Zsófia urgently, drawing a glare from her mother.

"Just a guy. She was always doing that." Valentin sounded almost jolly.

Alexa looked scandalized and leaned toward her brother. "Don't say that about Ilona, Val. Not in front of Zsófia. That's a horrible thing to say." She emptied the last of the bottle of wine into her glass, spilling some as she did so.

It struck me as odd that, unlike most people—who tend use the full name of a person they are admonishing—Alexa seemed to shorten her brother's when she was angry with him.

"What do you know?" mocked Valentin with the level of disdain siblings reserve specifically for each other. "You were just a kid. I remember you then. Daddy's girl, you were. Always following him about, doing whatever he asked you to do. Brownnoser. He didn't like me. He hated me. Oh, but he loved you." Valentin held his chest, mock-swooned, and put on a singsongy voice. "His ray of sunshine. The apple of his eye. All those loving things he'd say to you. Remember?" He dropped his fork onto his plate. "I do. I remember. Funny that, eh? For a guy who's losing himself piece by piece, I can remember that. Ironic, eh? But what did he ever say to me? Nothing loving, nothing supportive, nothing encouraging. Just criticism. Carping on and on about how I could do better. How lucky I was."

"It wasn't just you who got it in the neck, Val. Ilona always nagged at me about that, too," said Alexa angrily. "I was so *lucky* to be growing up in Canada, not Hungary. I could live *free and easy* in Canada, not like back here, where everyone had to follow rules and watch what they said and did. Always going on and on about it."

Valentin picked up his fork again and shoved mush around on his plate. It was almost empty. "Don't remember that," he said. Then he winked at me and added, "Doesn't mean it didn't happen, of course. Avoided each other like the plague, didn't we, Alexa?"

His sister shrugged. With about five years between me and my own sister, I could imagine the dynamics between these siblings when they were both teens.

Valentin pushed his plate away and let out a belly laugh. "You were a lanky girl, Alexa, all teeth and greasy hair. Spotty, too. Couldn't have pulled a muscle, let alone a boy. Even so, you were the favorite. When you were born it was as though they stopped seeing me. Like I ceased to exist. Especially for him. He always looked at you with love in his eyes. He only ever looked at me to know what I was doing. Always asking *why* I did what I did. Never asked you. Loved you. Quizzed me."

"I think that's unfair, Val. Ilona and Kristóf were *our* parents. They loved and watched over us both," said Alexa petulantly. "They saved us from seeing the true ugliness of the world, which I also do for my baby princess."

"You were a whiny little kid," snapped Valentin. "You wouldn't have been aware Ilona was a woman who liked men. Young men especially. I always knew when she was going off to meet someone; she had a particular perfume she'd wear. It was heavy. Musky. Like an animal's smell. And she'd put on her lipstick a special way. Lipstick, then powder on her lips, then lipstick again. That's what she did when she was going out for a good time. Ordinary days it was just one layer of lipstick. I used to watch her do it all, sitting there in her slip and stockings at her dressing table, anointing herself." He paused as if looking back down the decades. "Always left their bedroom door open when she was getting dressed. Clouds of hairspray would billow out into the hallway, hanging in the air forever, it seemed. I remember how it smelled. Sickly. Acrid. I always knew what she was up to. Kristóf did too. You didn't. You were too little to understand."

The exchange was fascinating and revealing, in more ways than one. I took my chance to find out more. "Is that why the original queen in your first two books paints her arms with red dye, then covers them with soil that's been blessed by the priest, then more red dye, before she goes to watch over a battle?" I asked Valentin.

"Whoever you are, you're clever," said Valentin, smiling. "Read my books, have you? Then I guess you know all about my family already." He waved his arms in the air, indicating himself, Alexa, and Zsófia.

"I think I do," I said, wondering what the reaction would be. "I was talking to your niece the other evening about the way your books could be read as more than just a fantasy, and I've found them to be intriguing. Am I correct in thinking you are both Zoth, the eldest son, and Frag, the middle one?"

Valentin stared at me, nodding slowly, a smile of admiration on his thin, pale face. "Indeed. I am both the scheming, evil son, and the pure son. The warrior, and the man of learning. I am the brawny, battling one, and the effete scholar. The one with the strength of arms, and the one with the strength of mind. You saw that, did you?" I nodded.

"I didn't see it, Uncle," said Zsófia. "I haven't read your work properly at all, it seems. I thought I knew it well, but I didn't understand it, did I? Who am I? Will you tell me?" She leaned forward, apprehension and hope on her pale, innocent face.

Valentin's expression softened as he gazed at his niece. "You, like me, are more than one character, my dear. Who do you think you might be? Who do you hope you are?"

Zsófia spoke quietly. "I hope I am Elba, but maybe I am Vanna too?" She'd named the most sympathetic female character first—a young woman of humble stock given to the third son of the family as a child bride, who'd then helped humanize the brutal young man by loving and nurturing him. Next she'd named the siren with the liquid voice every warrior desired, but none could possess, because she was a priestess of the weird religious cult they all followed.

Valentin smiled, looking suddenly tired. "Very good. I bet my sister can't pick herself out, though. Nor Kristóf. He'll never guess who he is."

Alexa moved uneasily in her seat. "Oh, Valentin, Kristóf's been dead for years. You remember that, I know you do. Besides, you're kidding, right? You don't mean to tell me the whole world is reading about our family? Not really." Her eyes began to dart about as the thought nibbled into her consciousness, and I could tell her mind was racing. "I can't believe you'd do that. What about Ilona's death? Oh!" She stood abruptly, scraping her chair across the antique wooden floor. "The queen is killed in the second book. And the *way* she dies! What have you done, Val? Val—what does that mean? Tell me!"

Zsófia tried to calm her mother, who was pacing about, muttering to herself. Eventually she said, "Uncle Valentin, don't be cruel to poor Mama. You have made her worry. Please explain what you have written."

Valentin stood, with some difficulty. "I'm tired now. Thinking about then and now, and there and here, is too much. I'm in too many places and times all at once. I should sleep." He pushed the little button hanging beneath his tie.

Zsófia moved to help him, but Martin arrived almost immediately.

"Mr. Valentin will sleep now," explained the nurse, helping the suddenly feeble Valentin.

"Do you have any pages for me to work on, Uncle?" asked Zsófia as the sagging man was being helped through the door. "Shall I come to collect them from you later?"

"It's done. All done. Finished it weeks ago," said Valentin weakly.

"But it can't be—I'm still editing the final battle scenes," said his niece, puzzled.

I saw Valentin's eyes twinkle when he turned to answer. "You think it will end with a great battle where everyone dies? Too simple, child. Those chapters come earlier. I have the rest written out. It's all finished."

"Let him sleep now," said Martin, and the two men left.

I'd stayed in my seat while all of this unfolded, and couldn't imagine we'd reconvene at the table, but I was wrong. When we were three once more, the two women sat and became lost in their own worries, contemplating new puzzles.

"I don't know where those chapters fit in," announced Zsófia after a few minutes. "I cannot imagine where he can take it all after that battle. There's almost no one left alive. The entire family's been decimated. There's only—oh, how clever. I wonder if . . ."

"That's of no consequence," snapped Alexa at her daughter. "What's important is what he's written about *us*. I'll admit I've only read his books once, when they were still just his handwritten manuscripts. I haven't really taken much notice of them since they were all published. Tell me, Zsófia, who am I? What does he say about Ilona and Kristóf?" She looked desperate. "Is Kristóf the king in the books, do you think? Is Ilona his first queen?" her eyes searched her daughter's face for an answer.

Zsófia furrowed her brow. "I think so. Or maybe Grandfather is the priest? Or the magician? Or am I being too literal about all this? Cait, you've read the books, what do you think?"

Their eyes turned to me, and I knew I was in a tricky position. Then I realized I had a great chance to find out more than Alexa might imagine about the circumstances surrounding her mother's death, so I decided to play along.

I knew I had to tread carefully to not reveal the secret of my eidetic memory, so I made an effort to sound much vaguer than I really was. "I think the king might well be Kristóf. Let's look at the evidence: he flees to lands far from his original home"—in my mind's eye I saw page

473 of book one telling of his decision to leave his homeland, then I ran through the next couple of chapters mentally, rapidly reliving the terrible journey he'd made with his wife across an unforgiving landscape in the dead of winter—"taking with him his young bride, and establishes himself in the new land, as ruler of all." *That's chapters eleven to sixteen in book one.* "He starts a family and rules with an iron will—through terror, not love." *Book two, chapters one to five.* "The queen is lusty, and dallies—and much more—with quite a few of the young men at the court." *Pages 335, 546, 681, 846, 932, 1056, and 1127 in book two.* "He tries to bully all of his sons into being warriors, even though two of them are far from warlike, and one, certainly, would rather be studious and thoughtful." The king's bullying ways were too numerous to recount, even to myself. "I do think this suggests Kristóf is the king, especially given what Valentin just told us about his father."

"The books are so very long and I got confused by them. But there is something I remember—the king ordered his first queen to be put to death," said Alexa staring into the bottom of her empty glass with dread in her voice.

"He did," I said quietly. "He had her tied to a stake and stoned by every woman in the town, then ordered her body chained behind a horse, to be dragged around the castle walls from sunup until sundown. Chapter twenty-six, book two." *It slipped out.*

Zsófia whispered, "Until now, I've always felt sorry for the horse in that part of the book, having to run all day like that. Now? Oh, Mama." She held her hand over her mouth, her eyes round with horror.

Alexa pushed her empty glass away from her and stuck out her chin. "That's just stuff Val made up, my darling child. Stop looking like that, Zsófia. Buck up. It's all rubbish."

"In the fourth book, the ghost of the queen comes back to haunt the king, and shows him her wounds. The wounds made by the stones,"

I said. "Might that be Valentin alluding to the time your father took you to see your mother's body, Alexa?"

The woman stood, grabbed the second bottle of wine that had been standing almost untouched between myself and her daughter, and filled her large glass. She drank it as though it were soda, and angrily wiped its red remnants from her lips with the back of her hand.

"Enough. That's it. I'll read his blessed books again. I'll have to. What more can there be in them?"

"I do have one question," I ventured. "Who do you think might be the model for the Listener, Alexa? The shadowy figure that never seems to sleep, hides in every corner, and hears every word. The character is never described physically, seems to be able to be in many places at once, and passes information to any and all parties. I've found the Listener to be a pivotal character in the entire saga. Was there someone in Valentin's, or your, early life who might have inspired that character?"

Alexa sagged into a chair. I was surprised she could manage even that. Her voice sounded distant as she replied, "There was a man who lived with us for some time. I don't know how long. It seemed like a very long time indeed. By the time Ilona died, he'd left. He went because of Valentin, I remember that much. Valentin didn't like him at all, and there were lots of times when I knew Ilona and Kristóf were arguing about him, but they'd stop when I came into the room. He always seemed to be where you didn't expect him to be, I remember. Maybe he made an impression on Valentin, and he put him into his books."

"You say he'd left by the time your mother was killed?" I pressed.

"Yes, a long time before," said Alexa airily. "Not the university, but our house. Kristóf said he'd found him a place in the halls of residence."

"Was he a student? The same age as your brother?"

She shook her head heavily. "Oh no, he was older. Like a man, not a boy. Always wore a suit or a sports coat. He was all grown up."

"I don't suppose you remember his name, do you, Alexa?"

Alexa burped, then slurred, "Of course I do. It was Mezey. Peter Mezey. He was from Budapest, like Ilona and Kristóf. He left. Suddenly he wasn't there."

I wondered if Bud might be able to find out more about this additional person in the family's home. It was possible this Peter Mezey was the lodger he'd told me about.

"Did the police question him at the time?" I knew this was something I could ask Bud about too.

Alexa looked vague. "I don't know. Why would they? By then he was just like anyone else living on campus. Just another man. I can't imagine my father would even have mentioned him. Why would he?"

"Do you recall when he arrived?" I didn't hold out much hope.

Alexa tried to focus on my face. "When he what? Oh. Yes. No, I don't know. Maybe he was with us for a year? Maybe less. I really don't know. I think he stayed on campus after Ilona died, but I don't know for how long." She slumped, then, almost immediately, seemed to rally. Her back straightened and she just about managed to control the movement of her upper body as she said loudly, "He could have killed her! Will you find out about him, Cait? Maybe *he* did it. I never thought of that idea before now. And tell me all about the people in his books. Do that too. Yes, that." Her eyes gleamed with what I judged to be relief.

I leaned forward and said, "You told me you didn't want me meddling in your family's affairs anymore." I felt it only fair to remind the woman she'd said as much just a couple of hours earlier.

Alexa shifted in her chair. Her daughter moved as if to save her from toppling, but she managed to keep herself upright. "Okay," Alexa mumbled with a sly grin, "you've got me. If Valentin is writing coded messages about my family, especially my little princess, in his books, and if they tell us something about who killed Ilona, then I guess I do want to know, after all. There might be clues in the books that point to that Peter guy. Or someone else. One thing's for damn sure," she made grand gestures as she spoke, her face working hard to form words, "if some geek living in his parents' basement is so into the books that he writes something online about my family, and manages to somehow link it all to Ilona's death—however much we're all sure no one knows who VS Örsi really is—I don't want to be in the dark and the last to know. So go ahead, Cait. Ask what you want. Dig all you can. You and your lovely husband in Canada." The sigh she let out shook her whole body. Her eyes were blank—I didn't know if that was because of the wine she'd consumed, or because she really didn't know what to think, or feel, anymore. "What can I do?" she said, completely without emotion.

I knew what I wanted, so I asked for it. "Zsófia, I'd like to read the manuscript for book six, if you have it."

"I do," said the girl, rising. "I think Uncle Valentin still has some surprises up his sleeve, if what he said here earlier is true, but I could bring it to you in the salon, if you'd like to read it now."

"That would be most helpful. And maybe, while I read it, you could gather together some old family photos and the like for me. It always helps me to see the people I'm researching."

"His books are too long; you'll be here for days. Zsófia, give it to her to take away." Alexa was becoming almost impossible to understand.

I looked at Zsófia and said quietly, "I am an extremely fast reader. I won't need more than a few hours. I'm happy to do it here, if that's okay with you."

"I'd prefer that," she whispered. Then, in her normal voice, she added, "Cait will come to my rooms to read it. We'll leave you in peace and quiet, Mama. Unless you'd like me to take you to lie down."

Thrashing arms dismissed us from the room, and I suspected Alexa would be asleep before we'd even climbed the stairs.

About four hours later I left the Takács/Seszták home and made my way back to my little apartment. I had a bag full of goodies to work with, and the entire final book to think through as I sat on the metro, then the bus. It had been quite a day.

Dinner Talk

THE FOLLOWING DAY SPED PAST, and almost before I knew it, I was getting into one of the buses they'd organized at the HUB to take us to the picturesque Vajdahunyad Castle. St. Martin's Day being such a big deal, this one had become an integral part of the celebrations marking the HUB's 380th, or possibly 360th—depending on whom you believed—anniversary. The original university had been established in 1633 in what is now Serbia, but it had moved to Budapest in 1653—hence the discussion about the number of years of existence the university could claim. The mirroring of my own university's peripatetic existence was not lost on me.

The castle sits in a city park, and as we approached it through the darkness, it looked for all the world like a medieval whimsy floating on a lake, its floodlit walls and turrets reflecting in still, ancient waters. In reality, it had been built in 1896 as part of an exposition that had celebrated one thousand years of the Hungarian State. Sometimes carefully constructed façades can trick us into believing a place is something it is not, and I was dwelling on that concept when a voice close by whispered my name and made me jump.

"Ah, Patrik, what a pleasant surprise," I said with a forced smile when I discovered it was him. Uttering the word "pleasant" required a particular effort.

As we walked—well, I walked, and he sort of minced and hopped, which was how he always propelled himself forward—it became clear the castle was a hodgepodge of architectural styles from different eras. I didn't know what to expect of the interior, and was pleasantly surprised by the large space where tables had been laid out around a gallery atop a wide staircase. I suspected it would be a rather drafty evening, but it wasn't too bad. Besides, I had Patrik's smile to keep me warm.

I decided I simply had to bite the bullet and accept his company for the entire dinner. As we all settled and chatted, and wine was poured, I decided upon my strategy; I put it into action as soon as the ceremonial carving of the goose had been performed by the HUB's chancellor, who opted for the 380th anniversary in his toast.

"Now that we have a chance to talk," I began, as conspiratorially as possible, "tell me all about your time in Canada. It must have been fascinating for you." I tucked into the plate of goose liver pâté in front of me, hoping it would be delightful, even if his company wasn't.

Patrik's chest swelled with pride. "Indeed it was. The academic culture there was a great change from that with which I was familiar. It was much more . . . open. That was it. Quite different."

"And you worked with Hollingsworth, you told me. I bet that's been a hard act to follow."

Patrik appeared to give my remark some thought. "Not so much. It was a pinnacle for me, of one sort, but my teaching has been rewarding in different ways."

"How so?"

"My students have excelled in their chosen fields, and I have set them on their path. That is as satisfying as taking the path myself."

I had to admit I agreed with him, and told him so. He'd put it elegantly, and I often told myself, while grading in the dead of a winter night, that what I was doing was worthwhile. I was surprised to discover I'd almost not noticed the main course of moist roast goose as I'd eaten it; Patrik and I had enjoyed a cogent conversation about the teaching life, as two colleagues. It was almost refreshing, and, as he spoke, I noted a light in his eyes I'd not seen before—the gleam of enthusiasm for the achievements of others. I wondered if my initial judgment of the man had been too harsh; maybe he just wasn't blessed with good social skills. Goodness knows Bud's told me on many occasions that mine are pretty appalling.

The dessert arrived, a glistening chocolate tart topped with a raspberry compote, and I was hoping I'd be able to accommodate it when Patrik said something that allowed me an opening to get onto the topics I'd wanted to press him about.

"I met some wonderful people when I was at your university. People from every part of the world, it seemed to me at the time," he said with a smile of reminiscence on his face.

I didn't miss a beat. "Did you know Professor Kristóf Seszták, by any chance?"

"Did you know him?" Patrik sounded puzzled and guarded.

Why didn't he just say yes or no? Any Hungarian on the UVan campus in those days would have known of, if not known, Seszták.

I aimed for "casually interested" when I replied, "He's quite famous at UVan for bringing the faculty of psychology from the HUB in the 1950s. It was quite a feat. It must have been difficult for all those people to leave their families behind and flee their country." I wondered if he'd bite. He did, but not as I'd expected.

"I was so young when all that happened," he said with an alarmingly coquettish smile. "I was only six years old when the Prague Spring uprising took place. With the exception of my short time in Canada, I didn't really know anything but Communism until I was in my forties." Was that a wistful look I spotted, or a pained one? "It was difficult for me to adjust."

I wondered which "adjustment" he was referring to. "Whatever is normal for us, when we are young, it helps us construct our life views and comfort zone," I said, hoping he'd be more forthcoming.

"You are correct, though we do not always see it that way. Since the Communists have left, my life has changed a great deal."

"For better, or worse?" I couldn't stop myself from asking.

Patrik hesitated only slightly before he said, "For the better, of course." He wasn't smiling anymore.

I decided to take my chance and said, "I understand Professor Seszták's wife was murdered not far from their home on the UVan campus itself. It was long before my arrival there, of course, but it's a case that's always fascinated me. Were you there at the time?"

A flicker of his right eyelid was his tell—I'd spotted it, and now it was as though he was winking, it was so obvious. "I heard about it."

It was the sort of reply that might have suggested he was nowhere near the university when Ilona Seszták was killed. I decided to play along as if that was what I believed.

"I bet you were glad to not be there at the time. It must be tragic to be caught up in a murder investigation."

He licked his lips just slightly before he said, "You should know."

My heart gave one almighty thump in my chest, and I stuffed a piece of chocolate tart into my mouth so I didn't have to speak for a moment. I tried to make my eyes smile. I didn't want this man to see he'd surprised me. Had the folks at the HUB checked me out before they'd invited me to visit? I reasoned that if they had, my head of department might have mentioned my arrest on suspicion of murder in the UK before I immigrated to Canada as part of some sort of "full disclosure" thing, but he also knew I'd been released. Since then, I'd been cleared by multiple Canadian law enforcement agencies as suitable to have access to their files. Surely if he'd mentioned one set of circumstances he'd have mentioned the other?

Wiping crumbs from my bosom-shelf, I decided to become Patrik's "victim," and whispered, "I expect you know all about my problems in the UK?" He raised his eyebrows above the frames of his spectacles, his mouth pursed, suggesting he did. "Well, although I was cleared—completely cleared, you understand—it was an upsetting experience.

I'd be grateful if you'd keep this between just the two of us. Unless, of course, everyone else at the HUB already knows."

His smile was small and sly. "Just the dean and I know of your troubles, I believe." He patted my hand. My skin crawled.

I feigned relief. "I'd be happy if it could stay that way, Patrik. Thank you. And I can tell you this, you missed nothing by being nowhere near the crime scene when that poor woman was killed."

"Less of the 'poor woman,' Cait. The professor's wife had something of a reputation around the campus. One she richly deserved."

"Really," I said, sounding as scandalized as possible. I leaned closer to my co-conspirator and hissed, "Details please." I even managed a little school-girlish giggle.

Hunching in, Patrik dropped his voice so I could barely hear him above the babble of the post-dinner chatter. "She wasn't a young woman, and she had grown children. One of them a son not much younger than me. But that didn't stop her. She made it clear she was interested in various men on campus." He paused and scanned our nearest tablemates. "It was a difficult situation. I was an innocent abroad—quite literally. I wanted to focus on my work, but she was a great . . . distraction. I didn't say anything to anyone at the time, of course. One must not speak ill of the dead."

I touched his arm in what I hoped he would take as the sympathetic act of a confidante. "Oh you poor thing," I gushed, "that must have been terrible for you. How embarrassing. And you say she had a son about your age? Did the son know his mother was pursuing you?"

Patrik puckered his entire face. "No. If I don't want someone to know something, they don't."

"Well done," I said, patting his arm the way I sometimes pat Marty's head when he's been a particularly good dog. "So you say she made a habit of chasing after young men? Do you think that might have been what got her killed? I believe they never solved the crime—at least, that's the gossip at the campus."

Patrik's eyes narrowed. "I thought you said you did not like gossip at your university."

Rats! "I meant when it comes to students, which I don't think is fair." I hoped I'd made a good catch. "But this is all ancient history." I forced myself to gush when I added, "I'm sorry, I don't mean to imply you are ancient . . . but . . . oh, I'm sure you know what I mean." My eyes pleaded with him for forgiveness. "My husband's also terribly keen for me to not gossip, you see—he doesn't like me to stick my nose in where it doesn't belong. He tells me this often. But I'd welcome any personal insights."

My colleague smiled like a naughty schoolboy. "I understand. Gossip can be divisive. But this was long ago, so what can it matter now? I was so young, and foolish, and some thought I cut quite a dashing figure."

I decided to rise to the bait. "You are still dashing, Patrik, and let's have less of the 'foolish' too. You must have been quite outstanding, even then, to have been accepted into Hollingsworth's team at UVan, and—thinking about it, and the times of which we are speaking—you must have received some extraordinary clearances from the Hungarian regime to be allowed to leave the country to study at all. How on earth did you manage that?" I hoped I'd played a convincing part, that he'd accept the flattery and give me the information I wanted.

Disappointingly, it seemed Patrik couldn't be so easily swayed. "You're right, I was always exceptionally bright, and Hollingsworth was happy to have me. As for going to Canada to study? Many tourists from all around the world came to Hungary during the 1970s. They opened the Hilton Hotel in the Castle District in 1976, and Hungarian students went to universities that were global centers of excellence throughout the Communist years. It wasn't so unusual. At that time education was seen as a linchpin in building a better world."

"You don't think it is now?" I couldn't resist.

Once again, the "normal" Patrik was back—the Patrik with the jovial, yet prudish expression. "I am an academic, Cait, like you, which means I have dedicated my whole life to furthering man's understanding of humanity. In my case, I especially focus on man's understanding of how he sees himself, and then presents himself in the company of others. Of course I believe education is critical to humanity's future. I would hope you do too. Or maybe you're in it for the money."

I laughed so loudly I almost choked. "The money, Patrik? You must be joking. I don't know of anywhere we academics are well paid."

Once again I saw that little flicker of his eyelid. He pursed his lips then replied quietly, "I know we are paying you thirty thousand Canadian dollars to be here with us. I think that's being well paid."

"I beg your pardon?" I couldn't make sense of what the man had just said. "You think I'm being paid thirty thousand dollars to work here for less than a full semester? What makes you think that?"

"I saw the dean sign the invoice with my own eyes." Patrik looked shocked that I would doubt him. "I agree the payment was to your university, not to you in person, but I assumed they would pass on the payment. This would be correct."

I was beginning to feel quite warm. "It would be correct, but it's not what has happened. I haven't received anything above my normal pay for my time here, Patrik. And that's a great deal less than the amount you stated. It seems my head of department has been less than forthcoming about the amount of money I'm worth in the marketplace. He appears to be using my skills and reputation to pad the departmental coffers."

Patrik sat silently for a moment while I fumed. I was absolutely incensed, but didn't dare utter a word. Once again I found myself seething about something in the company of this obsequious little man. But I was glad he'd let that little nugget slip.

I poked the last crumbs of my dessert around my plate, and Patrik seemed to be hunting for something to say. He pulled his wallet from his jacket and flashed a photograph of a woman with a good set of teeth she wasn't afraid to show off and four children who might well have had the biggest heads I'd ever seen on human beings.

"Yours?" I asked, as winningly as possible.

He gushed and beamed. It hadn't occurred to me Patrik would be married, let alone the father of four. My surprise must have shown, because he giggled softly and whispered, "Yes, the four children often shock people. I married late in life, but we are Catholic so—well, you understand, I am sure." He pursed his little mouth.

"Did that prove to be a challenge during the years of occupation? I understand religion was frowned upon at that time."

Patrik glanced around and moved even closer. "People find ways to follow their faith, even under tyrants."

I grappled with this new vision of Patrik. "I'm sure they do," was my glib response.

"You cannot possibly understand what it is like to live in this country, this city," he said, snapping the wallet closed and shoving it back into his inside pocket. "You'll be here for a little while and think you know the place, the people. You won't. As I don't really understand the experience of growing up and living in a country like Canada, or a city like Vancouver. You people take everything for granted."

I gave his words some thought, and felt my perspective on my entire time in Budapest shift in that instant. Other than the bizarre antics of the Seszták/Takács family, I'd focused on everything familiar—the similarities between the university life I knew in Canada and now in Hungary had been at the fore. But I was truly a stranger in an unknown land, adrift within a culture I didn't really understand at all; one built upon a complex mixture of Magyar nationalism, proudly free

Europeanism, and a still-seething anger at the hardships of the recent past. Hungarians had proved themselves an adaptive race throughout centuries of invasion and tyranny. Not unlike the Welsh, I supposed, though I couldn't pretend to truly understand the Hungarian brand of resilience in the face of adversity.

Even as I felt my world shift a little, it struck me as odd that it had taken one sentence from the unnerving Patrik to make me feel that way.

Patrik frowned at me as I sat there, reassessing my place in the universe. The furrows on his brow deepened as the moments passed. He cleared his throat, a little too loudly, and I snapped out of my reverie.

I rallied. "While you were studying at UVan, Patrik, there was another young Hungarian there, I believe. A Peter Mezey. Did you ever run into him? I gather he, too, was from Budapest."

Patrik looked surprised by my change of topic, then his eyes all but closed behind his spectacles. "Peter Mezey? It is a common enough sort of name, I suppose. Maybe it sounds familiar."

I had no idea if "Mezey" was a common family name in Hungary, so I couldn't really comment on Patrik's observation. But I certainly noticed he hadn't answered my question.

Any further chance at conversation was halted when the chancellor of the university rose to make a long, rambling speech, which Patrik unnecessarily translated for me. The moment the polite applause stopped, a great deal of chair scraping and coat wrestling ensued. Patrik began to chat with a colleague who collared him about something or other, and I was pleased to have the time it took to return to the waiting bus to consider not just what Patrik had said but how he'd said it. And, of course, what he hadn't said at all. I felt I'd spent the evening in the company of a man who was somehow playing a part. Was that why his bonhomie grated on me so much?

Word Is Passed Down

I'D WARNED BUD I'D BE late getting home that night, and, by the time I got back to the apartment, I was pretty tired. It had been a long day, and the rich food wasn't helping me remain alert. Even so, I brightened considerably when I saw my husband's face, until I realized something was wrong—other than him still having a nasty cold, that is. He was raking his hands through his hair and I felt my full tummy tighten.

"What's the matter?"

"Don't get upset." I hate it when he uses his "calming" voice.

"Something's up."

"It's this case. The Ilona Seszták killing. Seems you've caused me to stir up something of a hornet's nest at this end. Go figure—you, doing that, eh?" Bud rolled his rheumy eyes. "You're thousands of miles away, and you've still managed it."

I pulled a face designed to make my husband laugh, but it didn't work. "What have I done now? Just tell me all in one go."

Bud smiled wearily. "Okay, I admit it, it's not you, it's me—and Jack and his old pal. I know that. But this case? It just got a lot more complicated, and politically sensitive too. You'll need some background, because you didn't get to Canada until long after all this happened. I'll give you the highlights, but I can't send you any paperwork on it. This really is all hush-hush, so I'm working from notes and you'll just have to take me and my source at our word."

"Of course I'll take you at your word. Do you trust your source?"

"Absolutely. I have no choice but to trust this person. So should you."

"Good enough for me. Tell me what you can. I'll make up the rest. Go ahead."

"Don't go making up anything. Or telling anyone this. Got it?"

I smiled sweetly.

Bud settled himself. "Today's a holiday across Canada, so I was surprised to get a visit here in my parents' home this morning from someone whose name you don't need to know. It seems the informal inquiries Jack and I have been making have come to the attention of some folks with a lot of fruit salad on their chests, and a few whose stock in trade is to say they 'work for the government.' I'm pretty sure I haven't been given all the facts, but I've been given enough information to help me understand why I should back off."

"What do you mean, back off?"

"Don't get on your high horse yet. Hear me out."

"Okay."

"The first nugget of information is that Kristóf and Ilona Seszták's son Valentin isn't who you think he is."

I couldn't help but interrupt. "I know. I told you, he's VS Örsi, the author."

"Cait," Bud was using his professional voice, "if you keep butting in we'll never get through this."

"Yes, dear."

"I know about that. What I mean is he isn't Kristóf and Ilona's son at all. He was adopted."

"That's news." I sounded as surprised as I was. "No one's mentioned that."

"Nor would they. Apparently, the Sesztáks never planned on telling him. He was adopted when he was just two years old, and they wanted him to have a completely fresh start."

"That doesn't sound good."

"You're right, it's not. Valentin Seszták's real name is Colin Cook. He was the younger son of . . ."

"You mean Freya and Elmer Cook were his parents?"

Bud nodded.

"Oh my goodness me." I had heard about the case. "He was the toddler who survived the massacre of his entire Vancouver family in 1959. It was committed by his sixteen-year-old brother. That's so sad."

"Well, it is, and it isn't. At least he lived and had a good chance at a normal upbringing, and—given what you've told me about his recent life—it seems he's managed to find a creative spark he's shared with the world," said Bud reasonably.

"I can understand why they didn't want him to know who he really was. Maybe living with a psychologist was an advantage—Seszták could have watched for any psychological trauma resulting from early memories. But you know, there's been some recent research . . ."

Bud held up his hand. "Don't go off on a tangent, I haven't finished yet," he said firmly. I motioned locking my lips, and threw the invisible key over my shoulder. Bud continued, "As I'm sure you know, it's one of the grisliest cases in Vancouver's criminal history. The real problem for us is the older brother, the one who did it. The night of the murders the police found him a few blocks from the family home, drinking a soda. He never denied killing both his parents and his two sisters, though he was never found guilty of murder. He was sent to the Valleyview Institution for the Insane in Coquitlam at the age of seventeen, where he was diagnosed with schizophrenia. They released him when he was thirty-four, following 'successful medication.' He was never seen again. It was 1976."

I sat quietly for a moment. I wanted to say so much, but didn't know where to start.

"Before you say anything, Cait, I've been told there was a terrible political hoo-ha when it emerged he'd been let out. They managed to keep it from the press, because they didn't want the population to panic, but I gather several key people were dismissed. Three years later, in 1979, a report came out criticizing the gradual shift from qualified clinicians running the place, to administrators taking over the decision-making. Hence the political sensitivity. The multiple-murderer, Edward Cook, Valentin Seszták's biological brother, was supposed to report to one of the then-new outpatient facilities for those leaving the residential care of the hospital. He never showed up. Ever. Never got a script for his meds, or showed up at a clinic or a doctor's surgery. I guess the one good thing I can report is that he also never showed up on a police charge sheet. Not anywhere in Canada, in any case. There was a room organized for him at what they referred to in those days as 'an appropriate place,' in other words some sort of boarding house where people being turfed out of institutions were supposedly kept an eye on, but he never showed up there either. Once the cops knew he had dropped out of sight they put all the usual alerts, for the time, in place. He was never spotted—he essentially disappeared the moment he left the grounds of the hospital."

"When exactly in 1976 was that?"

Bud paused, and I could tell he was weighing his words. "Cait, it might mean nothing. He was released early in August."

"And the adoptive mother of his young brother Colin, Ilona Seszták, was found murdered just a couple of months after his release?" I couldn't help myself.

Bud held up his hand, trying to calm me. "Whoa there, missy," he said almost jovially. "I know where you're going with this information, so let me rein you in for a moment or two. There's more."

"Don't tell me the cops knew it was Edward Cook who killed Ilona all along and didn't tell the family to avoid a scandal? A lawsuit?"

"I knew that's where you'd go with it. Just let me pass on what I have been told."

"Now I get it. They've fed you some flimflam, and we're supposed to buy into the cover-up, right?"

"Cait, stop it." Bud sounded genuinely cross with me, so I did as he asked. "As you can imagine, when the news of Ilona's death came out panic among the higher-ups was rife. The decision was made to not pass the information about the relationship between the freed killer and the dead woman's adopted son on to the RCMP because the people who mattered felt the information was irrelevant to the case, and might have diverted the efforts of the officers involved."

"Good grief, Bud, who on earth are these people that they can make decisions about keeping information from the RCMP when they're investigating a murder? Did anyone tell Kristóf that Edward Cook had been released?"

"Cait, like I said, we've rattled some golden cages by looking into this case. I asked exactly what you've just asked me, but got no answer. And it was made clear that I'm not going to. I guess we can both understand why my digging about in such muddied waters has drawn down the wrath of some pretty important people. They've panicked, Cait. I'd like to think my reputation has something to do with the fact they've come to me with this information. But it's not information we can use. They've given me facts to persuade me to stop digging. They thought it had all gone away."

I gave the whole matter some thought. Questions swirled in my head. "Who knew about the adoption of the boy?"

"That question they *did* answer. My source says almost no one. The young child, Colin, was taken to the local police station the night of the murders; he stayed with a female police officer for a few days. It all gets a bit vague then—purposely, I suspect—because it turns out Professor Seszták was big buddies with someone high up in the child services department of the day, and I suspect the adoption was less formal than it should have been. This is me reading between the lines here; Seszták and his wife were quite the stars when they arrived at UVan, it seems, so their stock would have been pretty high in 1959.

I understand they named the toddler Valentin because they adopted him around St. Valentine's Day in 1960."

I supported my chin as I spoke. "I can't help but think of the graphic descriptions of bloodshed in Valentin's books. I wonder if the horror he witnessed as a toddler is the genesis for all that."

"I thought you would. You mentioned the rivers of blood often enough when you were telling me what the books were about."

"Yes. I thought he might have been referencing Magyar and Transylvanian myth and lore in those passages, but now? I recall from reading about the Cook killings that they found the young boy hiding under a bed, covered in blood. Maybe Colin/Valentin/VS's obsession with gore comes from a deeply personal place." I paused, thinking along Colin's timeline until he'd been Valentin for seventeen years. "Do you think it's possible the older brother, Edward, could have somehow tracked down his sibling when they let him out? Somehow worked out Valentin was Colin? Might he have somehow found out about his brother's new family while he was in hospital? Did the authorities think so at the time? Any evidence he did?"

Bud furrowed his brow. "All questions I asked. None of them were answered. We both know more or less anything is possible. But *probable*? Even if Edward Cook did somehow find out about his kid brother, which I have to be honest with you, Cait, I think is unlikely, why on earth would he want to kill Ilona Seszták? All she did was adopt the little guy and give him a home, and a life. Okay, I get it that Edward, the killer, was nuts but—"

"Not nuts, Bud. Don't say he was nuts. He was diagnosed as schizo-phrenic; I recall that from the coverage I read about the case. He was sick. Of course, the basis for the diagnosis has shifted somewhat since the 1960s, and there might have been other aspects to his condition, but we'll never know that. It doesn't sound to me as though anyone's going to let you, or me, read the guy's case notes any time soon. But I'm still confused—and annoyed, Bud. What you're telling me is someone over there doesn't want us nosing about in the Ilona Seszták case to such an extent that they've come to you with information you might never have otherwise uncovered to stop you going any further?"

"That's about the size of it."

"So they're sufficiently concerned you might inadvertently discover something about the poor management of the release of the murderer Edward Cook into the community because they know how brilliant and dogged you are?"

"Possibly."

"Hasn't this all been dealt with, in political terms, and in management terms too? Would the general population today be frightened of a man who's been, possibly, in their midst for the better part of forty years without coming to the attention of the police? He'd be seventy-one by now, if he's still alive. He might have tried self-medicating with any number of legal or illegal substances, might have lived on the streets, and used an alias. He could have survived like that for a long time. It's also sad, but true, that some people die and their remains are never found, or they aren't discovered until fingerprints have disappeared. He could have ended up as an unidentified cadaver on the coroner's table. Did you ask if they had anything on file from the hospital, or in their own records, that could have allowed for a DNA match with any bodies found?"

Bud puffed out his chest. "I asked those same questions and was told there wasn't any. So, you're right, he could be dead and simply recorded as an unidentified decedent in Canada."

"They'd have had his dental records though, surely."

"They would have. He was in the system, so they'd have been easy to find and match—so long as they hadn't been misplaced or lost."

"You're not going to tell me that happens all the time, are you?"

Bud shrugged. "It's not unheard of. Cops are only human, as are the civilians who work in some filing roles too. Mistakes can be made."

"You're covering for your source now, I can tell. They're telling us it's a closed avenue of investigation. I get it. Still, that's a lot of food for thought. Thanks. I'll bear it all in mind at this end."

"No, Cait, not 'thanks and I'll bear it in mind'—I told you, we've been warned off. Shut down. In no uncertain terms. The only reason this . . . person . . . came to my parents' home and told me what they did was out of respect for my record, and with a clear understanding of my security clearances. Cait—I've signed several sets of papers during my life that prohibit me from talking about this case now that I have been officially warned off it. My source understood I would have to divulge certain facts to you so you, too, would understand the situation we're in. We are not to inquire, pry, prod, or poke. I am not to have so much as an informal chat with an old colleague about this after this discussion. Nor are you. Got it?"

"Hmmm." My mind was racing.

"Cait?"

I smiled. "Of course, I get it. Don't do anything more. You're right, you shouldn't. Thanks for all you have done. I know they'll be grateful over here."

Bud stood up in his parent's kitchen and paced about, disappearing from the camera's range, then re-entering the frame. "You're not hearing me, Cait. It's not just *me* who has to stop, it's you too. I'm not happy about it, but come on—what did this girl think? That after thirty-seven years we'd be able to track down some guy walking a bike path at night, in a rainstorm, who got it into his head to smash her grandmother on the side of her head with a giant rock for no good reason? Because, given what I've been able to find out from the police records, that's about the size of it. The RCMP couldn't find one credible suspect in the woman's immediate circles, on the campus, in the general area, or even in the entire province. Short of writing 'A passing tramp must have done it' on the file, they couldn't have made it clearer. They were completely stumped. We all know someone must have done it, but there are, quite literally, no clues about who that might have been. Even with this new information, I don't see where it leads. We know little more that's of any help to us."

"It might mean they know who did it—Edward Cook—or maybe it's nothing to do with him. I don't know about that. I'll have to think it through. However, I do have some more insights of my own. I just had dinner with a man who told me he ran a mile because Ilona was all over him like a rash."

"What?" Bud looked aghast and sat down in front of his computer screen with a thump I could hear half a world away. "Tell me."

"Patrik Matyas, my overly jovial colleague and sometime shadow, told me Ilona Seszták made unwanted advances toward him."

"Was he telling the truth?"

I grinned. "See? You want to know, don't you? You cannot help but want to know what happened."

"It's not so much that as the feeling of injustice for the poor woman who was killed. She deserves better." Bud's expression became grim. "I felt like I was being railroaded today, all that political nonsense being spouted when there's a family living without answers. It makes me angry. But I have to comply, Cait. I have my suspicions that maybe some pressure was brought to bear to keep the case dormant over the years. It can't be closed, but there are ways and means of making sure a file doesn't make it to the top of the pile for a very long time. Yes, Zsófia Takács's family deserves to know what happened, but I'm not interested in what you've discovered just so I can solve some sort of abstract puzzle, Cait. That isn't what it's about—we're merely the means to an end. The end being justice."

"I know. And you're right. We're stuck in a difficult situation. We want to help, and believe we could, but the powers that be are shutting us down. We have to decide what matters more to us—morals and ethics, or abiding by rules being imposed upon us."

Bud sighed with resignation, his shoulders drooping. "What did the guy say, exactly?"

I replayed my conversation with Patrik for Bud, and he whistled his amazement at the end. "Not quite the bombshell I dropped, but pretty good. There's nothing I can do here, now, to try to find out if Ilona Seszták was the man-eater Matyas suggests she was, and all you have is his word, and what you've told me about him doesn't suggest you have a high opinion of him."

"You're right. He's a slippery one. But you know I'm pretty good at reading people, Bud, even when I'm far, far away from you and all on my own in the big, wide world. So, no, I'm not just taking his word for it, even though I believe he was telling the truth. What he said, when taken with the comments Valentin made about his mother, suggests she might have been the type to find dalliances with young men to be at least fun, if not deeply satisfying. Now you've told me Valentin was adopted I can consider the internal family dynamics in a different light. Ilona knew Valentin wasn't her son, even if he didn't know she wasn't his mother. If she was as drawn to young men as has been suggested, maybe there was some sort of Oedipal thing going on there."

"Hang on," interrupted Bud. "I thought Oedipus was all about a son killing his father and marrying his mother. Then, when the two of them found out who he really was, she killed herself. Or have I gotten that little gem from the Greek myths mixed up with some other jolly tale about happy families?"

"No, you haven't got it mixed up at all. I got my hands on some photos of Ilona and Kristóf from the family yesterday. She presented herself to the camera in a highly sexual manner—primed for action, if you know what I mean. I'm not sure the word 'cougar' was in common use back in the 1970s, at least, not in the way it's used now. But if it had been, she'd have been a woman with all the hallmarks. Knowing Valentin wasn't her son might have led to a tension in the household he wouldn't have understood, but his father would have. Let me get the pictures to show you." I heard a bell ring out somewhere in Bud's parents' house. "Is that your mum, summoning you?"

"Yep, gotta go. She might be getting a little more confident on her feet, but she's getting a whole lot more impatient." He looked at his watch. "It's late there, and I have to go help Mom down the stairs. Tomorrow for those photos?"

We said our goodbyes, then I was alone again—but delighted I had so much more to think about as I lay in my half-empty bed. Well, two-thirds empty, if I counted the space usually filled by Marty.

Worried Words

"TO SUM UP TODAY'S SESSION then, 'Sticks and stones might break my bones, but words will never hurt me,' is not something we believe to be true anymore. Not only can words can be extremely hurtful, but that hurt can cause psychological damage, which may present itself in many different ways. Psychological abuse is abuse nonetheless, and we'll consider its possible role in influencing behavior to go beyond social and moral norms in our next session. We'll also consider how it can result in both detrimental and seemingly positive defense mechanisms coming into play. That's all for today. If anyone wants to talk to me about their mid-course report grades, but hasn't emailed me for an appointment, I'll be in my office for the next hour."

I'd noticed I was running a bit late with my lecture, so I'd rushed through my last few PowerPoint slides. I could tell the students were eager to leave; it was a Friday, and over the years I've learned that even when a lecture finishes before lunch, students' minds are often out of the door long before their bodies when the weekend is calling.

Unusually, Zsófia rushed out but Laszlo stayed. I reckoned he must have a good reason not to trail after her, so wasn't surprised when he sidled up to me as I checked around the room getting ready to leave.

"Can we speak, Professor Morgan?" he asked politely.

"Certainly, though I'm happy to say I don't think you have much to worry about regarding your report. It was good. You deserved the A grade I gave you. Well done."

"Thank you," replied the young man, blushing, "but it's not about that. It's private."

I paused. "Very well, let's get to my office and you can tell me all about it there."

Once we'd both settled in the tiny space I'd been allocated, I looked across the desk at a young man in turmoil. I didn't say anything—I thought it best to let him begin in his own time.

"It's about Zsófia," he began.

"What about her?"

"I'm worried about her, and I don't know who to tell."

His sad-puppy eyes were almost irresistible, but I felt it best to respond with, "Before you say anything, do you really think I am the best person to confide in? I'm happy to deal with academic issues, but maybe the student counselors here could help if it's a matter of a different type?" I've found to my cost in the past that, because I'm a psychology professor, students sometimes seem to think this imbues me with special powers. It doesn't. I'm pretty hopeless when it comes to giving advice of a personal nature, so I try to avoid it whenever I can. Except when I truly think I can help, of course.

"I wouldn't do that to her. She doesn't trust them. She trusts you. She told me that. I don't know why, but she does. So I will too."

I respected his reasoning. "Okay. What's the matter?"

Laszlo shifted in his chair and broke eye contact. "I like Zsófia. I like her a lot. And sometimes she seems to like me too, but other times not so much." I began to panic, hoping I wasn't about to be drawn into problems connected with young love. "But that's not it." I was relieved. "She's doing something in secret I don't think is a good thing. And I'm afraid it will get her into trouble."

I wondered if Laszlo had, somehow, got wind of our inquiries.

"Could you be more specific?"

"She has a wonderful voice. You must know that. She told me you saw her sing at the New York Café. Her mother doesn't approve of the idea of her signing, but she does it anyway. She sings in a lot of bars, and she's popular. Tonight she's singing at a bar many students go to, and she told me there's a record producer coming along to hear her. If he thinks she's good enough, she might get a chance to record some songs. She's excited about it."

I imagined she would be. "And you think that's a bad idea?" I wasn't sure where Laszlo was going with this.

"No, not the idea. It is the person who is coming to listen to her who is bad. He's Russian."

Laszlo looked at me with horror. It seemed that to be Russian was enough for him to fear the man.

I pressed, "And that's a problem because . . . ?"

Laszlo's mouth became a thin, white line, and his eyes blazed. "It's not just that he's Russian, but he is a Russian who has lots of money, and a reputation for making girls into big hits."

I rather assumed those two things weren't necessarily so dreadful, and said so.

"But they all end up like shooting stars, then they become drug addicts with no friends, and some die," he bleated.

I had to find out if what the boy was saying was true, or just the baseless claims of a young man anxious to not lose the girl he adored.

"That's all a bit vague, Laszlo. Come on, give me some specifics."

He spent the next fifteen minutes showing me videos of female singers on his phone, the gossip magazine photos of them as they glammed up, then spiraled out of control. In a couple of cases he showed me the newspaper coverage of their tragic deaths. "They were all *his* girls," he said, vindicated. "Stanislav Samokhin was their record producer. Every one of them. If he likes Zsófia, he could do the same to her."

I knew I had to choose my next words with the greatest care.

"If your concerns are coming from a place of unselfishness, and you are certain of that, tell me what you think I can do to help."

Laszlo became energized. "Yes, yes, I am not being selfish. I know I don't stand a chance with Zsófia—she is up here, and I scuttle around down here." His hands displayed a great distance between the two positions. "I just want her to be happy. She has a wonderful voice, and singing is something she could easily do for a living. But more than happy, I want her to be safe. And she might . . . sometimes it's not easy to choose the safe path when you think happiness is along another road."

I was impressed by his surprisingly mature take on the matter. Hoping he would understand I said, "Sometimes a person will accept unhappiness and heartbreak in order to achieve their goals. It's a subject we were discussing just last week, if you recall, in the classes about deferred gratification and impulse control."

Laszlo sunk into his chair. "I know, it's as you said; we all make judgments about what we want most, and what we're prepared to put up with in terms of risk to be able to get it. Your examples about the risk-reward choices made by criminals of varying types were really helpful in that lecture. And I see how it applies here. You're saying it's Zsófia's choice to make. She's the one who'll take the risk, and get the reward. Not me." He looked wide-eyed across the desk at me. "You also spoke about risk assessment that day, and I don't think she's got that part right."

"Have you spoken to her about this Stanislav's history, as you have to me?"

"She wouldn't listen. She pushed me away. She doesn't want to know. Why wouldn't she want to know?"

I bit my tongue. Many years ago a barrister in Cambridge tried to show me my then-boyfriend Angus's criminal record when I went along to support him at a court hearing. I didn't want to see it. By refusing to face the truth that day, I allowed myself to cling to the hope I could help Angus become the person I thought he could be.

I allowed myself to continue to believe my love had the power to stop him being an abusive, often violent, man, with several addictions and a chip on his shoulder the size of a small planet. In other words, I'd sealed my own fate by not taking a chance to be in control of it by acknowledging all the information available to me. It sounded as though Zsófia was doing the same thing, in a different way.

Rather than telling the youngster in front of me that, sometimes, even bright people can make stupid decisions, I said, "Maybe if we're around when she meets this man, you and I can steer the conversation in directions that will force him to show his hand."

Laszlo shot out of his seat. "Wonderful! Thank you, Professor. I was hoping you would agree to help. Let's meet at the bar, so we can be on the spot when she talks to him. I can confront him with the facts about all these girls who have become addicts, and worse—then we can see what he says."

I stood too. "Maybe we should be a little subtler, Laszlo? Recall what I said in class about the role of rebelliousness in decision-making; I talked about the way some criminals undertake certain activities because a part of the reward is to shock those who have tried to control them. You remember?" He agreed, grumpily. "So let's play it more carefully. There's a saying I first heard when I was a little girl, sitting on my father's knee, 'Softly, softly, catchee monkey.' My dad liked that saying, and it's useful here." I smiled at Laszlo's puzzled expression. "It means that patience, stealth, and guile can help you achieve something that might remain beyond your grasp if you rush to grab at it."

His expression showed he understood. "I don't understand why it is about a monkey, because I think this man is a snake, but it works well as a saying in this case."

"Good. So, where's this bar, and when is Zsófia performing?"

I entered all the information into my phone, including Laszlo's number, then decided I'd better head back to my apartment to brief

Bud, and change into something suitable for a night at a student bar that, by the sounds of it, had a reputation for cheap beer, a positive attitude toward smoking, and no windows. Just my kind of place. At least, just the kind of place the old Cait would have loved.

I stood alone for a moment in my tiny office and acknowledged the changes that had taken place in my life, and in myself, since Jan, Bud's first wife had died. It's funny how loneliness can make you reflective, even when it's not naturally a part of your makeup.

I thought about how Bud had never tried to alter me. Well, he'd nagged me to pack in the smoking, but that was understandable, he was doing it for my own good. But other than that, he'd allowed me to settle into my new life without putting any pressure on me to do so more quickly. It hadn't been an easy time for either of us; he'd been grappling with grief, and then the challenges of retirement, and I hadn't been half a couple since my time with Angus. As I pulled on my coat I wryly admitted how poor a blueprint for a harmonious relationship that had been, and how very happy I was sharing my life with Bud. As I headed out to make my way "home" I longed for my *real* home. Someone needs to come up with another word for missing someone you love. Not even the Welsh *hiraeth* manages to sum it up. It's the most awful feeling to carry about, and it gets worse the longer you have it. Stages of grief? There are levels of loneliness a person only feels when they realize they no longer function well as a single unit, but require the presence of a particular other person to feel whole. It was hard for me to come to terms with the fact that that was now my reality. Me—independent, lead-with-your-head-not-your-heart Cait Morgan. No longer it seemed. Maybe I might as well have changed my name to Mrs. Anderson. That was now who I was in my heart, after all.

A Siren Song

THE BAR WAS PACKED, NOISY, and filled with a blue haze. Ancient stones formed the walls and vaulted ceiling, small candle-lit tables littered with beer glasses were dotted about the place, and I didn't think I stood much chance of easily locating Laszlo in the bustling crowd. Luckily, he saw me hovering uncertainly on one of the last of the precipitous stone steps I'd negotiated from the street above. He jumped to his feet and flailed his arms, catching my attention. I lost count of how many times I excused myself as I tried to wriggle between the impossibly close tables and chairs, but I finally flopped into a seat beside the young man, and was surprised to find myself facing Patrik Matyas.

"Look, Professor Matyas is here," said Laszlo in a tone that hinted at panic. "It is a surprise, no?"

"Yes, it is," I replied, smiling as brightly at Patrik as I could manage. Since no conversation could take place at less than a shout, I called, "What brings you here tonight, Patrik?"

He gestured with windmilling arms as he yelled, "I like the atmosphere, and the music is good."

I gathered from Laszlo's eye rolling that he'd never seen Patrik there before, and I wondered why the man would have come to the bar tonight, of all nights. I felt uneasy about the whole situation, and my anxiety level wasn't lowered at all when I noticed Zsófia waving at me from beside the small stage. She was calling me to her, pointing at the table she was sharing with who I assumed were the musicians who would play for her. The fact one was holding an accordion on his lap was the giveaway. If Patrik hadn't been there, I'd have gone to join her and would have dragged Laszlo with me, but, as it was, I realized I had to stay put, or else abandon Laszlo. I made a quick decision.

"Hey, guys," I began cheerily, "I can see Zsófia over there—I just want to wish her good luck. I'll be back in a few minutes. Keep my seat for me?"

I didn't see Laszlo's face as I left the table but could imagine his expression; I ignored the daggers that were likely to be heading for my back and writhed my way toward Zsófia's table. Once again I plonked myself onto a chair. This time I accepted a glass of beer the accordionist poured from the jug on the table, and downed it in one. It's hot work being quite a wide person orienteering across a room crammed with obstacles while still wearing a thick winter coat.

"What a lovely surprise to see you here," called Zsófia, then she moved her chair to be close enough to me to be able to save her voice.

"I came to wish you luck, or to break a leg; I'm not sure if that works for Hungarians," I yelled.

Zsófia and her three male companions laughed. "Break a leg is fine, but I hope I don't," she replied. "How did you know I was singing tonight?"

"Laszlo told me," I replied, honestly enough. "He's here too, as is Patrik Matyas, for some reason."

Zsófia looked surprised at the mention of Matyas's name. "Why would he come here? This isn't the sort of place I'd ever expect to see him. I've seen him at a few of my gigs before, but only when I sang in places where older people would go. This place is for the young crowd." She blushed, and added quickly, "You're young at heart, Cait."

I acknowledged her attempted catch and said, "It's busy. Are they all here for you?"

"Not all. Some, I hope."

I nodded in the direction of the only other person in the room over the age of thirty. "He looks a bit out of place."

Zsófia followed my glance and swallowed hard. "He's a famous record producer. He *is* here to see me." She leaned in. "The people at this table know about him being here, and a few others too. Don't say anything to Laszlo about him, please. He'll get upset. *Again.*"

"Why is he upset?" I wondered what she'd say.

"Because Laszlo's as bad as Mama; they are both like the people who kill beautiful butterflies just so they can pin them in a box and admire them. It's not fair. I want my chance. I want to fly free. I don't want to spend my days in that house and just be with my family, or studying, or working all the time."

It was interesting to know how Zsófia viewed her life—a mixture of work and family responsibility, with a touch of "imprisonment" thrown in for good measure. So, a normal teenager's perspective manifesting itself in a twenty-year-old girl. Not so unusual. Was her voice her only way out? Here was a girl whose life was all about words—the words to the songs she sang, the words she organized and rewrote for her sick uncle, the words she had read about her grandmother's death—and how they had impacted her. How could I use words to help her see the best way forward for herself, I wondered? Was I even sure she was in danger?

While I pondered all this, the man she'd identified as the record producer stood up and moved away. I suspected a bathroom break before her performance, but was taken aback to see him weave his way to the table where Laszlo and Patrik were sitting. Fascinated, I watched as the man bent to Patrik's ear, spoke a few sentences, with Patrik replying, then left, heading for the washrooms.

"I see your record producer knows Professor Matyas," I observed.

Zsófia was visibly shaken. "How could he? Why would he? Their worlds cannot possibly intersect."

She was right—I was having a difficult time putting the two of them together in any way. A Hungarian professor of psychology and a Russian record producer didn't, on the face of it, stand much of a chance of having anything in common. My interest was most certainly piqued.

I decided my time might be better spent with Patrik than Zsófia, so wished her and her fellow musicians luck, thanked them for the beer, and wended my way back to my original seat. Settling in I asked Patrik, "Who was that chap who came to speak to you? A friend of yours?"

Patrik pursed his mouth into his characteristically prudish bud, then smiled, tilting his head. "Laszlo was asking the same thing. As I told him, I do not know the man, he simply commented we were the oldest people here, and he was glad he wasn't the only person over fifty to enjoy the music of today."

His response was too smooth for my liking, and I didn't believe a word of it, but I chose to not comment.

"Another six months and I'll be joining you in that age group," I replied.

"Are you that old?" asked Laszlo, grinning wickedly.

Patrik and I shared a brief moment of strained bonhomie as we discussed the views of the young on what constitutes "old," then the general hubbub died down as the accordionist took the stage. I looked around; the Russian was nowhere to be seen. Would he miss Zsófia's performance after all?

I needn't have worried; the musicians took the stage alone and delighted the crowd with two stirring instrumental numbers that owed more to the roots of Roma music than anything else. The Russian was back at his table before Zsófia stepped up to the microphone, and I wondered what she'd sing. The crowd showed its delight by becoming almost unnervingly quiet for her first piece, which was a haunting ballad sung in Hungarian. Next the audience hummed along as she sang the Sinatra standard "One for My Baby," which I've always loved. She continued with a mix of standards in English, Roma songs, and a few pieces I recognized as being reinvented versions of up-to-date hits. Finally, after about fifty minutes, she wrapped up her set with a hand-clapping, foot-stomping local favorite to rapturous applause and a good deal of cheering. I was happy for her, and applauded madly. Laszlo was on his feet, glowing and screaming. Patrik clapped politely, his mouth pursed. The Russian was typing on his phone. I didn't know if that was a good or bad sign.

Following the general rush to get drinks after the performance, the audience settled again to a noisy level of conversation, and I decided it was time I made my way back to Zsófia. I leaned toward Laszlo, "I'm off to congratulate our songbird. Coming?" The young man shot up and we told Patrik we'd be back soon.

Finally able to talk to each other alone as we moved slowly across the room, I confirmed that Laszlo had no idea why Patrik had shown up, and hadn't heard what the Russian had said to him. We agreed we'd take things slowly with Zsófia and not mention the record producer until she did.

When we arrived at her table a good deal of hugging ensued, and we shared the jug of beer I'd brought so we could toast the performers. I was delighted, and apprehensive, when I saw the Russian approaching. Zsófia was on her feet in an instant and shook the man's hand as though he were royalty. The accordionist gave up his seat, then leaned in to listen to the man introduce himself as Stanislav Samokhin. He handed out cards, his fingers lingering on Zsófia's as she took one. I felt everything in me clench—not just because of the way his eyes were sliding across Zsófia's bosom, but because the way he presented himself wasn't endearing at all; there's only so much bling a person can wear before you begin to wonder why they need to have that much gold about their person at all times.

As a psychologist I'm aware that what many refer to as "gut instinct" is, in fact, the accumulated wisdom of their experience. As someone adept at reading people, I often find myself an impassionate observer; not on this occasion. I decided to trust my assessment of the man, and opened with, "Would you have worked with any artists an old fogey like myself might have heard of?"

Stanislav shrugged. "Maybe not."

He rattled off a list of names—some of which sounded like mere syllables rather than people—and I caught just enough to be able to reply, "Didn't a couple of those people die recently? One was a drug overdose, another a shooting, I believe."

Another shrug. "Sometimes people I represent early in career move away from me and become involved in lifestyle that I, of course, do not control. It is sad." His accent was a strange mix of heavy Russian and American twang.

"Sad, maybe, but surely you work with these artists, and their management teams, to try to ensure their wellbeing?"

"I am also manager for some. When I am, I do."

His responses seemed to be worryingly conditional.

"Do you have a manager, Zsófia?" I asked. I knew she didn't.

The girl's eyes opened wide. She looked panicked. "Not yet. But maybe if an experienced producer agreed to work with me, I might find a company to manage me." She lowered her eyes and bowed her head. *A lamb to the slaughter?*

"Surely you should attend to that before signing any contracts. And I bet Mr. Samokhin agrees with me when I say it's not ideal for a producer and manager to be one and the same—there'd be a conflict of interests."

The Russian didn't shrug this time. Tilting his head toward me he said, "Who are you? Her mother?"

"Cait's just my professor," snapped Zsófia.

I understood her reaction, but it stung. I'd been working on her grandmother's case, and I'd roped Bud into it back in Canada to the extent that he'd come to the attention of some government people I didn't like the sound of. I'd put many hours of reading, talking, and thought into the whole thing, and had even exposed myself to the infighting of her family. Now I was being cut off with a "just my professor?" *Nope—not going to happen.*

I stared her down as I replied cuttingly, "That's correct, I am just this girl's professor, and a visiting one at that, but I can tell you now that, even if you offer her a recording contract on the spot, I will do whatever I can to talk her out of either accepting or signing it. Career-making decisions shouldn't be made in the heat and enthusiasm of the moment. If you think she can be a hit, others will too."

Zsófia's mouth fell open. "Cait, you have no right to speak for me like this."

I silently admitted to myself she was right, but defiantly stuck my chin toward the Russian.

The man grinned. Even his teeth were gold. "You have someone to fight for you? Maybe this woman should be your manager. I do not talk business at venue, with person who is not a manager. Is too important. If you have people who are loyal to you this way, Zsófia, you listen to them. I think you have good voice. Others will agree. I want to make money from your talent, so will others. I believe I can handle your career so we both benefit. Call my number. I hope you call. You are good. I am best at making the good better. But I do not need confrontation like this. I am in Budapest two days more, then I go back to Moscow."

Stanislav stood, bowed, and left—his otherwise dramatic exit marred by the fact he had to wait while a boy carrying four jugs of beer passed our table.

I watched him leave, then turned to see Zsófia staring daggers at me.

"You did not catch any monkeys," said Laszlo to me quietly, looking worried.

I cursed inwardly, and set about rebuilding bridges between me and my student, whose chin was beginning to pucker. The accordionist looked at me as though he wanted to smack me over the head with his instrument, and his two colleagues both had their arms around the young singer's shoulders in an attempt to comfort her. They shielded her from me as though I was dangerous, and she accepted their protection.

Eventually, she wiped her nose and looked at me. Her eyes were red, her lipstick smudged, her eyeliner just a memory. She appeared about twelve years old. "You and your stupid words—you just made that man angry. Maybe you have destroyed my best chance to get away from here, to be a success. Why? Why would you speak to him like that? He is an important, successful man. He has made many great careers."

"And he's overseen some spectacular falls from grace too, Zsófia. He specializes in propelling young, solo female singers into the spotlight, working them until they collapse, then watching them slide down the charts until almost no one remembers them—and all this in about two years, according to his track record." I'd spent an hour doing my own online research into the man back at my apartment.

The usually meek girl's eyes glittered with disdain. "Fashionable performers have to make the most of their chances, then they will not be fashionable anymore. I could be a different type of star—I love the old songs, and I could appeal to more people. You saw how the audience at the New York Café liked me—they were all ancient. Like you. If they enjoy me, and my own age enjoys me, I can succeed. I can be better than his other girls. I can have a great career and leave this little city and everyone in it behind me. I won't have to perform in grubby student bars like this anymore—I can have great musicians on stage with me, people who really know what they're doing."

As she spoke, I noticed her three accompanists become rigid with shock. Laszlo's expression folded into puzzlement. All four of them were unprepared for Zsófia's display of self-belief. Having seen the girl so nervous before appearing on stage just a few weeks ago, and even earlier that night, I, too, wondered about the source of her seemingly newfound confidence. I didn't believe I was witnessing true bravado, nor hubris. I looked at her almost untouched beer—maybe she'd taken a few shots of something stronger earlier on for courage, and it had worked its way through her system to become aggressiveness? Maybe she'd taken a few hits of something other than alcohol. The idea scratched uncomfortably at the back of my brain, and I ran through the types of drugs that might have been at work. Her confidence, her railing at her family, Laszlo, and me as all trying to work against her . . . maybe cocaine, with its subversive cocktail of boosted energy and accompanying potential paranoia?

Of course I kept my thoughts to myself, and also watched my tablemates. The two young men who'd been comforting Zsófia had removed their arms from her and were nursing their drinks. Laszlo was speaking to her, low and fast, in Hungarian, assuring her I was just looking out for her best interests. The accordionist had retaken his seat and pulled out a running order of pieces of music to study. Zsófia pushed Laszlo away, and stormed off toward the ladies' washroom as best she could, given the crush. I mouthed to the distraught Laszlo that I'd follow her, and then I did, catching up with her at the doorway, which was blocked by a line of other females all keen to use the facilities.

Using an old-fashioned compact from inside her fire-engine red purse, Zsófia studiously ignored me as I spoke to her in tones as low as possible.

"You can't go rushing into things," was the summary of my speech, but it seemed to fall on deaf ears. As truculent as a teen, she turned her back on me, and I wavered. Then the dam burst.

Grabbing her shoulder, I spun her around and addressed her loudly, "Zsófia, don't you dare treat me this way. You are my student, but we crossed a line when you asked me to look into that matter back in Canada for you." Even now I didn't want to break her confidence in public. "You have brought me to meet your family, about whom you have told me many secrets—and you've encouraged me to unearth others. You trusted me to know all that, and about your uncle's work and your role in it. I have accommodated you, and I've dedicated more than a little time to helping you and your family, as has my husband. When I spoke out in front of that odious man, I did so for your sake—not mine. In a few weeks I'll have left here, and your future success or failure as a singer will be neither something over which I will have any control, nor something in which I will have any part to play. But while I am linked to you by a mutual trust, I will speak out when I feel I must. That man has a questionable track record when it comes to young women under his supervision, and I believe you have the chance to succeed with or without his controlling your future. You have shut out your family—except your great-aunt, from whom you are supposed to be cut off in any case—from this part of your life. In some cultures, you are seen as an adult; as a psychologist I know you are still developing your mental and moral map to manage your life. Since there was no one else to speak for you, I had to do so. So listen to me, will you?"

Zsófia sneered at me, "You have worked on my behalf? For my family? No. It is all for you. I knew about you and your love of puzzles before you got here. You think you are so clever, unmasking killers wherever you go, working with the police, writing papers that talk about victims as though you care. Now, I am finished with you. I do not want you in my life anymore. Good-bye."

I was speechless. She'd used me! She'd researched me, found my weaknesses, and just plain used me. And I'd fallen for it. I'd actually *liked* her. I turned, shoved my way back to my original table, grabbed my coat, and said good night to a confused-looking Patrik, who was still sitting there sipping a warm beer. I don't lose my temper often, but I knew I was at a point where I shouldn't say anything more, so leaving was all I could do. I silently cursed myself, the entire Takács/ Seszták clan, the weather—which was bitter—and the slippery streets. I eventually got to the nearest taxi rank, and then sat fuming the entire cab ride back to my apartment. I texted Bud, who said we could Skype. The minute I saw his face, I burst into tears and babbled the whole evening's events out to him.

"I'm so hurt, Bud. You know me—you're the only one who does. I've gone through so much of my life with walls built around myself, not letting anyone in. It was the only way I could cope after the way I allowed Angus to hurt me and grind me down into nothingness. Then you came along, and I allowed myself to open up a bit. Now this. See? I've been right all along to not trust anyone. I feel so stupid. So . . ."

"Human? Cait, don't cry. I can tell you're feeling fifty percent angry and fifty percent hurt, but try to make those feelings subside into realizing you're just another human being, please? You trusted someone. Isn't it better to trust and be let down occasionally, than to never trust at all? And it's me saying this—a cop with a track record of working out who to trust and who to use."

I wiped my eyes. "At this moment, Bud—no, I don't think it's better to trust and be let down. I think it's better to act as though everyone's going to be horrible to me, because they usually are. Eventually."

"Oh my darling wife, don't say that." I knew we both wished we were in each other's arms. "You might not see it yourself, but when we worked together and were just friends, one of the aspects I noticed about you was how you shut people down, and shut people out. It was something most people noticed—you didn't trust anyone. Of course neither I nor they knew at the time that was because of what you'd been through with Angus; we both know, professionally speaking, how devastating it can be to endure an abusive relationship . . . but

138

I don't think you've ever really come to terms with how very much he damaged you. Now I think you're beginning to, and you need to do that to heal. I know it's what you'd say to someone else in your situation. I'm right, arent' I?'"

I knew he was.

Bud reached forward and pointed at his wedding ring. "Look at this, Cait—look what we've done, what we've agreed to do. Our rings tell the world we've committed to one another. But we also have to commit to ourselves, to be whole for each other. I like to think our love has allowed you to let people in, to see people for who they can be beyond a collection of traits and behaviors like you usually do. As I say, you might not really have noticed how much you've opened up, but I have. And it's not a change I want to see you unmake. Your life, *our lives*, can be so much richer if only you share your true self with others. I'm sorry this girl has let you down, Cait. But listen, she's young; she probably doesn't realize how hurtful her words were. Maybe she'll apologize. It doesn't mean you have to climb back into your protective shell and hide from everyone for the rest of your life."

As I blubbed aloud in my suddenly bleak apartment thousands of miles from the man I loved, I gave Bud's words some thought. The bottle of Bombay Sapphire gin in the fridge, the packs of cigarettes dotted around the place? They spoke of the new Cait trying to act like the old Cait because, finding myself alone again, I didn't know what else to do. Old patterns of behavior can be tough to break. In my heart I knew my husband was right; I'd changed a lot during the past couple of years and now was not the time to backtrack.

Finally, Bud's kind, gentle words had helped me calm down, and I listened to his soothing tones as he wound up with just what I needed to hear.

"Don't worry, Cait. I know how much you care. However high you might try to build those walls around you, you *still* care. But this?

This *is* something you can walk away from with a clear conscience. You and I have done all we can."

"Yes," I sniffed. "We have."

"I love you, Cait Morgan."

"Even when I wear horizontal stripes just to confound the fashion police, like I did tonight?"

Bud smiled, which was all I needed to set me off again. "Even then."

"Love you."

"Love you more."

"Love you most, Bud Anderson."

Silent Terror

SATURDAY DAWNED BRIGHT AND CLEAR—and well below freezing. I dawdled over my coffee, did a little final polishing of my research paper, which I'd finished, and sat in front of the window taking in the view below me. Other than being herded about to HUB-organized events I'd seen relatively little of Budapest, so I decided I'd take a day for myself. I reckoned I deserved it, and hoped doing something a bit selfish would help me shrug off the terrible weight I was carrying on my shoulders after the events of the night before. The weather forecast suggested the temperature would be a balmy forty degrees Fahrenheit by noon, so I decided to head out by then, giving me about four hours before the thermometer began to plummet toward the promised low of twenty degrees.

Despite knowing I could get a bus at the end of my road that would take me almost directly to the Fisherman's Bastion—another of Budapest's legacies from the 1896 Millennial celebration—I decided, instead, to take myself off to the aptly named House of Terror. I suspected I'd find it much more interesting to muse upon man's inhumanity toward man, than to find myself mooching about in the chilly climes with hundreds of other tourists, all trying to take grinning selfies with the Danube at just the right spot in the background.

By a little after one o'clock I was surrounded by all manner of exhibits telling the tale of two reigns of terror in Budapest—that of the far right under the Nazis for a year or so, and that of the Communist regime, which had lasted four decades. It was a grim museum, but fascinating too. Portraits of proud military types overlooked the tools of the most dreadful torture. The dark, dismal basement filled me with dread; I had the certain knowledge I could leave whenever I wanted, so I shivered alongside my largely silent fellow visitors at the thought that, for so many, it had been the last place they'd drawn breath.

I watched the videos of the remnants of the Communist army leaving the city in the 1990s, then walked solemnly through one of the final parts of the exhibit—which showed row upon row of simply framed photographs of the Hungarians who had supported the Communist regime and helped it retain its iron grip on the populace. Grainy shots of the days when the false hope of the Hungarian Spring flourished were also displayed. The good people of Budapest had dragged the secret police and the informants—their neighbors and fellow citizens—out of hiding and strung them up. Knowing I was standing in the very building the secret police had used as its headquarters during both the Nazi and Communist occupations made the display seem even more viscerally real.

I paused, recognizing a face I'd seen in the photos Zsófia had given me. Smiling down at me was a man named as Tamás Örsi, Informant. Here was the man I knew to be Zsófia Takács's great-uncle, husband to the singer Klara, and brother of the woman whose death in Vancouver had become such a large part of my time in Budapest. It seemed fitting that in this bleak place I'd find a connection with the blackness I was feeling in my heart—remorse for having let loose at Zsófia the night before. I must have lingered in the same spot for several minutes, trying to decide if it would be wise to contact Zsófia to apologize; I had her cell number, after all.

"They blight our lives, even now," said a voice cracked with age from behind me. I turned and looked down into a wizened man's face.

"The informants were never charged?" I asked, knowing the answer.

"It is our national shame," he said quietly. His strong accent told me he was Hungarian, his worn, old clothing, bowed back, and gnarled hands spoke of a heritage of hard, physical labor.

"It must be difficult to cope with, especially if some of these people still live in your city," I said.

A smile showed two blackened teeth, and gums. "Difficult for us. Almost impossible for them."

"They are known and victimized?" I guessed that was what he meant.

Showing tremendous shock and dismay he replied, "No, they are not victims. Two wrongs do not make a right. They are known and they are watched, as they once watched us. They are reported upon, as they once reported upon us. They know what it is like to have no privacy—a luxury we were all denied for so long. It is a type of justice."

I was thinking it sounded more like a form of retribution, but said, "Are many still living?"

Beckoning me along the wall he pointed high. "Her? She was active until 1991. She was still young then, as you can see. She now lives on the Buda side of the river in a good house. When the Communists left she began to work for a Western advertising agency here, now she is in charge of it. Today she is forty-eight years old, has two daughters, one of whom has just married and will soon have children of her own—or maybe not. A dozen of us attended her daughter's wedding and held up copies of this photograph. Some were the children of the people this woman informed upon. Their parents could not be there because they died under the Communists, some in this very building. We did not speak, we simply bore witness for ourselves and our loved ones."

I pondered the tragedy of which he spoke. "You think the children of those who informed should have their lives impacted even though they had nothing to do with their parents' crimes?"

"The children of those who died or suffered have to live with the results of the informants' actions, why should the lives of the informants' children be any different? Injustice has long arms. It reaches out and touches those who come afterward. Justice should do the same." He didn't sound bitter; it was clear he felt he was stating simple facts.

"Justice is a complex concept," I said. "Sometimes retribution wears justice as a mask. It takes wisdom to know the difference."

"Wisdom? Maybe I am not so wise then. I could not escape the clutches of those who held me here and beat me for a week, trying to make me tell them which of my friends had marched in the spring of 1956. We were happy in those days—we thought the Communists had gone for good. Why would we not smile and cheer at the young men and students with movie cameras who were waving our flag, themselves a part of our throngs? When the Communists came back, they seized those films and used them to identify the people who had marched. It was terrifying. We hid in basements, attics, or barns for months. Like rats, we lived. Someone told them where I was hiding. I never found out who did it."

He stared up at the rows of photographs. "Maybe it was one of these. I wish I knew." His tone suggested the outcome for the culprit might not be good if he gained that knowledge.

Turning back to me he continued, "After I was picked up, I was tortured, then sent away to a camp. I managed to survive for ten years. I was young and strong when they sent me there. They broke my back, but I wouldn't die for them. They starved and froze me, but still I lived. Then they were done with me. I did not go to the streets to cheer when they finally left for good. I stayed at home, alone, and cried for the good friends I once had who were not alive to see that day. Now I am here, to bear witness. We must do it, or it will be repeated. Our government even now spies on us, and listens to everything we say and do on the Internet and on our telephones. How else can these people we keep close watch on suddenly change their plans so our observers lose them?"

The bitterness in the man's voice told me he wasn't just feeling the pain of old wounds. These were fresh sources of anger.

He thrust his chin, as best he could with his bowed back, toward the photographs. "Right, left—Nazi, Communist. It doesn't matter what you call them. Victors, despots, even elected officials, they are all the same. Their currency is information. This place should be called the House of Terror and Information, because that is what they have always used to control us—our own words."

A group of five other people had joined us, and were silently listening to the elderly man with grim expressions, transfixed by his tale. When he paused, it was as though the spell was broken, and they turned away, peering watery-eyed up at the walls, not knowing what to say.

"You have my sympathy for all you have been through. I hope that, sometimes, you are able to see the beauty of life, and enjoy it. Thank you for sharing your memories." I shook the man's hand warmly, and made my way outside into the bustle of a Saturday afternoon on Andrássy Avenue, trying to free myself from the shadow of the twentieth century's horrors.

After a few deep breaths of the chilly air, I decided to find myself a bar where I could get a coffee, a brandy, and maybe something sweet. I strode out, trying to put as much space between myself and the ominous House of Terror as I could as quickly as possible, heading toward the major crossroads area known as the Oktogon, which had the advantage of offering a choice of bars and a metro station.

It also meant I was walking toward Zsófia's home, but I told myself that was pure coincidence. I stopped in my tracks and had a silent conversation with myself. I knew I'd have to pass her front door to reach my destination, so why was I going that way? I thought about Bud's words the night before, and him telling me that Zsófia might regret what she'd said to me at the club and want to apologize. I tutted as I realized I should be the one apologizing. Yes, she was young. I wasn't. Not anymore. I was staring fifty in the face and I should act it. I strode on, deciding it was time Cait Morgan held out an olive branch to a girl who, given her family circumstances, could probably do with one.

As I got closer to Zsófia's imposing home I found myself forming sentences I could use when I faced my student. Since I'm not used to apologizing I found it difficult to come up with anything more than a string of platitudes, and I knew I had to do better. What had Bud said? "Allow yourself to feel with your heart, Cait, not just think with that huge brain of yours." Amid everything else he'd said, that was the suggestion that struck home at that moment. I had to allow myself to feel with my heart, and speak from it to Zsófia. I tugged at the bell pull, my nerves jangling, and waited.

Nothing to Say

I STOOD THERE FOR WHAT felt like an age trying to imagine a scenario in which there wasn't a single person in the house, then I tugged at the bell pull again, and even tried the door itself. Of course it was locked, so I knocked. I could hear the family's little dog yapping inside, and imagined it slithering across the marble floor to ward me off. I seemed to be there for hours, but I supposed it was only a matter of five minutes.

Alexa was surprised to see me when she opened the door. "Cait! Were we expecting you?" She reeked of alcohol, though she looked steady on her feet, her eyes bright and focused.

"Hello, Alexa. No, you weren't. I was passing by and wondered if I could have a word with Zsófia. Is she at home?"

Alexa seemed unsure. "I think so. I think she was with Valentin. Maybe it's not a good time." She didn't open the door and invite me in, and I wondered if I'd get the chance to be magnanimous, as I'd planned.

Both Alexa and I started as a piercing scream reached our ears. It was followed by a clattering of feet on one of the upper floors. I wasn't sure how to react. Was this another everyday occurrence at the house? I watched Alexa to take my cue. She blanched.

"That's Zsófia, I'm sure of it," she said, turning and abandoning me at the open door. She raced to the stairs and began to run up them. I hovered for a second or two, then decided it was best to follow her. I slammed the door behind me and followed my "hostess."

It took every ounce of energy I had to run up the stairs, and I silently cursed each cigarette I'd smoked in the past few weeks. The door to Valentin's rooms was open and I dashed inside, panting. Both he and

147

Zsófia were on the floor, each in some sort of medieval costume. Zsófia was half sitting up, rubbing her throat and moaning, her mother at her side. Valentin had a gash on his forehead, and a silvered helmet lay on the floor beside him, badly dented. He wasn't moving.

I could see Zsófia didn't need my attention as well as that of her mother, so I focused on her uncle instead. I tried to find Valentin's pulse, but to no avail. A moment later Martin ran into the room.

Alexa was wailing rather than comforting her daughter, who was trying to get up, though her mother seemed to keep pushing her down. Martin managed to find Valentin's pulse, then called for the help of his colleague. It took about half an hour, but eventually Valentin was put to bed under the watchful gaze of his two nurses. I sat with Zsófia and her mother in their salon, taking tea; it was a bizarre scene of normalcy, save Zsófia's odd costume and some blotchy marks on her throat.

"So you have no idea why Valentin tried to strangle you, Zsófia?" I asked. It wasn't a topic I'd expected to be discussing when I'd rung the doorbell with an apology on my mind.

The girl was sipping tea into which I'd stirred three spoonfuls of sugar—I'd heard my own mother's voice when I'd handed it to her saying, "There, there, that'll help a bit."

Zsófia was still tearful, but trying to put on a brave face. She half smiled. "He's sick. He doesn't know what he's doing, and there certainly doesn't have to be a reason for him doing it. Not this, not many things. It's not his fault."

I knew it wasn't my place to comment upon how poorly the family seemed to be dealing with a man whose illness was making him a danger to others, and possibly himself, and—for once—I managed to say nothing. I'd arrived ready to apologize for speaking out of turn—I didn't want to leave having created another situation that demanded I eat humble pie.

The only reason I was still there at all was because I'd felt I had to request tea be served by the cook, rather than the large brandies Alexa had suggested, and then had to stay to drink it myself. Alexa was in a state of nervous exhaustion—something I believed she was on the edge of at the best of times, so the fact that I didn't know how Zsófia was now feeling about the events of the previous night hardly seemed relevant. It was clear the family had reached a crisis point in their "management" of Valentin's condition, and I thought it would be best, once the two women were as settled as possible, to leave quickly. I drank my tea as fast as I could. Of course I was desperate to know what precipitating event could have led to Valentin trying to choke the life out of his niece, but I bit my tongue.

Having drained my cup, and scalding the roof of my mouth doing so, I said, "I'll show myself out."

Zsófia insisted on accompanying me to the top of the stairs, much to her mother's chagrin.

When we were finally alone I said, "I know you have Martin here, so you'll get the proper attention you need from a healthcare professional, but I also know you have your final exam for my course on Tuesday. If you need a medical exemption, I would be prepared to assess your course grade on the basis of the work you've already turned in, and your participation in class. I'm sure it can be sorted out within the department, and it won't jeopardize you getting the credits, or the marks, you deserve."

Zsófia smiled weakly. "Thank you, Professor. I'll see what Martin says, and I'll see a doctor if I need to. Maybe I will feel well enough to take the exam. At this moment, however, I believe I will accept your offer. This has shaken me, and I am greatly concerned about Uncle Valentin."

The student I'd come to admire in class was back; the harpy from the night before had been replaced by a sweet, vulnerable girl. I was pleased, but deeply puzzled. I weighed the risk of asking her what on earth was going on against the need to know.

"Last night . . ." I began.

Taking her hand from the bannister, against which she was steadying herself, Zsófia waved away my question.

"I wasn't myself last night. I am now. I—" she paused for at least ten seconds, "I did something very foolish last night. I took some pills that were supposed to calm me before my performance. I was so terribly nervous, you see, and I didn't want to spoil my big chance. They seemed to work, but they had the opposite effect afterward." Her eyes dropped. "I shouldn't have listened to the person who advised me to try them, and I certainly shouldn't have drunk beer at the same time. I know that now. I will never do it again." She looked back at the room we'd left. "Please, don't tell Mama. She'd be angry with me. It would hurt her."

"Was it Stanislav who gave you the pills?" I was immediately angry.

"No, it was someone else. Someone I know a little at the HUB. They meant well, I believe. But I learned my lesson. Truly I have."

I thought about all the stupid choices I'd made in my life and decided to be mature about it—Zsófia didn't need me nagging her to "just say no."

Zsófia's face brightened when I nodded my acceptance of her contrition. "Maybe something good came from last night," she said. "What you said, about not just one record producer thinking I am good, has helped me decide to talk to my mother about my singing. I will invite her to a performance. We will discuss what I should do after that. I was caught up in the emotion of last night. I apologize for speaking foolishly, and rudely, Professor. You have shown nothing but kindness to me and my family."

Her eyes were downcast, her lip trembling, hands shaking. I suspected she was suffering shock after the attack, and knew it wasn't the time to give a speech, so I said, "Zsófia, I'm glad something I said has made a difference, but, in all honesty, I am the one who should apologize. I had no right to speak as I did. I came here today to say that, and want you to know I acknowledge it."

I let myself out onto the street glad I'd had the chance to speak as I had, but wondering what had precipitated her uncle's attack. The fact that she was dressed as a medieval princess wearing a leather battle-bodice was also something that hadn't been broached . . . which might have been for the best.

Chilling Words

ALTHOUGH I'D TALKED ALEXA OUT of force-feeding me brandy, I knew I felt like a drink. I found the bar I'd been heading for before my detour to the Seszták/Takács house in just a few minutes, managed to get a window seat, and allowed myself to give in to the guilt-ridden joy of a cigarette. When I caught the eye of a waiter I ordered a large gin and tonic; I don't really care for brandy, and I didn't need more tea and certainly didn't want a coffee—my entire body was still vibrating from the "excitement" I'd just experienced.

A couple of drinks, a plate of cold sausage and cheese, and several cigarettes later, I was feeling much more composed and a good deal less sweaty. I knew I wasn't far from a metro station, and that I could get back to my apartment within an hour, but I didn't want to do it in the dark. With the end of the day not far off, and temperatures dropping, I decided I'd better make a move.

Just as I was pulling on my coat, my phone rang inside my purse. Of course, by the time I found it, it had stopped. I checked to see who'd phoned me. I didn't recognize the number; it was local, which I thought odd. The phone played its little tune again before I'd reached the door to leave, and I paused in the warmth of the café to answer it.

It turned out it was Laszlo—using his friend's phone because his battery had died. As he blustered on about Zsófia, I contemplated the never-ending ability of young people to allow cars to run out of gas, phones to lose their charge, and printers to run out of ink halfway through printing out a class assignment. The gist of his heartfelt bleating, which I only half listened to, was that he was worried about the girl.

I wondered if I should tell him this was the beginning of a lifetime of worrying about some girl or other, but decided I shouldn't be so cynical. I also decided I shouldn't heighten his concerns by mentioning that a family member had just tried to strangle her, so used my closest approximation to my husband's calming voice to try to get him to be a little less agitated. He seemed convinced Zsófia was about to disappear on a private jet to Moscow. I assumed he'd made a leap of vivid imagination to supply the record producer Stanislav with such a mode of transportation, but I only managed to put his mind at rest when I told him I'd just shared tea with Zsófia and her mother, and she'd told me she was going to talk to Alexa about her dreams of a singing career.

As I pressed the screen of my phone to disconnect, I noticed a man sitting in the corner wearing a dark coat with the collar turned up (despite the warmth of the bar), who touched the screen of his phone at the exact moment I did mine. He was holding the phone close to his face, a wire leading from it to a single earbud. His eyes met mine as we mirrored each other's action, and he forced a smile, as did I. As I pushed my phone back into my purse I couldn't help but think of the little room back at the House of Terror featuring the headsets and telephone-bugging machines the secret police had used. Why was that? Was I so discombobulated by the goings-on at Zsófia's home that I was now allowing the soup of secrets and lies I'd come to know existed within that family to infect my own outlook?

I tried to push the connection I'd made to one side, and headed out to the metro. At the bottom of the steps that led from the street I walked along the platform and turned to peer into the tunnel—*because that always makes a train arrive faster.* A short, skinny-legged young man wearing a dark peacoat with a turned-up collar sauntered onto the platform. He didn't look at me at all, which I judged to be odd, because there were only four of us in the whole place, and everyone else seemed to be looking about at their fellow travelers. It wasn't long before a train arrived, and I got a seat with no problem. The peacoated young man sat in the next carriage along.

When I got off at my station I stood outside the doors of the train and watched to see if the man with the upturned collar got off too. He didn't, which gave me a ridiculous sense of relief. As I continued my journey I told myself there was no reason on earth why anyone would want to either listen to my telephone conversations or follow me.

Unfortunately, any sense of security I had managed to build for myself was dashed when I arrived at the front door of my apartment. It wasn't shut, and I knew it should have been.

Everybody's sat in front of a screen and shouted—even if silently, or muffled by a pillow—"Don't go into the attic, basement, or closet because that's where the monster, serial killer, or vampire is hiding." I also know that a door that should be locked but isn't, is not the one you walk through calling, "Hello? Anybody there?" That's just asking for trouble. I know this because I watch TV and movies.

The weird thing was, that was exactly my instinct—to walk right in and assume the best; and that's quite normal. Human beings possess an extraordinary desire to protect ourselves—we'd die out as a species if we didn't. However, we also have a level of confidence, often misplaced, that we are safe in familiar surroundings. The apartment wasn't my home, but it had been a place where I'd spent a good deal of time, and I felt comfortable inside it. It was also surrounded, on an open balcony set around a courtyard, by other apartments full of individuals, couples, and families going about their normal early Saturday evening business. I didn't feel as though my safety was threatened—I just hoped there might be some perfectly good explanation for my front door being unlocked and ajar.

In the two seconds it took me to assimilate all these thoughts, I didn't move, didn't touch the door at all, and didn't make a sound.

I'm not sure I even breathed. Then my self-preservation instinct took over, and I looked around at the other apartments on my landing to see which ones were obviously occupied. I scampered around the balcony to the third apartment along, where the loud zither and violin music I'd heard so often late at night was playing. Lights shone through the long casement windows into our shared space. I knocked and waited. When a raven-haired woman in her thirties answered, a dishcloth in one hand, half an onion in the other, and a cigarette in her mouth, I introduced myself and explained hurriedly, in my Welsh-accented Hungarian, that I thought someone had broken into my apartment. She threw the grubby cloth over her shoulder, took the cigarette from her mouth, peered around the balconies with wild, dark eyes, and hauled me through her door. I felt completely safe, and even more convinced I was in no danger, when I saw the size of her husband, who dwarfed me in every dimension.

A hurried conversation followed wherein the pros and cons of calling the police were discussed. I gathered the couple—Abigél and Andras—preferred to not do so, though they agreed it was my decision because it was my apartment. Eventually I agreed that, much against my better judgment, Andras could go into my place and check if it was safe. He retrieved a long, heavy wrench, which worried and comforted me in equal measure. I stayed with Abigél, hovering in the couple's doorway, as her husband lumbered to my apartment and disappeared inside. We held each other's hands, which was comforting. Ludicrously, it made me worry I might smell of onions for the whole evening. Several anxious moments later, Andras poked his head out, smiled, and called us over. Slamming her door, and locking it behind us, Abigél and I joined her husband, as he showed us into every room of my little place—I was glad I'd spent a bit of time clearing up before I'd gone out earlier in the day—and he was right, there was no one there. I also couldn't see that anything had been moved or was missing.

The couple invited me to join them for dinner, but I declined. Whatever Abigél had been preparing when I arrived had smelled wonderful, and certainly involved the liberal use of paprika and onions, but I wasn't feeling hungry. I was anxious to lock myself in and talk to Bud. I explained all of this, and also agreed we should meet for tea at some point. They left, first making sure I had their phone number, and that I understood I could phone them at any time of the day or night if I had a problem.

I allowed myself some time to walk slowly around the apartment using my eidetic memory to assure myself nothing had been moved or taken. By the time I was entirely satisfied nothing had been so much as disturbed, it was almost time for my 8:00 PM get-together with my husband. I acknowledged I was beginning to feel the strain of what was supposed to have been a "quiet day off." I tried to sound calm as I recounted the day's events to my spouse. He wasn't impressed.

"So let me get this straight," said Bud testily when I let him get a word in edgeways. "You've rescued a girl from the murderous clutches of her uncle, you think someone is listening to your cellphone conversations, you believe you've been tailed across Budapest, and your apartment has apparently been broken into. Have I captured all the highlights of your day in there?"

"None of it was my fault, Bud. All I did was go to a museum."

Bud scratched his head. Hard. "I don't know what to say, Cait, really I don't. No sooner have we both agreed to walk away from a problematic investigation than you're on the radar of who knows what sort of person thousands of miles away from me, so I can't do anything to comfort, help, or protect you. I'm not happy, Cait, not happy at all. I feel so useless." Bud cursed quietly. "Why am I not there with you? Can't you just stay in the apartment until I get there on Saturday? Can't someone cover for you at the university?"

"Please don't worry so. Poor Zsófia was in the wrong place at the wrong time when her uncle suffered an episode, and I'm probably seeing suspicious characters where only other tourists exist. Nothing was so much as disturbed here at my apartment, trust me on that; my special memory at least allows me to be able to tell you that with complete conviction. Maybe I just didn't lock the door properly, and it blew open," I said—almost convincingly, I thought.

"You're hopeless, you know," said Bud, sighing. "Thank goodness. I'd hate to have a wife who was a good liar."

"Thanks?"

We stared at each other silently for a moment. Dark circles beneath Bud's eyes told me he wasn't sleeping well, the mess he'd made of his hair informed me he was deeply stressed, and the look of resignation on his face spoke volumes. He wiped his dry-skinned, pink nose with a tissue. He was still far from well.

"Bud, I know we both feel completely helpless—but we're not. Like I said, I'm probably imagining things, and you know I can be a bit forgetful of routines, like remembering where I've put my keys or Marty's treats, for example." I noticed at least a faint smile play around my husband's lips at this. "I might have a photographic memory, but if I'm not paying attention to what I'm doing—and that's often the case when I'm doing something repetitive—I don't recall things too well. I promise to keep an eye open for anything odd—anything at all, and report to you. Or the local police, if need be. There are good locks on the front door and casement windows of this place and I've checked them all; they're in perfect working order, not a scratch on them, and they are all currently in use. They will be at all times. I *will* pay attention to that. I really have stepped away from the Seszták case, as have you. Besides, I don't believe there can be any link between the folks in Canada telling you to back off, and my front door being open in Hungary."

Bud's jaw clenched. All he managed was a grunt. Not a good sign. "I'm taking Mom to the surgeon's office on Wednesday, and we're hoping she'll get the all-clear. Then I can allow Dad to look after her himself. I'll be there with you on Saturday. Please keep yourself safe until then?"

It was late; we'd been talking for a long time, and I knew I needed to get to bed, which I did after one final check that the front door and all of the windows were locked.

I was surprised that the next thing I knew it was gone nine in the morning; it's unusual for me to sleep right through the night. I suspected I was exhausted, and my body was grabbing the rest it needed while it could. Of course, once I was up, I was wide awake—though sore all over.

Standing in front of the bathroom mirror I looked myself up and down—not something I do often because it's just too depressing— and told myself my aches and pains were all connected to stress, and nothing to do with the fact that I was staring fifty in the face, or that I'd been smoking my brains out for a few weeks after having given it up, cold turkey, just over seventeen months earlier. I conceded to my pitiful reflection that maybe my getting through a bottle of gin a week by way of "rewarding" myself for a job well done at the end of each day might also be taking its toll. Apparently my body didn't like me living the life I'd been quite comfortable with before Bud and I started dating. I told myself it had to stop. And I meant it.

I'd brushed my teeth, then allowed the water to run hot so I could wash my face. It took a while. As the steam finally rose up and enveloped the mirror, I felt suddenly cold. Something was written on the glass in such a way that it could only be read in a steamy room.

DO NOT MEDDLE appeared across the bottom of the mirror. I could see my reflected mouth hanging open, my eyes wide—then the steam rose farther, and I felt my whole body begin to sway. LISTEN TO YOUR HUSBAND was written higher up.

There was nowhere to run, and no one to battle, so the adrenaline just shot around my body until my entire being began to tremble. As I stood there staring, the words dripped into nothingness. It didn't matter that they were gone; they were seared onto my mind's eye. As was their meaning.

Someone *had* been inside my apartment, and they'd chosen to leave a message in such a way only I would see it, and fleetingly at that.

Do not meddle? Many people might be in the know that I was looking into Ilona Seszták's death.

Listen to your husband? Chillingly, only someone who'd heard Bud telling me to back off the case would write that.

That could only mean one thing—someone had been listening to our Skype conversations. Listening to us when I believed I was alone in the apartment.

As the realization dawned upon me I felt utterly exposed, and it wasn't because I was naked. I grabbed a towel, pulled on my robe, and went to sit on my bed. It didn't take long before the adrenaline coursing through my veins won out, and I was sobbing like a child. I hugged my knees. It was around one in the morning in Vancouver, so phoning Bud would rouse the entire household.

I desperately wanted to hear my husband's voice—to listen to him explain away the message on the mirror. But how could he? How would knowing about it make *him* feel? It wasn't as though he could do anything to help me.

I rocked myself back and forth as my mind darted about. Should I phone the police? What would I tell them? The message had disappeared completely. I knew my neighbors had invited me over, but I didn't want to bother them. Finally, I stopped crying and decided I was a big girl and I could cope on my own. I left the bedroom and sat at my desk looking out over the city beneath me. I glared at the cigarettes beside my computer. "Not even you can help me," I told them.

Whispers in a Church

I HONESTLY BELIEVE I'M AN optimist, but I had a hard time seeing anything good about my situation. I checked all of the locks in the place again, then finally ventured back into the bathroom. I discussed with myself the alternatives of staying where I was and stewing until I could talk to Bud again, or leaving and seeking out crowds into which I could disappear. Neither prospect was appealing.

After an hour of attempting the sitting and stewing option, I knew it wouldn't work. I couldn't settle, and I'd drive myself nuts if all I did was prowl around the apartment for hours; it wasn't that big. Eventually, I gave myself a good talking to, made myself look presentable, and headed out hoping activity would help with my jitters.

I decided to take the bus to the Fisherman's Bastion; I wanted to be with as many people as possible, and reckoned it was just the place to go. I tried not to look over my shoulder as I walked down Gellért Hill, nor to stare at the people on the bus, but once I alighted at my destination I felt a little more comfortable; as I'd expected, even on a chilly November Sunday morning, the Bastion was buzzing with tourists.

Once I was a part of the throng I felt able to take out my phone and hold it up, pointing it in every direction as though I was taking photographs—so I could study the people around me. Everyone looked innocent enough—cold, but not paying more attention to me than they should be. After about an hour of wandering the seven-turreted neo-Gothic walls, on both the upper and lower levels, I was chilled to the bone. I found the arch-covered walkways lined with statues in niches were slightly less frigid than the open spaces, and there was a pretty constant stream of people coming and going, so I lingered, seemingly entranced by the detail of the sculpting. I pretended to be taking photos and offered to do so for several couples who were delighted I could help capture them together in front of the imposing carved figures.

I knew the Matthias Church opened its doors to the public at one in the afternoon, after services, and I was counting on it being a good deal warmer in there, with the result being that I was about the fourth person in the line to buy an entry ticket. I was delighted to get inside and feel my extremities begin to thaw. I took the chance to sit on one of the wooden pews that lined each side of the aisle. It was impossible to keep track of everyone around me, so I decided to push my paranoia aside, as far as I could, and take in my surroundings.

It was a magnificent sight: every surface, including the pillars, the vaulted roof, and every inch of the walls, was painted in rich hues, and the gold detailing shimmered in the pale winter sun streaming through the stained-glass windows. Groups of tourists whispered in hushed tones so the entire building seemed to hiss with secrets. The devout crossed themselves as they approached the chancel steps. I couldn't imagine how many years you'd have to sit there just to be able to take it all in. It was somewhat overwhelming, and yet, to my frazzled senses, it didn't feel sacred—or safe.

My rear end is quite well padded, but the unyielding wooden pew was too much to bear after about half an hour, so I joined the shuffling masses, and peered around as I moved through the imposing, historic structure. Beyond the main body of the church are side chapels, separated in some cases by pointed Gothic arches. I peeped inside, with my fellow visitors, and all were empty, save one. A short, portly man wearing a coat with a turned-up collar was wandering aimlessly. Our eyes locked for a moment, and he turned away—too quickly.

It wasn't the man I'd seen at the metro station the day before, of that I was sure, nor the one I'd seen in the café. Was he just another tourist trying to keep himself warm? Or had he followed me into the church? I suspected the latter wasn't true, because a second or two after he'd looked into my eyes, he turned on his heel and walked out into the main body of the church. I moved to sit on a pew where I could keep an eye on him. I had to bob my head about a bit to not lose sight of him, so I saw him go directly to a much taller, slimmer man and speak to him—quietly enough that the other man had to bend his head to listen. They both turned their heads in my direction, and I instinctively ducked out of sight.

Sitting there, hunched on a pew, surrounded by the whispers of people oohing and aahing at the décor, I checked my watch. 2:18 PM. It wouldn't be long before I could phone Bud. I looked up and swept the church with an unblinking gaze. No sight of either of the men. I pulled on my gloves, and left the warmth the church had offered, venturing out again into the throngs.

It seemed I'd chosen a particularly busy time to descend the stone steps to the bus stops along the riverbank below. Shoals of tourists were being led up from their luxurious, heated coaches by guides waving flags, umbrellas, and, in one case, a cockerel on a stick. I wondered if that group might be French. I felt as though I was swimming upstream, even though I was walking down the steps. As I passed between two bustling groups I lost my footing and tumbled forward into open space.

I caught a whiff of cigars beside me, felt the touch of a padded jacket beneath my gloved hand as my arms flailed, and saw the flashes of cameras out of the corner of my eye as I tumbled. I know I screamed—as did others about me. For an instant I was airborne—then something painful was digging into my arms and I stopped flying. I dropped to the ground.

The first thing I was aware of was the searing pain in my right elbow. The second was a man with a stump of a cigar in his mouth bending over me, dropping ashes and screaming in Italian that someone should call an ambulance. The crowd was pushed back from me by a woman in her thirties wearing a sensible coat and shoes.

"Okay?" she asked.

I nodded. The motion hurt. It seemed I'd twisted my neck, so I reached around to rub it. The leather of my glove was torn, the flesh on my fingers scraped and bloodied, my fingernails ripped. I pulled off the remains of the glove, and felt the back of my neck. I'd make it. Some discussion ensued—loudly, and in several languages—about whether I should be helped up or forced to remain sprawled across two steps until a medical professional arrived. I decided I wanted to move, and chose to ignore the multilingual assurances I'd be too heavy to lift. A few men helped, and I made it upright. I placed my weight on each foot in turn, and moved each arm carefully. Then each wrist. Everything worked. Nothing was broken. My thumping heart slowed a little, and I asked who had grabbed me to save me from a much worse fall. A tall man wearing an impressive full-length sheepskin coat timidly raised his hand, and received a spontaneous round of applause.

I declined all offers of help, and moved to the side of the steps so I could lean against the balustrade. It took me about ten minutes to feel confident I could make my way again, by which time all but the sensibly clad woman, who'd turned out to be a French nurse, had gone. I was lucky a nurse had been on hand, and she was confident I hadn't knocked my head at all, so I was "allowed" to leave.

I took my time descending the rest of the steps under the watchful gaze of the helpful Frenchwoman, and finally stood on the banks of the Danube looking back up toward the conical turrets of the Fisherman's Bastion. I searched the crowds for the face of the person whose hand I was almost convinced I had felt in the small of my back just before

I slipped. No one except the nurse was paying the slightest attention to me.

I couldn't shake my suspicion that someone had pushed me down those steps, but who? I also realized if it hadn't been for the lucky grab a passing tourist had made, I could have been in much—*much*—worse shape than I was. As it was, all I was suffering was a badly grazed hand, a sore neck, and an acidic panic in the pit of my stomach. I turned up my collar, kept my eyes working the crowds around me, and headed for the bus. I had to get to a public telephone as soon as I could—only then could I get hold of Bud and tell him about my concerns, and plans.

Stolen Conversations

HUMAN BEINGS ARE FASCINATING CREATURES; the question of why we do what we do has been my chosen field of study for the better part of twenty years. Sadly, as I sat on a crowded bus that frigid November afternoon in Budapest, I realized I was still none the wiser. I've faced killers and accused them of their crimes. I've been in dangerous situations and have found my way out of them. I've watched police interrogations of people who have committed heinous acts and seen them smile as they admit to them. But I'd never felt as scared of every other person around me as I did on that bus journey.

Back in September I'd laughingly said to Bud, "It's not paranoia if they really are out to get you." At the time I'd been referring to the cloak and dagger shenanigans in my department at UVan; now the words swirled around my brain for an entirely different reason. Was that all they were? Just words? I told myself to breathe deeply and think rationally: if "someone" was out to get me, then who? And why?

I realized I'd lost track of where I was on the bus route, and the windows were so steamed up it was impossible to see what was outside. I decided to get off at the next stop, and head for the nearest hotel, whatever it was.

It turned out I'd been on the bus a lot longer than I'd thought, and the nearest hotel was the Gellért. I told myself it was perfectly acceptable to believe that returning to a place I'd already visited would also make me feel just a little less vulnerable, and, on a more practical note, that it was certainly large enough to allow me the chance to find a public telephone.

In the weeks since I'd first walked through the front door of the grand old hotel two things hadn't changed—the uniformed doorman was just as glum, and the heat still hit me like a wall when I entered. On this occasion I found both things to be oddly calming. I felt my spirits rise as memories of family gatherings came to mind, summoned there by the scent of pine in the air. Then the sight of a massive Christmas tree, recently installed in the center of the lobby, made me feel *almost* festive. I scoped out the open areas, searching for a payphone, but I couldn't spot one. Eventually I asked the concierge, and was told there weren't any coin-operated payphones, only house-phones, which could be used to call up to guests' rooms. He added—a bit snootily—that the *public* spa baths had several *public* phones. I thanked the man, and made my way to the baths, as I had when I'd visited Zsófia there.

When I inquired at the front desk of the spa, I was directed to an area beyond the staff room where I'd chatted with Zsófia, and, sure enough, there were four little dark-wood booths with bifold doors housing old-fashioned payphones. I pulled open a door and was delighted to smell wood polish, and to note the entire booth was spotlessly clean. A tall stool allowed me to rest my aching body as I punched in the number for Bud's parents' house. I suspected I'd be waking people unpleasantly early on a Sunday morning, but I couldn't wait any longer.

Bud sounded sleepy when he answered, "Hello?"

"It's me."

Silence. "What's wrong? Something's wrong. What's happened? Are you okay?"

I knew I had to keep the call short, so I went for it. "Bud, I'm fine," I lied. "Don't talk, please, just listen." I told him about my discovery of the message on the mirror, and what it had said. "I have to believe my apartment is bugged. Someone's been listening to our Skype conversations. When we talk this evening, don't pass me any more information about the Seszták case. Let's just talk as though we've both packed it in."

"I thought we had." Bud sounded angry and worried.

"Of course, I know we *have*, but I want to make that clear to whoever is listening. Otherwise, let's stick to family stuff, university stuff, that sort of thing. Keep it light, okay?"

"I don't like it, Cait." I could picture his face. Grim.

"Nor do I. But you'll be here in less than a week. I'll be fine."

The frustrated tut Bud let out in Canada almost deafened me in Hungary. "Cait, just move out. Get yourself booked into a hotel. That's what credit cards are for. Move to a hotel, lock yourself in, and live on room service. It's the only safe thing to do. That, or go to the cops."

"There's nothing to go to the cops *with*, Bud. Nothing substantial. And I don't want to tip them off by moving out of the apartment. I'm staying."

"Tip *who* off?" Anger bubbled in his voice.

"I don't know." I tried my hardest to stop my voice from trembling.

Bud cursed softly. "I love you, Cait. I can't lose you. I lost my first wife, I won't lose you too. Just stay away one night, tonight, in a hotel, I beg you."

I sighed. "It's my final session with the students tomorrow before their exam on Tuesday. I don't see what good it will do to not go home—I slept there just fine last night, but okay. I'm next door to the Gellért; I'll find out if they can fit me in—and if I can afford it."

"Good. Put it on the card. Don't worry about it. Your safety is much more important than money. Phone me and tell me what's happening when you're sorted. Call my cell."

"I'm only going to use public phones now. If the apartment is bugged, they might have some way of intercepting calls and texts from my cell. And yours. Landline to landline only from now on, if we want to have private conversations."

167

"Okay, but why not buy a pre-paid cell? Whatever version they have there."

"I didn't think of that."

"Brain the size of a planet, with only half an ounce of common sense tucked into a corner. Buy a phone and only use it to call this number. Mom and Dad's house. No one else gets your number, right? When you get any calls on your usual phone, believe every word is being listened to by someone other than the person who called you. Got it?"

"Got it. And I'll only use the Internet at Internet cafés. If I use the computer in my office, or the Wi-Fi on my normal phone, it'll just be for work stuff."

"And we need a tip-off word, Cait. A word or phrase you can use to tell me you're in danger—or that you know someone is listening. Something that sounds innocent, but something you can easily avoid during the normal course of our conversations."

I gave it some thought. "How about I ask how Marty's doing?"

"Good idea."

"How is he, by the way?"

"He's fine. Still enjoying doggie paradise with Jack and Sheila, and their dogs."

"Good. Now I won't ask about him again, unless I need to use that as a code for other reasons. Though what you can do about anything from there, I don't know. Anyway, I'll see if they have a room next door."

"Where exactly are you now?"

"Gellért Spa Baths."

"Where Zsófia works?"

"Yes, but she isn't here now. She only works in the mornings at the weekend. Besides, I really am off that case, and I don't expect to see her until tomorrow in class, if she's up to it."

"You should go, but I don't want to stop hearing your voice."

"I know what you mean." Silence. "This is silly. I'll go and see if they have a room, and work out where I can buy a phone. I'll ring you later."

"Okay."

"I love you."

"I love you."

I hung up. I'd never known before that feeling isolated was an emotion with such depths. I didn't care for the discovery.

I wrangled my way out of the phone box, and headed for the exit. As I pushed open the door to leave, it was pulled open by Zsófia, entering.

"Cait!"

"Zsófia."

"What are you doing here?"

"I needed to make a phone call." I let my mind race. "My cell has a few issues, and I wanted to tell Bud so he didn't panic if he couldn't reach me. But that's not your problem. How are you?" A red scarf, that exactly matched her lipstick, was swathed beneath her chin. I wondered if her uncle's attack had marked her throat badly—the early signs had been that it would.

Zsófia seemed to be aiming for "bright and cheery" when she replied, "Just fine, thanks. What happened to your fingers?" She looked at my scraped, bloodied hand with horror. I didn't think it looked that bad.

I tried to laugh it off. "Oh, I slipped on some steps, that's all. It looks worse than it is. Maybe they'll have some bandages in the little shop in the hotel. I'll ask. So, no ill effects after yesterday's incident?" I wasn't going to let the question go unasked, or unanswered.

The girl's right hand rose, unbidden, to touch her throat. "I'm fine, really, thank you." It seemed she wasn't going to offer an explanation for the events I'd witnessed. Maybe there wasn't one.

"So—will I see you in class tomorrow?"

"Yes, Professor, I will be there for class." She didn't make eye contact with me, and she licked her dry lips once too often for me to believe she was speaking the truth. "I must get on. I didn't come in to do my shift today, and there's something I need to collect from my locker."

I detected an underlying tone in her voice that suggested panic. *Why?* I weighed our rocky relationship and decided I had nothing to lose. "Something's wrong. Can I help?"

Her eyes darted furtively, then settled on my face. Tears welled. "I've lost Uncle's manuscript."

"The manuscript for book six? The one I read?"

"I've searched everywhere. I don't usually carry it about with me, but my locker here is the only place I can think of that I haven't looked." Tears rolled. "It's my last hope."

"You've misplaced that huge pile of paper?"

She hung her head, shoulders drooping. Tears fell onto her scarf, making darker red blotches on the fabric. A picture of abject resignation, I felt I should hug her—so I did. I swear I haven't a motherly bone in my body, but I am human, and Zsófia Takács was a person in need of comfort. "I tell you what, how about I come to your locker with you, and I can hold stuff while you empty it out to check what's there. Okay?"

The girl's muffled voice close my ear was quiet. "That would be kind. Thank you."

Pulling back from each other, I followed Zsófia. Ten minutes later we'd emptied, searched, and repacked her tiny locker. The manuscript wasn't there.

Trying to be helpful I asked, "You said you don't carry the manuscript about with you, as a rule. I can understand why you wouldn't, but might you have? Are there any other places you visit regularly? Might it be in your locker at the HUB, for example?"

"I've checked. I went there first, then came here," was her bleak reply. A change in the light in her eyes told me she'd thought of something. "It might have been in a big bag I have that I took with me to Klara's house."

"Your great-aunt's home?"

"Yes."

"Why would you take it there?" I didn't understand why she'd ever take it out of her own house at all.

"Sometimes I need to get away. Mama has kept me away from Klara and Tamás all my life, but I go there anyway. It's not like our house—it's old, and out in the countryside. You can hear your heart beating if you listen. I stay over. Mama thinks I'm at a friend's house. She doesn't know I don't really have any friends. She thinks I'm normal. It's Klara and Tamás I spend time with, not people my own age. Young people are so—I don't know, they just don't seem to have much to talk about. Because they haven't lived much, I suppose. And most of them don't have the same interests as me. I really like the old music, and the stuff Uncle Valentin writes about. I know he dresses it all up, but a lot of it is based on historical Magyar stuff."

I agreed. "The seven turrets at the Fisherman's Bastion representing the tribes that conquered the area in the ninth century are based on the shape of the Magyar tents, and your uncle used similar design ideas in his books; the battlefield scenes in book three are full of cone-shaped tents, I recall."

"You have a good memory. That's one of the details all the Bloodliners pull out."

"Bloodliners?"

"It's what the hard-core Bloodline Saga fans are called. They have memes, blogs, game-boards online. I'm sure you know what I mean. The shape of the tents is only mentioned in one sentence—it's one of their favorite bits of trivia. Why did that stick in your mind?"

I decided I'd still prefer to keep my special memory secret from Zsófia. "Maybe seeing the same shape at the Bastion today sparked the thought," I lied.

She nibbled her lip. "I might have had the papers in my overnight bag when I visited Klara. I put it away in there sometimes when I'm working on it late at night and I don't want to leave my room to store it. I don't like Janis to see it."

"Who's Janis?"

"Just the cleaning lady."

I began to wonder how many people worked at Zsófia's home in total. Maybe someone had sticky fingers?

"A lot of people seem to come and go through your home. Do you trust them all?"

Zsófia locked the little door to the long wooden cabinet that was her locker, and pursed her lips as she popped the key into her bag. "There aren't that many. At least, it's a number I am used to being there. A cook, with two helpers. A handyman. Janis, the cleaner. Uncle has four nurses on rotation. And of course there's me, Mama, and Uncle. Uncle's doctors change a good deal, and seem to come more frequently now. People deliver food and supplies all the time, of course, at the back of the house, but it's only really Janis and the nurses who have the chance to wander about the place."

I couldn't help but chuckle. "That's a lot of people coming and going. I know you might not like to think about it, but could one of them have taken the manuscript? I'm assuming they, at least, all know your uncle is VS Örsi."

Zsófia looked surprised. "They do. They all had to sign legal papers when they took their jobs. Uncle pays them well, too. But why would they take it? What could they do with it?"

My quick answer was, "Put it on the Internet. Sell it. Ransom it."

Her brow furrowed. "If they tried to sell it, or put it out into the public domain, everyone would think it was just a piece of fan-lit—there are all sorts of stories out there, often written by Bloodliners, about how they think the lives of the characters should move forward. Or end. Unless it's coming from Uncle's publisher, no one would believe it was real. Though I see what you mean about demanding money for its return. If we didn't pay up they might—I don't know . . . shred it, burn it? Then where would we be? I type it on an old typewriter. Uncle did that to start with. There's no copy. That's a terrible thought—but no one has demanded a ransom. They could ask for a lot. It's not as though Uncle doesn't have money. He has so much he doesn't know what to do with it all."

"I could think of a thing or two," was out of my mouth before I had a chance to press my internal edit button. Luckily, instead of shocking Zsófia, it made her giggle, and I felt the tension between us subside a little. I didn't mention how stupid I thought it was to not have kept a copy.

"I'll give Klara and Tamás a call and ask them to look for it at their house. Maybe I did have it with me during the week. I don't know." At least the girl's tone was more suffused with hope.

"Sounds like a plan. I am guessing you've been through your house, from top to bottom?"

Pulling out her phone Zsófia answered easily. "Yes, everywhere. Except in Uncle's rooms. I went in there to look yesterday and—well, you saw what happened."

I was glad of the chance to find out more. "He found you hunting about and didn't react well?"

"Depending on what sort of day he's having, he can be extremely touchy about people coming into his rooms. I went there, knowing I wanted to search, but I ended up putting on one of his costumes so he could see how it moved when I ran. Of course, I indulged him. I always do. Then, when he went off to make some notes, I had a bit of a dig about. He found me looking inside one of his drawers, and became angry. He didn't recognize me, you see. And sometimes he thinks everyone is spying on him."

I managed to stop myself saying, *I know how he feels*, and said instead, "If he's finished the books, why does he need to be making notes about how clothing moves?"

"Yes—that's another thing. I know he's finished the books, because I've put all his handwritten pieces together now and can see it's the end. He seems to think there's more to do—but there can't be. It's not possible. Unless he's going to start something new, and he hasn't said so if he is. Besides, the costume was the one I wear when I'm being the first queen."

"But she died in book two, didn't she?" I knew she had.

"She's back again in book six, right at the end. You didn't see that bit. Almost everyone is dead, and they all meet up in the afterlife. Uncle outdid himself. It's fascinating. The queen has her chance for revenge on her family, and the entire bloodline. That's what I mean about it all being finished. I could tell you about the bits you missed, if you'd like. Just let me call Klara, and I'll fill you in. We could have a coffee next door, in the espresso bar. The terrace would be too cold, but it's cozy inside."

I agreed with her idea and waited while she made her call.

"Tamás answered," she announced as we left. "I told him I was with you and he said he'd like to meet you. He's going to come here to collect me so I can go with him and look for the manuscript myself."

Coffee Chatter

BY THE TIME WE WERE settled on comfy red-upholstered chairs in the warmth of the Gellért Espresso, I felt more than ready for a Turkish coffee and a gargantuan slice of something called Esterházy torte, which Zsófia assured me I would enjoy. Its spider-webbed topping, the pinstripe layers of vanilla- and cognac-flavored butter icing studded with crushed walnuts, and macaroon pastry were just what I needed. Mentally, I justified my indulgence as I devoured it by telling myself the nuts made it healthy.

Ten minutes later I was dancing on a sugar high, topped off with richly caffeinated coffee, and in heaven. I didn't even mind that it was a non-smoking café, and told myself maybe nicotine would be just one chemical too many for my body to bear.

I felt able to focus more clearly on Zsófia's problem, and suggested, "Might Valentin have taken the manuscript, to work on it some more, and not told you?"

"That's why I wanted to hunt about in his quarters," agreed Zsófia nibbling a dismally plain-looking sponge finger. "After the incident yesterday, Martin gave him something to quieten him down, but I didn't feel up to having a look for it right then, and his nurses have been buzzing around him all day today. He's having a quiet day—which means he's feeling rather weak and is confused about where he is, and when it is. When he's this way, in his mind he can be in Canada as a child, or even in the world he's created in his books as any one of the characters. It's as though he 'remembers' being them all, you see. He tells me he's lived every life he's created. It makes for a challenging situation all round when he's out of step with the world about him, as he is today."

"It's a difficult disease, for all concerned."

"It is. Mama copes as she can—usually by turning up the volume on her music. She wears headphones a lot of the time, so she doesn't disturb Uncle. But she's alone in the house all day, and she doesn't mix much with anyone really. She tries to lose herself in her music. She has a particular fondness for Liszt and Bartok."

"Did your home used to be a social meeting place? Before your uncle's illness?" I said.

Zsófia's laugh was genuine. "Oh no. Never. I was not allowed to bring friends to visit when I was young."

You're still young, I thought. "Me neither," I said. "I didn't have a lot of friends, and those I did have didn't visit often. I don't know which came first—the not having friends, or the not visiting. It just all seemed normal to me. My friends were all in books."

"Me too," said Zsófia, grinning. "Since I can remember, Uncle's characters have been like real people to me. I suppose I have lived their lives too, like he has. Even the weird ones."

"Did you have a cat that raided the hen house?" I asked.

"You mean like in book three? No. That was Grandmother's cat, Uncle said. It got out of their home when she and Grandfather were still living in Budapest, when they were just married, and it got into a neighbor's hen house. In those days many people kept hens for the eggs. It was in the 1950s, so they needed all the food they could manage to get for themselves. Uncle said there was a big fight about it. Of course, that was a long time before he was born to them in Canada, but she told him about it, it seems."

"I enjoyed reading your uncle's books. Even though I know you don't want me involved in your lives any more, it's been a pleasure and a privilege to meet your family. I hope you all find peace with each other, and your shared history. Real, and fictionalized."

Zsófia put down her dainty coffee cup. "It's been a difficult few weeks for us all. I don't know how to say this, but I really would like to know what happened to Grandmother. But now . . . I daren't ask again. We have been . . . hot and cold about it. That's correct?"

"It is, and you have been. I suppose it's understandable, in some ways. To want to know, but to be afraid to uncover the truth." I made a decision. "Zsófia, I have stood down. If you want me to step up again, I think I should wait until Bud arrives at the weekend. He's the one who's been doing all the work back in Canada."

Pink-faced, Zsófia pulled at the scarf she still had wrapped about her neck. The loosened folds revealed red welts from her uncle's grip. Bruises were setting in too. I felt sorry for her, but took her motion to suggest she was not only getting overheated, but she trusted me enough to allow the marks to show. "I said some terrible things to you at the club the other night, Cait." It was the first time she'd called me anything but "Professor" since then. "I was on a high. Those pills I took. And the adrenaline. You talked about how that can make human beings do some strange things in one of your lectures. Stanislav Samokhin is the best person in the world to help me have the career I want. I know I could have many hit songs with him behind me. Having him in the room was the most thrilling thing that's ever happened to me. Then you said what you did, and, I admit it, I hated you for doing it. Now I see things differently. You were right. I had lost perspective. I know his reputation, and I truly believe it would be different for me, that I am strong enough to avoid the temptations such a life would place before me. I am still not sure you had the right to speak to him as you did, but I am certain I absolutely had no right to speak to you as I did. I am sorry."

"Words can never be unsaid. They ring in our ears forever—sometimes when we least want them to. But I understand what you're saying. If what I said has helped you decide to share your hopes and dreams with your mother, then maybe it was for the best. With her support you might be even less likely to founder in your career. Has there been an opportunity for her to hear you perform yet?"

"Not yet—though I have sung for her at home, and she enjoyed it. I didn't sing the old songs, of course, and I still haven't told her I've been spending time with Klara and Tamás. That might be too much for her all at once. However, in time, that will come too. I must be more mature in my dealings with her."

I couldn't help but smile as I asked, "Tell me why your mother is so set against you mixing with your great-aunt and uncle. Is it solely because of your great-uncle's role as an informant under the Communist regime?"

"Since Mama told me the news about him, we've talked about it a few times. It's been difficult for her. What she said was he could have got another job—that he didn't have to help the Communists do what they did. Klara stood by him; he was her husband, she loved him, so she would. Mama understands that. When Grandfather brought Mama and Uncle Valentin to Budapest, that was when they found out about Tamás. It seems Grandfather Kristóf and Tamás had been in touch with each other, in letters, over the years, but not so much since Grandmother's death. They weren't family, not *blood* family, though Grandfather treated him like a brother, Mama said. When Grandfather found out Tamás had been on the side of the Communists, he said he was done with him and Klara. In fact, the only reason they didn't all go straight back to Canada was because Mama had met my papa. They married quickly, because Grandfather was sick by then. After that, she wanted to stay because my papa was from Budapest and his life was here, so Uncle stayed too. When Papa died, Mama stayed on because I was doing well at school, and Uncle Valentin was working with the Hungarian publisher on his books. He'd been working on them since the time Grandfather died, but it took him some time to be ready to show them to anyone. I like my country. I've never left it, yet, but I'd like to travel. I'd especially like to go to Canada, where Mama and Uncle Valentin were born. Stanislav said my voice could take me anywhere I wanted, even Canada."

Knowing he'd said nothing of the sort at the club I asked, "When did he tell you that?"

"I called him yesterday morning to tell him I had taken your advice and spoken to my mother about my career. He was angry. He told me many things my voice could do for me. He talked about money a lot. He has no idea who my uncle is and how much money he has, so he would. Most people want money, don't they?"

I said I suspected they did, then asked, "How angry was Stanislav? Has he told you he's not interested in working with you anymore?"

Zsófia didn't answer, instead she shot to her feet as a short, round, extremely aged man approached. "Tamás, you're here." She looked at her watch as she pulled her scarf about her throat. "I didn't realize time had passed so quickly. Cait, this is my great-uncle, Tamás Örsi. This is my professor, Cait Morgan, Tamás. She's the one who's visiting from Canada. The one I told you about." Zsófia's flushed face glowed even more with excitement and apprehension.

The little man looked to be about ninety. He spoke gravely, "You are the one who has been digging into the death of my sister. I have told Zsófia, I do not think this is a good idea." It was a strange greeting.

Tamás peered at me, then at Zsófia, through his round, wire-rimmed spectacles with lenses so thick his eyes looked like raisins. He unbuttoned his coat but didn't sit. "Whatever you have been doing, I think you have been wasting your time. I do not believe we will ever know who killed my sister. The book is closed on this matter."

Zsófia looked at me, her cheeks flushed. "I have explained to Tamás and Klara that it would mean a great deal to me to know the truth about my grandmother's death." She glanced at the elderly man. "Klara agrees with me. Tamás does not. We have reached an impasse."

I held my tongue. It's not my first choice as an interrogation technique, but I've seen it work for Bud in the past, so I thought I'd give it a go. We all sat. "Zsófia tells me you are a very clever woman. So, do you have new ideas about this old death?"

I shrugged.

"Cait's husband was the one doing the research in Canada, I told you, Tamás. Cait cannot do more when she is here. Grandmother's death will be solved in Canada, not in Hungary." She sounded certain.

The old man's rheumy eyes twinkled with—what was it . . . curiosity, or condemnation?—as he replied, "Sometimes it is enough to know a person is dead. To know why they died is not necessary. Know the life, not the death. That is all that is important."

I was fascinated that here was another family member quite happy to not know who had killed Ilona. Alexa, Valentin, and now Tamás were all urging Zsófia to back off. Why on earth wouldn't they want the truth to come to light? What was it they all suspected—or knew?

I was intrigued by Tamás's comment. "What do you mean, 'Know the life, not the death?'"

Zsófia leaned forward in her seat as the elderly man opposite me shrugged and replied, "I don't know how much your mother has told you about your grandmother, my dear," he smiled at his great-niece, "but I believe not much. That is because I do not believe she knows a great deal. When my once-dear friend and brother-in-law Kristóf returned to Hungary he listened to rumors about me. After one terrible confrontation, he cut himself off from me and my beloved wife forever. Since that day, your mother has not spoken with me or Klara. It is her choice. All based on a misunderstanding."

Zsófia whispered, "Do you mean you weren't an informant for the Communists?" She looked excited.

Tamás looked at her with sad eyes. "No. That much is true. I did inform."

"Tamás," hissed Zsófia, "speak quietly. People will hear you."

Tamás surveyed the room. He reminded me of a tortoise peering out of its shell with his head swiveling slowly on his leathery neck. "Tourists, only tourists. What do they care? And the girl behind the counter? She's your age. She and you live for now. We older ones? We all still live for back then. We have no choice. For us, me and my Klara especially, our neighbors would not allow us to forget, which is why we left the city. They all condemned me. Would you condemn me, Cait?"

I decided to come clean. "I saw your photograph at the House of Terror yesterday, Tamás. It was on the wall they reserve for portraits of informers. However, what that photograph didn't tell me was whether you informed because you believed in the party line."

Zsófia studied her fingernails.

"The party line, ah yes," replied the old man, his head high, "those were the days." He snorted. "What choice did I have but to inform? None. My darling wife, Klara, has Roma blood. The Communists wanted the Roma to work in their factories—to do the dirtiest, most dangerous jobs. By doing what they wanted me to do I made sure her extended family had cleaner, safer jobs. Her family cast her out because she married a non-Roma. Me. I saved them from bad lives, though they never knew this. Like my brother-in-law, they too cut us out of their lives. Klara and I have each other. Only each other. People who did not live my life do not understand what it was like back then. They cannot understand. To do nothing was wrong. To do something was also wrong. It seemed no one could do anything that was right. I believe that to help those you love to live as well as they can is right. Maybe I did wrong, but it was what I did."

His logic contained a certain fatalistic harmony, and he was correct—I had no idea what it must have been like to be squashed by the Nazis, then the Communists, so I decided it was best to just say, "I'm sorry, Tamás. It must have been difficult for you. Sometimes the only choices available to us are bad choices, but they still have to be made. Now you have another choice to make—to tell Zsófia what she has asked to know, or not. To tell her about her grandmother, the sister you knew. It might help her work out whether Ilona's death was because of the woman she once was here, in Hungary, or because of the woman she was in Canada. Because, let's be honest, it must have been one or the other."

He cackled at me. "You do not understand what you are saying."

"Tamás, please don't laugh at Cait, she's right," whispered Zsófia. I could see she was close to tears. "I'm so tired of all the lies and secrets. What you just said about having to do things you didn't want to do to save Klara's family—that's the first time you've said something like that to me, or even in front of me. Why does everyone treat me like a child? I'm not. I'm old enough to be told things. I want to know the truth about my family, not to have people trying to protect me from . . . who knows what."

Tamás pushed his spectacles up his nose with a wizened finger and looked at his great-niece with what I judged to be a mixture of affection and pity. "You are correct, Zsófia. When you are old like me, it is easy to forget how it feels to be young, and to want to know everything. I know too much. You believe you know too little. I accept you have the right to know about your grandmother, but we should not speak of this here. Come home with me for dinner. We will speak more of this with Klara. She also knew your grandmother when we were all young." He looked at me. "You come too. You are the sort of woman who always wants to know more." The thick lenses of his glasses glinted.

I hesitated. "I'm not sure if I should. I would need to get back here afterward, you see."

"Here?" Zsófia was puzzled.

Rats! "I was thinking of having a night of luxury, here, tonight," I lied.

"Here? Luxury?" scoffed Tamás. "You'd need a suite for that. This place was fitted out by the Communists, and I don't think they've changed much."

"Tamás, look around you, the new owners are spending a good deal of money here. It's becoming fashionable again," chided his great-niece.

Leaning in Tamás said, "The higher-ups in the party would stay here. Beyond the means of normal people. Of course they allowed the Western tourists to stay as well. Fancy food here. Always. But I hear the beds are bad. Stay with us. We have a room. It is better than a hotel. We have country air."

"Klara and Tamás live in Budakeszi," explained Zsófia. "It's about twenty minutes away, in the forest. It is popular for people to visit."

The first thought to cross my mind was that I didn't fancy Tamás driving me anywhere—let alone out into the forest, in the dark, on a night I was sure would become slippery with frost and possibly ice. He didn't look equal to the task. His eyesight was pretty questionable, I reckoned. I reminded myself he'd driven here, and had managed all right, but I still wasn't keen.

Bud's always telling me my face gives away my inner thoughts, so maybe Zsófia picked up on my concerns because she added, "Tamás allows me to drive his car. I can drive us there tonight, and I'll drive all three of us to class in the morning, then Tamás can take his car home again. We wouldn't be late for the lecture, Cait, I promise."

I weighed my concerns about being driven by an inexperienced driver or a nonagenarian, and realized I'd probably prefer to stay put. However, I admitted to myself my curiosity was piqued. It seemed Tamás had judged me correctly—I do always want to know more.

I agreed to the plan to dine and stay over, then excused myself to nip off to the little shop in the hotel to get some overnight necessities before we departed. As I was hovering beside the emergency toothbrushes I realized I'd done nothing about finding an untraceable cellphone, but decided to not worry about that—they certainly didn't have them for sale at the hotel in any case.

Eventually, I squeezed into Tamás's tiny Skoda's back seat, buckled up, and hoped we'd reach our destination in one piece. As Zsófia sped along the still-busy roads, I held onto the seat as tightly as I could. The lights of the city were a blur, and I finally shut my eyes and tried to swallow my terror.

Safe to Talk

THE CITY WAS FAR BEHIND us when I opened my eyes again. The darkness was almost a relief, because I was less aware of our speed. There was one final, bone-jarring surprise in store for me though—we bounced over a metal grate in the road that I was laughingly informed was in place to prevent the local animals from straying.

"It is Tamás's job to make sure the animals stay where they are, in the park," said Zsófia over her shoulder.

Not knowing anything about where we were, I asked Tamás if he was now a farmer, though he seemed too old to me to have any job at all.

"I am a warden here. This is a wilderness park," replied the man seriously. "It is a big responsibility to keep the humans safe from the animals. I have done this for many years. I now have young helpers."

I wondered what sort of animals he meant, but then we arrived at the Örsis' home, so all conversation stopped. The house at which we'd arrived was small, traditionally built with white stucco and dark wood features, and every window and door was arched, showing a yellowish light. It made me think of illustrations in library books I'd seen when I was a child, when families of squirrels, or other gentle woodland creatures, were shown living in little homes set into the roots of trees, safe from the dangers of the forest about them. I was pretty sure there *was* forest all around us—because there were no other lights to be seen, and I could hear the wind whipping through bare branches in the darkness.

As we walked into the house, Tamás hailed his wife with a raucous croaking sound. She replied with a deep-throated trilling. It was a little unnerving. Not quite as unnerving as the row of rifles in a wooden case hung on the wall inside the front door.

"You have a lot of guns," I couldn't help but remark.

"We have a lot of wild animals," was Tamás's cryptic response.

Klara emerged from what I judged to be the kitchen, at the rear of the house; the woman I'd met when she was dressed in her finery was now in an old-fashioned velour dressing gown, printed with lurid red roses and butterflies. It swamped her tiny, wizened frame. Upon seeing her great-niece, the woman's face lit up, and her little arms fluttered around Zsófia's ample frame. She greeted me like a long-lost family member. We three were shooed into the main room where we sat at the dining table. Tamás disappeared for a moment, returning with three little shot glasses and a bottle made of black glass that bore a circular red label with a gold cross on it. It looked for all the world like a spherical comedy bomb with a neck. He assured me, with a sly smile, that Unicum is a drink that should be taken before every meal. I knocked back the shot-glassful he'd given me and the flavor was more disgusting than anything I've ever tasted. All I wanted to do was lick something sweet to get rid of the terrible aftertaste. Zsófia came to my rescue and offered a glass of soda water, which I accepted with gratitude, then she rushed about the house hunting for Valentin's manuscript, eventually deciding that it wasn't there after all. We all agreed it would be best for her to try to hunt through Valentin's rooms the next day, but when she was able to do so without his being there.

I was keen for the conversation to turn to Ilona, but it seemed that wasn't about to happen over dinner, which was a bowl of steaming goulash served with homemade bread and a glistening chunk of butter. It was a hearty meal, made with love and experience and, judging by the specific ingredients, on a pretty tight budget. After we'd finished, I felt warm and full. It was a lovely sensation, but it wasn't why I'd come.

Eventually, with a nod of agreement from Tamás, Klara opened a cupboard and produced a large leather-bound photograph album, which she plopped on the table in front of me and Zsófia. Tamás settled in his armchair beside the open log fire and worked on his pipe, which eventually gave off fragrant billows of smoke. We opened up the album and Klara showed us a few photographs of her and her husband as small children. Zsófia showed more interest when we were shown a picture of a foursome, who turned out to be Zsófia's grandparents with Klara and Tamás.

Ilona had been a pretty young woman, and her husband, Kristóf, looked much older than her. Tamás and Klara hadn't changed much, despite the folds of age on their faces.

"Were these photographs taken after the war?" I asked. Their ages suggested it must be the case.

"Yes, after the Nazis had left Budapest in rubble. It must have been about 1952. We were all still young, as you see. Good friends," said Klara.

"Wasn't it difficult to take photographs at that time? Having access to a camera, film, and getting it developed must have been a challenge." I said.

Klara smiled with pride. "Tamás had a good position at a newspaper, so we were able to use the camera he had for his work. The machine had a timing device. He would set it up, then run to be in the photograph himself. Tamás was an artist with the camera." The aged couple exchanged a tender glance. "And words. He would take photographs and write the stories to accompany them. We met because of that. He was taking photographs of the Roma performers in the streets, and I was singing. It was love at first sight." Her face creased into a smile as she spoke.

"Love at first sound," said Tamás, his pipe clenched between his teeth. "At first it was her singing voice, then her speaking voice. It was rich, round, and I was bewitched. Her beauty was beyond compare to my ears, and my eyes. Then I got to know the woman inside, and I loved her even more. Fate decided we should meet, and choices have kept us together."

"Tell me about Ilona. She was my blood," said Zsófia calmly. "I *feel* as though I know her though no one will tell me about her. Not properly, as though she was a real human being. Mama just dissolves or gets angry when I ask her about Grandmother. Please, talk to me about the person she was."

"Very well," said Tamás, removing the pipe from his lips. "She was my sister, so it is my tale to tell. I will be brief, for it is impossible to tell you everything I know. Ilona was brilliant. I was her brother, and brothers do not usually think well of their sisters I have found, but even I had to admit she was beautiful, intelligent, and had a great gift for languages. Here, in Hungary, Cait," he looked at me over his spectacles, which gleamed in the firelight, "we have people from many parts of Europe. It has always been this way. In the 1930s and the 1940s this was also the case. Yes, Hungarians have often left their homeland for new places, but many people have come to Hungary to find a new life also. Living in Budapest we heard many languages spoken on the streets and in the cafés each day. Ilona was like a sponge. By the time she was a teen she could understand almost any language of Europe, and could speak, read, and write many of them too. I was born in 1924—so I will reach ninety next year. Ilona was born in 1930. My baby sister. The princess of my family. You know how it is for girls in Hungarian families, Zsófia."

He arched his eyebrows and Zsófia grinned. "It's nice to be always pampered and attended to when you are a small child, Tamás, but I am a young woman now. Mama cannot see this. She still wants me to be a child. Being a princess can last too long."

Klara patted Zsófia's hand. "Enjoy your youth, my dear. It will pass soon enough."

"This is true," said Tamás. "When the Nazis arrived in 1944 Ilona was still a child, but like you, she acted like a woman. The photograph you saw? It was taken before Ilona married Kristóf in 1954. It was hard here then. The war was over, but there was so much destruction all around us. Uncertainty, too. We were glad to have the Nazis gone, and many people believed the Communists would be our saviors. Klara and I joined the Hungarian Socialist Workers' Party. Most of our friends did the same. It was common, and we did not think it was a bad thing."

"It was much better to be a socialist than a Nazi," added Klara.

Tamás nodded and sucked on his pipe. "Kristóf would not join, and Ilona didn't either. This led to pressure being put on them, and on me. I worked for a newspaper, as Klara told you, and my job was at risk because they did not sign up. Kristóf worked at the university, and Ilona was told she had to work for the government doing translation work, or else she would be sent to work in a factory, far from Budapest. In those days you never knew if you were safe. If someone, anyone—maybe a neighbor who didn't like you for some reason—wanted to get you into trouble, all they had to do was say you were a right-wing person, and the Communists would send you off to a place where you might live and work hard, or you might die. This even happened to leaders of the party itself. For it to happen to little people like us, it was nothing."

"I've read a good deal of the history of that time, though it's always hard to understand how the great events of the day, which are what history books tell us about, impacted people on a personal, and daily, basis." I'd done my homework before traveling to Hungary, and didn't need a full-on history lesson from Tamás. I was much more interested in the specifics as they related to the Örsis and the Sesztáks. Luckily, Tamás took the hint.

"Personally, I was not a political animal. I was simply concerned about keeping Klara and myself safe. I think this is natural. I tried to persuade Kristóf and Ilona to join the party. I had grown up through the war years and knew how to keep myself safe. Kristóf had different views. As a psychologist he said any repression was bad, and I believe he worked with some of the anti-Communist factions before he left for Sopron. They were lucky to get out. I know that. I forgave Ilona for not telling me of their plans. I only found out she had escaped a year later. For all I knew she and Kristóf had been taken and sent to a camp in 1956. Through a newspaper contact, I got a photograph from Canada of the faculty arriving at the University of Vancouver in 1957. She and Kristóf were in the photograph. I knew she was safe, but *not* safe. You see, when she was forced to work for the party she translated conversations that were recorded by the Communists. She and I would talk about this. I do not think she ever told her husband. He would have been angry. She worked on sensitive materials, you see. When she and Kristóf fled, I was taken and interrogated about her. It was bad. I thought I would become one of the people who disappeared, sent to one of the camps. But then they let me go. I managed to say nothing about what she had told me, but, after that, it was clear I had to help the Communists to keep everyone I loved safe. I was marked by them. I had to inform on my friends and neighbors. I had no choice."

Klara was crying silently. She didn't react to the tears rolling down her face at all. I could only try to imagine the terror she and her husband must have felt at the time.

"And that is why you are now remembered as an informant," I said quietly. "It seems unfair."

"We do what we have to do. We cannot blame people for thinking the worst when they do not know all the truth."

Zsófia looked horrified. "This is so cruel, Tamás. The people who persecuted you should have given you the chance to defend yourself."

"Why would anyone want to listen to me?" asked Tamás. "I did what I did. They knew that. No one cared why I did it."

Zsófia picked at her fingernails as she said, "Do you think the Communists might have sent someone to Canada to kill Grandmother because she knew something she shouldn't have known, because she translated it here?" I saw hope on her face. "Oh no, wait, that doesn't make sense, does it? She would have been working here in the 1950s, so why would anyone want to kill her because of that in 1976? Why wait that long? Why bother then? What could she have known that would matter all those years later?"

Tamás, Klara, and I shared a look of almost-pity.

"When you're as young as you are, Zsófia," I said, "a couple of decades or a quarter of a century is a lifetime or more. But in the world of politics, and power plays, it's not long at all."

"You are correct," said Tamás. "In 1975 we had elections. I know with certainty of two people who were elected then, who had been listened to by Ilona. If the knowledge Ilona had about their activities during the war had been made public they could have been ousted from power, or worse. Some stood for election because they were true believers, some because they saw a better life for themselves and their families that way. All the candidates were puppets of the party, and all did it because they wanted power and influence at any price—and under any regime. They didn't really care about parties or ideologies; they just wanted to be in charge. As their rulers changed they adapted their views. Ilona knew about that."

"So you think men who were Nazi sympathizers became members of the Communist government?" said Zsófia, surprised. "It seems unlikely they would change allegiance like that. And why would it be only Grandmother who knew this? Wouldn't everyone know? The people who'd been around during the war, for instance, who knew their opinions and actions then?"

"Who can be certain what a man believes in his heart when they look at him from the outside?" asked Tamás gravely. "Was I a true

Communist, informing on my friends and colleagues, and doing hateful things because I thought they were correct, or was I just a loving husband? The things we do, the words we say, and our true feelings are not always in line with each other. Ilona knew the public words and acts of these men, but she knew the private truths about them too. Yes, they were supported by the new regime, and took power within it. Because the new regime had listened to their private conversations it had leverage over them."

I had a thought. "Once these people themselves had power, they might have taken steps to eradicate that leverage. They could have been executed if Ilona had talked." I looked at Zsófia, my mind whirring. "I'll be honest; I've been thinking of Ilona's death as something that arose from a family dynamic. However, it could be she was killed to shut her up, forever, by someone who'd acquired power here."

"You mean she was assassinated?" asked Zsófia, her eyes wide.

If Tamás was speaking the truth, it sounded as though the reason for Ilona's murder could well have been connected with her work in Hungary before she fled, rather than with her family life in Canada. As both Zsófia and I came to terms with this new idea, I could see the girl's face light up with fresh hope.

"All of that is good news, Tamás. It means Grandmother wasn't killed by anyone in our family." She looked happy at the thought.

Klara laughed throatily. "You thought Kristóf killed her? Or Valentin? Or maybe your mother? Oh, child, they would not have done that. Your mother was too young, and your uncle and your grandfather were not ever men with murder in their hearts. Kristóf was a pacifist, through and through, even though he himself was an angry man. He used words, not fists. Valentin has his mother's brilliance, and his father's nature. He would never do such a thing."

I felt suddenly hot; I didn't like knowing more about Valentin's background than the three other people in the room, who all believed they were related to him by blood. It suddenly seemed terribly dishonest of me to not tell them the truth about him—however much Bud had insisted I keep those secrets. But what impact would the truth about Valentin's background have? Especially for Zsófia, who obviously loved the man a great deal.

"You are a quiet guest," said Tamás, catching my guilty expression. "I think you have ideas about all this you are not telling us. What do you know that we do not?"

I hate it when people spot that I'm lying—even when it's just by omission. I didn't reply immediately. Eventually I said, "My husband found out something about Valentin's background that I don't believe any of you know."

Zsófia tossed her head suggesting she wasn't worried about what I might say next, but I was keenly aware I was about to shift her entire perspective on her world as she had known it up to that point.

"Valentin wasn't Ilona and Kristóf's natural son. They adopted him when he was just a toddler."

Three pairs of eyes stared at me; one in utter disbelief, two displaying surprise, but not shock.

"Valentin isn't really my uncle?" cried Zsófia. "That's nonsense. We act alike. We even think alike. He's never said anything about this. It cannot be true."

"They didn't tell him?" asked Klara. I shook my head. "Why not? Did he come from a bad, or sad, background?"

Impressed by her perspicacity I gave her the answer she deserved. The truth. It took a while, but, when I had finished, all three of my companions looked stunned.

"This is a tragedy," said Klara. "For a little one to see such things. To know his brother did this to his parents."

"But he does not know," Tamás corrected his wife. "It cannot harm him because no one has told him."

"In one of my classes—not yours, Cait, one with a different professor—we studied early childhood memories. There's research that says we remember things from times before we can speak. Do you think Uncle . . ." she paused, almost catching back the affection with which she'd used the word, ". . . Valentin remembers seeing his whole family killed?"

"I have no idea, though I am aware of the research to which you're referring. Early-life trauma can be recalled under hypnosis, though often the subject cannot clearly explain what they have seen—because they had no frame of reference at the time. However, they can recall how the experience made them feel. It might be that Valentin holds such memories of emotion within him, hidden deep somewhere."

"What if Uncle lost it, somehow, and bashed Grandmother on the head in a fit of temper?" whispered Zsófia, as though she was afraid to hear the words she spoke.

"He has no temper," replied Klara. "Zsófia, you have spoken about him to us so much, so often, and you have always told us that, despite his writing, he is a gentle man."

Zsófia pulled open the scarf she'd kept around her throat through dinner. "He did this to me," she said sadly. "He didn't mean to hurt me, I don't think. Or maybe he did. In any case, he did it."

Klara's face creased with a warm expression. "He is a sick man, Zsófia, my dear. He is raging against things in his head over which he has no control. It is normal. We must forgive him."

Tamás said, "Sometimes a man hides his true self. But it will show. Like a wild beast, he cannot help but follow his nature."

I half-raised my hand. "Not all Alzheimer's patients become violent. It's not unheard of, but it's not a part of the 'normal' course of the disease. Maybe we should consider the trauma of seeing his family killed when he was a very young child, his drug use as a teen, and the fact he might have been jealous of his mother showering her affection upon young men he was studying with. All these things could have accumulated to provoke outbursts long before his disease took hold."

"Ilona and young men?" asked Tamás, surprised. "What are you saying? She was just a girl herself."

"In 1976? No, Tamás, not a girl. The sister you never saw after she was in her twenties was a woman of forty-six by then. She was the mother of two, and living on a campus that I know from first-hand experience is a breeding ground for gossip and lies. She had a reputation for eyeing up young men; I have this on good authority not just from Valentin himself, but also from another source." I looked at Zsófia directly as I added, "Patrik Matyas was at UVan during the 1970s and witnessed her approaches, even having to fend them off himself."

"Professor Matyas was in Vancouver when my grandmother was killed? Is that when he worked with Hollingsworth on that paper?" asked Zsófia. When I'd explained the timeframe, Zsófia added, "I had no idea it was then."

"Matyas?" Tamás hissed the name. "You know a man by this name?"

"He's one of my professors." Zsófia sounded puzzled.

"You have never spoken of him," pressed Tamás.

"He'd just be one of many professors Zsófia has at the HUB," I said. "Why do you ask? Do you recognize the name?"

Tamás looked thoughtful. "It might be the same one. Patrik Matyas. Maybe there are two? Who knows. One Patrik Matyas works for the people who follow old informants like me around, trying to make their lives uncomfortable, even unbearable. But he's not only working for the group involved—he passes information to us so we can avoid them when we want."

I took a moment to think through what Tamás was saying. "You mean Patrik Matyas acts as a double agent, working within one organization, but passing information to another?" If it was true, it made sense.

"We are not an organization," sulked Tamás. "We are people who had to do what we did. Sometimes we are the only ones who understand the full picture. We talk, tell each other things. He helps."

Zsófia looked at me aghast. "It can't be the same person," she said hesitantly.

"Think about it, Zsófia. Think about the nature of the man. Might he be keeping an eye on you because you are related to Tamás?"

"You mean that's why he follows me about? Do you think all the people who follow Valentin, Mama, and me are part of the same group?" I nodded. "And then he tells—he tells the . . . what, the Communists about us?"

"No, child," replied Klara quietly. "The people who follow us are not Communists. They are the families of those who were informed upon. They think we are Communists, and the people who still support the Communist ideals do help us out from time to time. It is a strange situation, to be helped by the people who, for so long, were our sworn enemies, and made us do things we hated doing." Her intelligent eyes looked at me. "Matyas is still working for the party—or what's left of it."

"He told me he remained a devout Catholic throughout the occupation," I said thoughtfully. "Maybe he was acting as an infiltrator then, too. Passing information to his masters about the religious community."

Zsófia's eyes lit up with excitement, "His field is group dynamics— that's a good area to be in if you're doing that. Maybe it is him. Maybe that's why they recruited him in the first place." The light in her eyes changed. "So *he* could have done it. He was there, in Canada, when Grandmother was killed. Maybe he was a hit man for the Communists."

Tamás said, "I know of people who were forced to infiltrate and inform upon all sorts of groups, not just religious ones. Like me they often had no choice. Like me, their assigned tasks were designed to spread discord within closed communities, to make those who might have become allies against Communism become enemies of each other. We didn't just gather information; we were also used to spread disinformation. Undermining from inside. It was hard to do. But not as hard as being told to kill someone."

"Were ordinary people made to kill people too?" asked Zsófia angrily. "If they were, I bet Patrik Matyas would have done it. He's the type." She gave me a challenging sideways glance.

"I do not know if the Communists sent Matyas to Canada to kill Ilona. And, whatever my husband says, I do not know of anyone who was sent anywhere to do such a thing. Unless it was their job. They had enough people who did that for them, without having to use amateurs, I would think. They certainly sent people away wherever they wanted, and whenever they wanted," replied Klara sadly. Her head tilted as she looked at her husband. "They sent my darling Tamás away twice, didn't they? Once for weeks, the year after the big elections." She looked at us again. "He wasn't the same man when he returned. It took years for him to be my Tamás again."

I was desperate to ask what she meant, but Tamás's reply of, "It was a time when there were many special stories I had to write, but it is not a time of which I will speak. Ever," shut me down.

Zsófia dropped her chin onto her arms, which were crossed on the table. "Knowing what I do now, I almost wish it was Patrik Matyas who killed Grandmother. But it seems so fanciful, like something out of an old movie. If it wasn't an assassin, it *must* have been a stranger. The brother they let out of the hospital. The sick one." Her head shot up again. "The one who killed Uncle Valentin's parents. *He* must have done it. He was already a murderer."

"We could speak like this for many hours, but this is an old wound. We cannot make it heal tonight," said Klara. "We have spoken of much. Maybe too much. Do not be in such a hurry, child. We are old, but we have time yet. We can talk like this, in the firelight, many more nights. I suggest we all sleep now." She sounded wise—and tired.

I had to admit I was flagging, too; I'd had an exhausting couple of days, what with one thing and another, and I had to be up early to get back to the city and deliver a lecture. After Zsófia and I made plans for the morning, I phoned and left a message for Bud about where I was staying for Bud using the Örsis' landline, then I fussed about in the tiny bathroom for as short a time as I could manage.

I was finally glad to let my head hit the pillow and I could feel myself drift off. I was warm, full, comfy, and in a proper family home for the first time in weeks. I knew I'd sleep well.

A River of Words

I WAS WRONG. I COULDN'T SETTLE. The place was too quiet, and the few noises I could hear—the shrieking of owls, the rustling of branches—were all making me feel completely overwhelmed with loneliness.

My mind was awhirl, and I couldn't stop thinking about . . . everything. Especially Patrik Matyas.

I sat up in the narrow bed and tried to get comfy. There was nothing for it but to do my best to organize my thoughts, or they'd keep me awake all night.

Sometimes, when I allow everything to fly about and take its own shape, I can understand the connections between places, people, and happenings more clearly. In a strange bed, in a strange part of a strange country, I closed my eyes and allowed myself to float . . .

I am on a boat on a river I know to be the Danube, even though it seems to be flowing through Stanley Park in Vancouver.

I peer across to one bank where I see Ilona, Kristóf, Alexa, Valentin, and Zsófia. They are all dressed in medieval clothing, and are beating each other with giant inflatable hammers. On the other bank I see thousands of men, two armies facing each other, one wearing red uniforms, the other black. Patrik is at the head of one army, Tamás at the head of the other. They are cheering and jeering at each other.

I know I must make a choice—do I try to paddle my boat to the side of the river where there is just a family with all its infighting, or do I paddle to the side where there are armies? I cannot decide, then

I realize I have neither paddle nor any rudder on my boat, so I can do nothing but drift.

As I float along the river, unable to steer, the scenes on the banks change. Where once there was Zsófia's family, now there is only Ilona, dressed in regal robes, surrounded by young men, all wearing sports jackets and bow ties, who are spraying her with aerosol cans full of perfume. The mist they are creating becomes a shower of tiny little stones, which land on her and explode into clouds of blood. There's so much blood, Ilona disappears.

The air clears, and I see Ilona standing with Kristóf, Alexa, Valentin, and a man I somehow know is Valentin's blood brother Edward Cook. They are all holding hands, as though in solidarity with each other, but then, as a frightening flapping sound approaches, each raises an ancient shield above their head.

They are warding off a flock of eagles descending upon them from a blackened sky. I see two of the eagles are carrying people—Patrik Matyas is on one, Tamás Örsi on another. Both men are throwing rocks from their flying steeds; the noise of the rocks on the shields is like thunder. Both men are wailing, "No, no, I do not want to do this!" They are each weeping tears of blood.

I see that all of Patrik's eagles are wearing clerical collars and bearing signs that say WE LISTEN. Tamás's birds all have cameras mounted on their backs. The eagles grab at the humans below them, plucking away their shields and finally carrying their bleeding bodies into the darkness.

Then there is Bud, silently weeping beside a gravestone. I know it is the grave of his late wife, Jan. He turns to me and begs me, without his lips moving, to be safe and to make good decisions. I must avoid all politicians, he says.

Inside my boat I see a telephone housed in a little wooden box. It's ringing so I answer it. It's a Russian voice telling me I can get lots of money so I can live happily ever after with Bud if only I sign a paper that says I am not Zsófia's mother. I say I will not sign, then the telephone changes into a giant bee, buzzing in my hand, its stinger close to my face. I don't know what to do with the bee—I don't want to hurt it, but I know it wants to hurt me. I throw it over the side of the boat into the water and it disappears.

A hand appears from beneath the water holding two quill pens dripping with blood-ink. Patrik's head pops up and he's laughing like one of those hideous laughing policemen you see at the funfair. He shouts with the sort of voice you expect to hear from a ventriloquist's dummy, "Write two times faster with two pens—it's the best way. Everybody's happy when you write things twice."

I'm no longer in a boat; I'm at the top of a hill, looking down a raging torrent I know is the bicycle path where Ilona died at UVan. She's there, dressed as the queen from Valentin's books and she's shouting at me, "I am my daughter." Then I see a man who has no face but who is wearing a kingly crown rise up from the torrent and lift Ilona's now-lifeless body, exactly as the character of the king had done in Valentin's final book. The man has no legs; they are below the waterline. He screams with grief.

I snapped back to reality, and knew I'd worked out quite a few things. I also knew I had to tell Bud what I'd deduced without delay, so I crept downstairs and dialed his parents' house again. There was still no answer, so I left another message. I spoke as fast as I could until the machine beeped, then I rang back again, and again. I had to tell him about Patrik Matyas and his work as a double-agent, and my belief he and Peter Mezey had been one and the same person. I poured out all I could in terms of the examples of how Patrik had wrong-footed me since I'd arrived, how he'd used insinuation, lies, and carefully framed true information to make me doubt myself, and others around me. I told him all about the conversation at the Örsi house earlier that night, and I finally told him that I had a suspicion Tamás Örsi might have been in Canada when his sister was killed. I admitted I was going out on a limb a bit with that idea, and begged him to look into it because Tamás's absence from Hungary only *might* have coincided with the time when Ilona was killed, but it was worth a shot. I didn't know what else to do.

As I replaced the receiver for the final time, I thought I heard a floorboard creaking above my head. Had someone been listening to my whispered messages? I crept back to my room, but couldn't tell if anyone else had ventured from their bed.

I finally settled for what was left of the night and told myself to go to sleep. I'd need my wits about me the next morning.

The Sound of Silence

IT WAS GONE SEVEN WHEN I awoke, feeling fuzzy-headed. The heavy silence of my surroundings was punctuated only by birdsong, and made me realize how far from civilization I was. I pulled back the floral curtains at the small casement window and peered out; having arrived in the dark I had no real sense of exactly where I was. The Örsis' house stood on a hill and was surrounded by open countryside, with forested areas of bare trees and some evergreens. Fat flakes of snow were falling, and it looked as though a few inches had already settled, rounding the edges of the landscape the way only snow can.

Luckily, the house was warm and cozy, and I was pleased no one was in the bathroom. I cleaned up and pulled on my clothes. I did the best I could for my hair with Zsófia's hairspray, which was as close to glue as I'd ever experienced. Finally, I bravely used the tube of red lipstick Zsófia had donated to me at bedtime the night before. I usually opt for more neutral shades, so I took my time with it, because I wanted to make the outline look as smooth as possible, which I know makes a big difference when you're wearing a really noticeable color. Eventually, I reckoned I was presentable enough to deliver a lecture—especially when my students would really only be interested in quizzing me about the exam the next day.

I made my way downstairs quietly, not knowing when the aged Örsis usually rose. No one was about. I made my way through each room downstairs to find they were all empty. I crept back up the stairs and risked knocking on then opening the door to the room Zsófia had told me she'd be using. It was empty. The bed was unmade, and had been occupied, but there was no sign of Zsófia herself.

Maybe she'd gone for a walk? I noticed the door to Klara and Tamás's room was open. Their bed, too, had been slept in, but was now empty.

I couldn't help but think of those episodes of *The Avengers* when Steed and Mrs. Peel would show up at a completely deserted English village and have to work out where everyone had gone. My rising panic told me I knew full well I was neither of those characters, and this was horribly real.

I raced downstairs again and began to hunt about for a note. I found one pinned to the back of the front door, and cursed myself for not having spotted it earlier.

> 4:00 AM Gone to help Mama. She needs us. Uncle Valentin is very sick because he has tried to kill himself. I will return to collect you by seven. Did not want to wake you. NOT your problem. Zsófia.

I let the news sink in. The note didn't answer most of the questions tumbling around in my head, so I ran to the sitting room and grabbed my phone from my handbag. It didn't have a signal, but at least I could access my contact list. I picked up the old-fashioned telephone handset to call Zsófia's cellphone. The handset was dead. That was new; it had worked a few hours earlier. I checked the wire leading to the box on the wall. It looked just fine to me. I reasoned maybe the snowfall had led to the landline being out of order. There probably wasn't a sinister reason for it at all.

I checked my own phone again for a signal; the Örsis had assured me there was none in the area, and Zsófia had even giggled the night before about how proud they were they didn't even know what Wi-Fi or cellphone signals were. Even so, I told myself it wouldn't hurt to check. I walked around the entire house holding the phone up, down, and sideways. Not a single bar.

The car wasn't in front of the house where it had been parked the night before. It was almost eight in the morning, and Zsófia hadn't returned. I had no way to get in touch with anyone. At all. Anywhere. I felt completely cut off from humanity, but I had a responsibility to deliver a lecture at ten o'clock at the HUB, so I knew I had to make a choice: wait, or walk.

I hate the snow. Luckily for me, living in the southwest corner of British Columbia, I don't have to contend with it often, and even when it does fall it usually clears up pretty quickly. So setting out to walk who knew how far, in shoes not made for the job, wasn't something I decided to do lightly. I found an old umbrella inside the front door that I hoped would shield me from the still-falling snow, and left a note pinned next to the one Zsófia had written, telling whoever might find it what I was doing. I allowed the door to lock behind me, reasoning the Örsis must have their keys with them, and set off.

I only had one useful glove, the other being in tatters after the events of the previous day, so I pushed my messed-up right hand into my pocket. It seemed my left arm wasn't equal to the task of keeping the umbrella over my head. The wind buffeted it, making it all but useless.

I headed back the way we'd driven the night before, toward what I hoped would be a proper road, rather than the slushy track that led to the house. Although it was cold and the snow slippery, the ground wasn't frozen, which was good. I was about halfway along the track from the house when my tummy clenched at the sound of an almost unearthly howl. When a shot rang out moments later, my entire body flinched. A flock of screaming birds scattered from the trees where they'd been roosting. They wheeled and reformed in the grey skies above the blackness of the forest. I put my head down and kept going, checking my phone in case I could finally get some sort of reception.

It took about fifteen minutes before I reached the paved road, during which time I mentally sifted through the previous night's conversations, and my wakeful dreaming session. The hill I was walking down fell away pretty steeply, and I stuck to the snow-covered grass shoulder, which I hoped would be less treacherous than the slippery asphalt. The sky was leaden, the sleety snow icy on my exposed skin. It didn't look as though it was going to stop anytime soon, so I hunched and hoped to spot a passing vehicle. In the near-distance a pitiful howl sliced through the silence again. This time I told myself firmly it must be a local dog, but I picked up my pace. The snow suffocated any sounds around me. That was probably why I didn't hear it—or maybe they really are as stealthy as people say.

Finally, I saw it. I knew right away what it was, even though a part of me didn't want to believe I could be seeing it. It was a wolf. It looked huge, and it saw me just as I saw it, though I suspected it had smelled me long before and had probably been stalking me. I didn't blink, I just ran . . . heading for what, I didn't know. I was simply running *away*.

I suspected the wolf would be quicker than me, because my short legs weren't built for running, but I resisted the absurd temptation to look back as I ran—I hate it when they do that in movies. *Just run, you idiot, just run,* pounded in my head as my heart thumped in my chest. I saw trees ahead of me. *I can't climb a tree!* I thought. *You'll have to try,* I told myself.

The sleet stung my face, and the air I was sucking in was so bitterly cold it hurt my lungs. They say your life flashes before your eyes when you're dying, but no one tells you what goes through your mind when you're running for your life. It's nothing, I discovered. The ground was extremely slippery, and I lost my footing as I ran downhill. I was so close I could almost reach out and touch the tree. But no, instead of trying to climb out of harm's way, I was skidding and losing my balance, and it was all I could do to remain upright.

As I finally fell, several things happened almost simultaneously: I saw I was tumbling toward a rocky ditch, and suddenly realized why

Valentin had written about the king lifting a dead body from a river, as well as who'd killed Ilona Seszták; I also spotted a rifle and a shooter. It looked to me as though the barrel and scope were pointing right at me. My body I hit the ground, my hands sprawling and my head turning to try to save my face from smashing into it. A whizzing, popping noise rang out, then I heard a pitiful howl and a whimper behind me.

From my prone position I lifted my head to see my savior in the distance. I pushed myself up with my arms, wiped the snow from my face, and stared at the redness it contained. Was I bleeding? No, it was the red of the lipstick I had borrowed from Zsófia. *Thank goodness.* Then I looked at the person holding the rifle. All I could make out was a camouflage-patterned hood and jacket, with dark gloves holding a camouflaged rifle. Then I saw the shooter was reloading and taking aim at . . . *What? Me?*

This time the howl came from my own body, as I screamed "No!" I pushed myself to my feet and ran back the way I'd come. I spotted the writhing, bloodied body of the wolf in the ditch as I sped past. Something inside me—a recollection I couldn't quite grasp—told me to duck, zig, and zag as I ran. *All the better to escape a bullet.*

My gloved and ungloved hands flashed across my line of sight as they pumped. I noticed my right hand was bleeding again—this time to such an extent that a spray of blood flew into the air every time that hand helped propel me forward. Each crunch of my footfalls seemed to be sucked into the sound-muffling snow.

I must have run for about a minute. Such a short amount of time, but so many racing thoughts. Bud's face appeared in my mind's eye as I labored up the slippery hill, then I felt as though I'd been kicked in the back. I didn't feel any greater pain, so I told myself to keep moving. Pretty soon, though, my legs stopped wanting to work.

I fell to the ground onto my back, wondering at the beauty of the snowflakes I could see so clearly against the dark skies above me.

Different Person, Different Voice

THE UNIFORMED GUARD LOOKED UNBLINKINGLY at the man's passport photo, then at his face. Glancing at the console in front of him he said, "And the purpose of your trip?"

"I'm here to spend some time with my wife. She's been teaching at one of your universities and now I get to join her for a while."

The official's expression remained unchanged. Handing the document back to the man, he said flatly, "Welcome to Hungary, Mr. Anderson. Enjoy your stay."

The white-haired man moved urgently along the winding, carpeted corridors, which finally delivered him to the area where haggard passengers were being met by gleeful greeters. He scanned faces as he stood his ground, his eyes steely under the fluorescent lighting. Reacting to a handwritten notice held high on an umbrella point, he weaved his way through the throng with some difficulty.

"I'm Anderson," he said to the man holding the sign bearing his name.

"Welcome to Budapest, Mr. Anderson. May I take your luggage? Your car is not far away. Allow me," said the dark-suited chauffeur politely. A man in his fifties, he was a good decade older and a head taller than anyone else holding a nameplate.

Bud Anderson ceded control of his suitcase, but gripped his carry-on. With his bags finally stowed in the trunk of a sleek car, Bud slid into the rear seat of the sedan.

"To your hotel, sir?" asked the driver loudly.

"Yes, please, I believe the service told you which one." The chauffeur shut Bud's door, took his seat, and eased the car into the knots of airport traffic.

"How are you holding up, old friend?" asked the driver. "I'm sorry we're meeting like this."

The two men's eyes met in the rearview mirror. Bud managed a wry smile. "I've certainly been better, John. Didn't think I'd be seeing you again so soon after our little reunion in Amsterdam. Thanks for all this. You know it means the world to me."

"Not a problem, Bud. We still can't grasp what Cait's mixed up in. I've had a couple of chaps working on it since you phoned yesterday but there are no concrete leads. There's been no answer to any of our calls; her phone's been without a signal. Can't even locate it. Either the chip's been removed, or her phone's in an area with no coverage. There are a few hereabouts. We've established she's not at the university; she didn't show for class today. No answer at her apartment. She didn't check in at the Gellért last night as you suggested she might. My chaps are checking with other hotels, as well as the hospitals and police stations. Covering all bases, you know the drill. We've got about thirty minutes before we get to the office. Glad we were able to help get you here so quickly. And informally."

"Me too. Thanks for everything. You've been thorough, but I'm going to try her cell myself in any case." Bud checked for reception.

"Local systems can take a while to pick up. Use the phone in the package I put back there for you. It's untraceable."

"Thanks, John." Bud dialed. "Voicemail. Where can she be?" He cursed quietly. "Guess I'd better let my parents know I'm here safe and sound."

"The dutiful son."

"John Silver, you old goat, watch it. I'm not in the mood. I told them Cait had been taken ill and I had to get out here fast, but I don't want them to be worried about me, or Cait. Not fair on them. You've been doing this multiagency, undercover stuff long enough to know how it is with our families; keep 'em happy by keeping them in the dark."

"You're right. Go ahead. I'll be the dumb driver for a few minutes."

Bud dialed, spoke, listened, hung up.

"News?" John Silver nudged the vehicle forward, changing lanes.

"Cait called my parents' house yesterday. They reckon it must have been around one o'clock local time there, because that's when they were out having Sunday lunch. I'd have been at the airport at the time, waiting for my flight to get here. Cait left a few messages for me. Dad's given me his passcode so I'll call right back to pick them up, but he told me one thing he could remember—he said she was staying the night at the home of Tamás and Klara Örsi in a place with a name he couldn't pronounce but he said he thought it started with a B. I know they're Zsófia Takács's great-aunt and uncle. Can you get someone to trace the call to my parents' number and get an address?"

"No need. We have it already." John loosened his tie, then indicated to change lanes again. "They're out in Budakeszi. It's a village not far from the city. Near a game park."

"A game park? You mean with giraffes and tigers?"

"No, not that sort of game. Wild boar, lynx, wolves, and the like. Areas with no cell coverage out there. Might explain a lot. If that's her last known location, I'll head in that general direction. The tablet in that package is completely clean, except for what we've put on it. Örsi, Tamás, will be on the contact list; if you could pull up the specific address, that'll help."

"Okay," replied Bud pulling out the tablet, "but then I'll pick up her other messages—that might give us some critical information."

He did as he'd said, and listened, twice, to the messages his wife had left, tapping notes into the tablet as he did so.

"So?" asked John when Bud had finished.

"She's mixed up in something big, I think, John. Does the name Patrik Matyas mean anything to you?"

"It does. Though he's had a few names over the years. Always kept the same initials. No idea why they do that."

Bud allowed himself a wry chuckle as they took a sharp turn and his tablet slithered across the back seat. "This coming from John Silver, aka Jack Simmons, aka Julian Stirling?"

"Not my choices, Bud. Not my choices. Maybe, like me, our Patrik Matyas has overlords with poor ability for invention. To be fair, your chaps weren't much better. I recall I was first introduced to you as Brian Andrews."

"So who is he, this PM guy?" asked Bud, gathering up the tablet again and tapping in Matyas's name.

"As far as I can recall we have him on file as likely KGB. Or FSB now. I don't have your wife's photographic memory, and we do tend to keep tabs on rather a lot of people. Found him on that thing yet?"

"Yep. More likely to be SVR than FSB, it says. But you and I both know how the world has changed, John. The old alphabet soup doesn't count for as much in these days of digital terrorism and global threats. Whichever agency he answers to, he might have any number of handler affiliations. I think the main thing is, he's not who he pretends to be, and never has been. And Cait reckons he's been keeping a close eye on her." He recounted his wife's messages to his colleague.

"I still don't see how a professor's wife getting her head bashed in at UVan in 1976 connects with a KGB operative embedded in an academic institution here," said John. "Unless he was sent to shut her up. As I recall, assassination isn't on the list of PM's accomplishments, though."

"No. He looks to have always been an infiltrator, disseminator of misinformation, and all-round bite-the-hand-you're-pretending-to-feed-from kind of guy." Bud's voice cracked with worry. "Got a file here on the Seszták woman?" he asked, tapping again.

The weak daylight was fast disappearing, as were most signs of civilization. "Not long now," announced John, checking his GPS screen. "And yeah. That one I did read up. Örsi was her name before she married."

"I see she was a low-level listener and translator for the workers' party. Brother was, what? Informer under duress?"

"That about sums it up. Worked for a newspaper that was nationalized. So essentially was a propagandist and information manager for the party. However, as the file says, a few periods unaccounted for."

"Which is another thing Cait asked me to follow up on. Any ideas? There's nothing here."

"If it's not there, then no. Sorry. I can get the chaps at the office onto it ASAP. In fact, why don't you call them and put it on speakerphone. I can get them to haul in Matyas and dig into Örsi."

Bud made the call, then the two men remained silent for a few moments while he read the file. "Ilona Seszták unlikely to be a viable KGB target, your file says."

"We don't believe she'd have had high enough clearance to get to hear, or see, anything worth killing her over. Though, to be honest, those listeners and translators can happen upon some juicy stuff when it's least expected."

"You calculated her security clearance by checking her salary?"

"It's a technique that usually works. Okay, now we're getting pretty close. Heads up."

The sleek car's tires left deep tracks in the slushy snow as it squelched along a muddy track. The headlamps eventually threw their ghastly light upon a small house. It appeared to be deserted.

"If anyone's in there they'll have seen us coming a mile off," observed John. "Might as well use the lights to our advantage now. Ready?"

"As I'll ever be," replied Bud. "This is the first time one of these ops has been personal for me. Though I know I shouldn't really call it an op."

"I know," answered John, sliding from his seat. "And you're right. Not an op. One friend helping another find his wife, who said she was here. All above board."

"Got it."

John made his way to the rear of the house, moving with an economy of motion borne of experience. Bud waited a moment, then knocked at the front door. Ten minutes later, the men had searched the entire small house. "Back door lock was easy to pick. They won't even know we've been here," said John as they stood inside the front door, his tiny flashlight playing on the worn carpet of the hallway.

Bud shone his light on the two pieces of paper pinned to the back of the door. "The note left by the Takács girl tells us they left Cait here alone, and why they did it. It looks like they never came back. Cait's note tells us she was planning on walking to the main road to try to get a ride, or a bus, around eight this morning. So why didn't she make it back to her place, or to the university? Why didn't she just phone for a cab?"

"Landline's dead. I checked." John continued, "If this Valentin Örsi chap is deathly ill because he's tried to top himself, might Cait have gone there? You know her, Bud, what would her priority have been? Work, or this family?"

"Work," replied Bud without hesitation. "She was due to deliver a lecture. I've seen her drive off to do that when she was so sick she should have been in bed. She's utterly professional in that respect. Something must have happened to her. I know it, John." Not for the first time, Bud's voice cracked with emotion.

Bud's friend and sometime-colleague laid a hand on his shoulder and said quietly, "We'll sort this out, old chap. Rely on me for that. You've saved my life twice in the past decade. I owe you at least this much. Come on. Let's follow the road we've just traveled, the one Cait must have walked along, and see what we can find."

Taking the front passenger seat, Bud strained his eyes as they progressed slowly, their full-beam headlights bouncing off the remnants of the snow, which had begun to freeze. "Stop!" he shouted.

John slammed on the brakes. "See something?"

"Don't know," said Bud, leaping out of the car. "Pull back a bit and shine the lights over this way, will you?"

John complied and Bud walked slowly, bobbing his head, bending and crouching at times. Finally, he gestured for John to join him.

"Here." Bud pointed at the side of the road. "Blood. See it? There." John crouched too. "Yes. I see it. It's not much. Which is good."

Bud played his flashlight along the ground, indicating a trail. "Something was bleeding, and was dragged along here. See the disturbance?" He pounced forward and grabbed something from the inner edge of a small ditch. Holding the item in the beam of the flashlight, he sniffed it, cursed quietly, then turned to his friend. "It's Cait's glove. Look, it's torn. Ripped. There's blood."

"How do you know it's hers?"

Bud pushed it under John's nose. "Smell it. That's Cait Juice— Coco Chanel. Her perfume."

John sagged. "That might not all be her blood. In the glove? Probably. On the ground? Maybe not."

Bud's jaw tightened as he regarded his friend, who was no more than a silhouette in the headlamps. "She was on this road, and here's this glove. I'm not dumb, John. Chances are that blood is hers. Question is—is she dead, or alive? And, either way, where is she?"

"Let's see if there's anything else around here that can help. Tracks, marks of any sort, some indication of the type of incident we're talking about."

"Right. We'll use the headlights and work a grid."

An hour later the two men were inside the car, heading toward Budapest. The evidence they'd seen had puzzled and worried them both. Three bodies had been dragged through the snow a little way, then lifted into what looked like two different vehicles, both with wide-tread tires. Cait had been on the scene. Bud was keenly aware he'd found her glove near the area with the most blood.

Photographs of the tire treads had been sent to John's team for analysis, and the report had come in that a full sweep of Cait's apartment had revealed no listening devices or bugs of any sort. The tech team also confirmed her computer appeared to not be infected with any spyware at all.

"I wonder how whoever left that message in her bathroom knew what you two had been saying to each other in her apartment on Skype, Bud. Any ideas?" asked John as he drove through the darkness, the lights of the city now in sight.

Sitting next to him Bud shook his head. "None. Maybe they went back into the apartment and cleaned up after themselves?"

"My guys said if they did, they were the best in the business at doing it, because they hadn't left a single trace of having been there. Place was clean as a whistle."

Bud snorted. "Don't tell me they said the place was tidy. Because if it was, then someone other than Cait has certainly been there. She goes for organized chaos. She'll remember where everything is, so she doesn't need to have it sorted out."

"Heck of a thing, that memory of hers."

Bud was deep in thought. "I wonder if they've contacted all the hospitals yet."

"They'll call when they have."

"Yeah, I know. Look, if she's not at her place, like your guys said, why don't we try the Takács/Seszták house in town instead? The girl, Zsófia, or the Örsi couple might know something, if they're still there."

"Okay. Let's try that. Tell the office we're going there. Don't want them to lose track of us. And get me the address from the file will you? I know the street, but can't recall the number."

Speaking About the Dead

THE SMALL DOG BARKED FURIOUSLY as Bud Anderson introduced himself to the short, round woman wearing a cook's apron holding open the impressive door. With the greatest reluctance she finally allowed the two men to enter. Insistent they not leave the spot they were occupying on the mat inside the door, she ran up the soaring staircase, throwing suspicious glances in their direction as she went.

A few minutes later a tall, slender woman with sleek, dark hair, pale skin, and puffy eyes appeared at the head of the staircase.

"You're Cait's husband?" she called. Her voice echoed in the marble entryway, making her sound disdainful, if not disbelieving.

"Yes," replied Bud, daring to leave his designated place and move toward the foot of the stairs. "My friend John has kindly brought me here this evening. I can't seem to find Cait anywhere, you see, and I wondered if she might be visiting you. I understand there's been a family emergency, so I thought maybe she'd popped by to help out?"

Resting on the bannister, the women looked puzzled. "My brother killed himself last night. That's not the sort of thing you let strangers get involved with."

Bud took this revelation as his cue to make his way up the stairs, to offer a heartfelt handshake. "Mrs. Takács—it is Mrs. Takács, isn't it?—I'm sorry for your loss. What happened?"

The woman looked him up and down, her arm slipping, her gaze wandering. "Overdose. They pumped his stomach, but they couldn't save him." Her arm slithered off the bannister. Bud reached out to catch her before she tumbled, his eyes not registering any surprise when he was close enough to smell her breath.

"Can I help you upstairs? John, maybe a hand?"

Alexa's dark eyes peered at him from within pink folds of flesh. "Thanks. Appreciate it. Come meet the family." Her voice carried no emotion.

Bud and John helped the unsteady woman across a wide carpeted landing into a brightly lit salon-lounge where the décor was sumptuous. "It's Cait's husband, everyone. Come to find his wife."

"Come, sit, Alexa. You are exhausted," said a small elderly woman who stood with surprising alacrity and helped the reeling Alexa into an armchair.

"Drunk as a skunk, more like," whispered John into Bud's ear as the two men smiled politely and introduced themselves to the family group.

A young woman with unkempt red hair and a blotchy face stood. "I'm Zsófia Takács. Cait stayed with me at my great-aunt Klara and great-uncle Tamás's house last night," she waved toward the elderly woman, "but we had to rush here in the early hours. I feel terrible that we abandoned her, but it wasn't her problem to deal with and—" Zsófia blushed, "I couldn't wake her at all. She was absolutely sound asleep."

"She can get that way. Sleeps like the dead sometimes," said Bud, his voice wavering with his final words.

Zsófia smiled weakly. "I tried to phone her to tell her I couldn't leave Mama and that I needed to stay to help with the police, and the ambulance, and so forth, but she didn't answer. She phoned you last evening—oh! I thought you were in Canada. You're not due until Saturday, are you?"

Bud managed to make his voice sound almost cheerful. "I managed to get away sooner than I'd planned. I thought I'd surprise her, but it seems the surprise is on me. She did get a message through to my parents, though, and in it she said she was at your home." He nodded at the elderly woman. "But John and I were there earlier, and the place was deserted. Has she, by any chance, gotten in touch with any of you? I'm getting kind of anxious about her whereabouts, what with the weather, you know."

"She'd have phoned for a cab, I'd have thought. That's what I would do. She was due to give a lecture today, and I'm sure she must have managed to get there somehow. It's really not that far. The people at the HUB should know where she is." Zsófia's face was puffy and her eyes raw. She made an effort to conjure up a smile.

"She's not at the university, or her apartment. This was the last place I could think of to check." Bud managed to keep the panic from his voice.

"This is a difficult time for my family," said Alexa sharply. "We do not know where she is. It's unfortunate, but not something we can help you with. My brother's death has been a great shock to us all. We must grieve. Alone."

"Mama, stop," said Zsófia softly. "Uncle Valentin's beyond our help now. Cait's not. She was trying to help this family, maybe now we can help her."

Bud's shoulders straightened. "Is there anyone else you can think of she might turn to, Zsófia? Her cellphone isn't doing anything other than going to voicemail, and I think it might be switched off. Is there anything you can tell me?"

Zsófia sighed deeply. "I don't think so." She pulled at her lank, vivid hair. "I feel so bad about this. I should have made more of an effort to wake her. We should have brought her with us, but Mama needed us to get here fast, so . . ."

"Don't blame me," slurred Alexa. "She's none of my concern."

"Oh, Mama, please be kind. Cait was kind to us." The girl's voice was rough from crying. "She spent some time with Patrik Matyas, one of my other professors, but they weren't really friendly. Maybe she'd turn to a colleague if she were in distress? But why wouldn't she just go home to her apartment? It makes no sense unless—do you think something has happened to her?"

"You mean an accident? On the road? In the snow?" asked Klara, her deep voice crackling with age and tiredness.

"Yes, maybe an accident. I don't suppose you've seen anything on the news today?" asked Bud sounding almost hopeful.

"The news? The news?" wailed Alexa. "The only news in this house today is that my brother is dead. He tried to strangle my daughter a couple of days ago when he was having an episode, realized what he'd done, and, last night, took his own life. He's gone. My brother is gone! He killed himself because of what he did to you."

"Mama, please," cried Zsófia, her chest heaving with sobs.

Bud strode toward the young woman and comforted her. "Hey, come on. It's not like it was your fault. Cait told me what had happened with your uncle. He couldn't help what he did. You know, maybe he realized what was ahead of him, and made a decision to not take that path. Nothing to do with you. So don't carry this guilt with you through your life. It's not yours to bear. I'm sure he wouldn't have blamed you."

Alexa waved her arms, gaining everyone's attention. "He didn't blame her—oh no, left her the lot, didn't he? Wrote his suicide note on the back of a codicil to his will, which he got his nurses to witness, if you please, swearing he was in control of his faculties when they did it. All the money from the final book, the sixth book, will be hers, that's what he said. And after all I've done for him, all these years."

"Mama, you're upset. Please don't shout at me," pleaded the woman's daughter. "The manuscript for the last book is gone, it's missing, so it doesn't matter, Mama. The Bloodline Saga will never end—people can work out their own finale."

Alexa let out a whooping laugh as she struggled to her feet. "Gone? Has it gone?" She giggled like a naughty little girl, snorting as she laughed, and scampered unsteadily across the room to a large bookcase. "Where do you hide a book when you don't want anyone to find it?" she said with a wicked grin. "Right where everyone can see it—among a load of other books." She pushed her hand behind a collection of tall volumes and pulled out a thick wad of paper. "Ta-da!"

Zsófia leapt to her feet. "Mama, you had it all the time? Why didn't you say anything? I was looking for the manuscript when Uncle got mad with me. Why have *you* got it? What have you been doing with it?"

Waving the manuscript above her head as though it were some sort of trophy, Alexa weaved her uncertain way back across the room. "What was I doing with it? Reading it, dear child. My ever-loving brother told us we were all in it, and that he would tell the truth about us all—so I wanted to see what he'd written. And do you know what? He did tell the truth. And that's not right. There are some things in life from which I can still protect you, Zsófia. So this is where it's going . . ." Twirling on the spot in front of the fireplace, Alexa swooped down and dumped the pages onto the roaring flames.

Zsófia screamed, "Mama, no!" She tried to pull her mother away from the hearth, where pages were curling, singeing, and flying upward, ablaze. Alexa laughed throatily as she blocked her daughter's flailing arms like like a football player protecting a quarterback. She was enjoying the game, and her daughter's anguish.

Klara was aghast, while Bud and John stood frozen, their faces conveying a mixture of uncertainty about trying to save the pages, and general impatience with the scene playing out before them. In moments the sheets of paper were no more than ash coating the crackling logs. A couple of pages had escaped the flames, and Zsófia, finally able to push her giggling mother aside, gathered them up, weeping.

"His story will never be finished now, Mama," she sobbed. "Why did you do that? I never thought you could be so cruel. All his work, gone. Like him. Oh, Mama." She sat down on the floor, hard, the ragged sheets in her lap, her face in her hands.

Bud moved to comfort Zsófia, and helped her to her feet.

John pulled his ringing phone from his pocket. "Excuse me, I must take this." He stepped away from his colleague, who was attempting to pacify the sobbing girl.

John pushed his phone back into his coat. "Bud, we need to go. They've found Cait."

Bud's face contorted with a mixture of joy and panic. "Is she . . . ?"

"Alive. She's at the Péterfy Sándor Hospital."

Bud's head and shoulders dropped, his eyes closed. Before he spoke aloud, his lips moved silently for a moment. "Do you know what kind of shape she's in?" His voice was quieter than the crackling of the fire.

"Sorry, old chap. Unconscious is all I know. But I also know the hospital's less than ten minutes away. Coming?"

"I'd like to come too," shouted Zsófia as the two men made for the door.

Bud stopped and turned on his heel. "You're welcome to come, Zsófia. But we need to go right now."

Zsófia didn't hesitate; she grabbed her purse from the floor, stuffed the pages of the manuscript inside, and yelled over her shoulder as she ran to catch the men, "Sober up, Mama, for once. I'll phone you to tell you what's happening, Klara."

Dumb, But Lucky

I COULDN'T MOVE. I COULDN'T SEE. The first thing I was aware of was Bud's voice. *Am I dead? Dreaming?*

"You're safe, Wife." *The sweetest words I've ever heard.* "Don't try to move, and don't try to talk. There's a tube in your throat, a mask over your mouth. If you can hear me, try to move a finger."

I wiggled the fingers on my right hand.

"Cait? Go on, try to move at least one finger if you can hear me. Either hand, I can see them both. Just let me know you can hear me."

This time I wiggled the fingers on both hands.

"Maybe she's still unconscious," said a voice I wasn't expecting to hear.

John Silver? What was he doing here? Wherever "here" was. The last time I'd seen him, Bud and I had just handed him a case on a platter in Amsterdam. *Am I in Amsterdam again?*

"Her readings tell us she is likely to be awake now." *Doctor? Nurse?*

"Do you think she can't hear me then? Has her hearing been affected by the overdose?"

I can hear you, Husband. What overdose? I began to flap my hands about until my wrists hurt.

My body felt as though it was floating in jelly. I was comfortable, and so happy to know Bud was with me. I felt warm, and loved, but confused. A few moments later I could make out shapes, but I felt I was seeing the world about me through a voile curtain. Was that Zsófia Takács's red hair? *So I'm still in Budapest.*

"The lack of reaction is normal for an overdose of fentanyl, as is the difficulty with her breathing, and the seizures she's suffered. We've been giving her doses of naloxone since she got here. The man who brought her in was able to show us exactly what she'd been injected with. He's been distraught. If fact, he's still here, outside, waiting. You must have passed him in the corridor. I have assured him he did all he could. Unfortunately, we couldn't pump the fentanyl out of her system, because it was injected into her back. It would have helped a great deal if we could have given her the antidote sooner, but . . . We still can't be sure of all the effects the seizures have had upon her nervous system."

I've been injected with fentanyl? That's a painkiller. *Is that why I don't feel any pain?*

"So the ventilator is helping her breathe, I can see that," said Bud urgently. "When do you think she'll be able to breathe for herself?"

I can't breathe for myself?

"I'm sorry, Mr. Anderson, I cannot say."

I could see Bud's hand sliding up and down my face, but I couldn't feel a thing. *I don't like this. This is scary.*

Moments later the doctor asked Bud if he would meet the man who'd brought me to the hospital, then I heard a voice I recognized. It was Tamás Örsi.

I couldn't hear everything that was said, all I caught was, "She kept changing direction. I was trying to shoot the wolf with a tranquilizer. I had already got one down, but there was another one. There usually is. She was running toward it. I don't think she knew it was there. I feel very bad about this. I did not mean to hurt her. The fentanyl in the tranquilizer rifle is very dangerous, I know this. I also know I should have taken a dose of the antidote with me, but I could not find it when I left the house. It is supposed to be with the darts. I was called out when I was very tired. I know they have given me a younger man to help me, but he had taken a short break. We had been on the trail of the animals for a long time. It is very bad, all of this. Very bad. I am grateful the dart only scraped her. She was moving about so much, you see. I couldn't help it. Honestly I couldn't." *Tamás Örsi shot me? There was another wolf?*

I wanted to shout to Bud, "Keep him here. Don't let him go, ask him about the wolf," but I couldn't speak, I was so tired.

I have no idea how long it took me to close and open my eyes, but eventually I heard Bud whooping, "She blinked at me. John, you saw it, didn't you? Cait? Cait—if you can hear me, blink again. Can you do it twice?"

I knew I'd managed it when I saw Bud and John shaking hands and patting each other on the back, which is all I'd ever seen them do, even though I knew they'd been through some tough times together, and thought the world of each other. It appeared I'd made some sort of breakthrough, and I allowed myself to feel pleased about it. But it seemed blinking was exhausting, and I decided I'd just close my eyes for five minutes to recover.

I woke from what must have been forty winks to hear Bud talk with the boring old doctor, who, it turned out, looked much younger than he sounded.

Bud was saying, "I don't understand. There must be hope, surely." I could see his hand raking through his hair. *Have you lost weight, Bud?*

"As I keep telling you, Bud, even after all these weeks, we just don't know."

Weeks?

"She's healed in all respects but this—and while we can keep doing scans of her brain, all I can tell you is it is not damaged. She's not responding as she should be. Whatever she is eventually able to do, it will take time. Months, or maybe years."

I wanted to scream at the man and tell him he was talking nonsense, but all I managed to do was reach out and smack a plastic cup off the little table sitting across my bed. Bud's face broke into the biggest smile I'd ever seen.

"There she is—she's back. My Cait is coming back. That's right, isn't it? You're fighting your way back to me in there, aren't you?"

I nodded. Slowly. I knew I'd really done it because Bud cried, sobbed, like a child. He held me as close as all the equipment attached to me would allow and I could feel his entire body juddering against mine. "I thought you'd gone, my love. Thank you for coming back to me."

His body felt odd against my skin, which was hypersensitive. Pulling back, he looked into my eyes, and I looked into his. I winked at him, and that set him off again.

When he'd rested me back against my pillows he sat on the edge of my bed and held both my hands. I could feel his skin warm against mine. I had missed that feeling so much.

"Oh Cait. These have been the worst weeks of my life, watching you lay here, helpless. But now you're on your way back. I can see you in your eyes. We can work on getting you well."

Echoes from the Cold War

THE SUITE AT THE GELLÉRT Hotel was wonderful; wood-paneled walls, elegant furnishings, and a canopied bed in a separate room made for luxurious surroundings. I'd come off the ventilator just a week earlier, but had already been given clearances to travel by the medical staff at the hospital, who'd all been astounded by my recovery. Bud and I had agreed to splash out on one night of indulgence before we left Budapest.

"It's absolutely marvelous to see you here, like this, Cait, my dear," said John Silver when he arrived with a box of pastries. "If Bud had told me a month ago this would be what we'd be doing today, I'd have done my best to bring him down from cloud cuckoo land without a bump. You've made wonderful progress." He was beaming.

The room was warm—maybe a little too warm, but Bud wouldn't have it any other way, so I was glad to be able to sip iced tea with the pastries.

"Yes, I'm just fine now, thanks," I said, munching a delicious chocolate tartlet topped with raspberries.

John patted my hand. "Wonderful." Looking across the coffee table at Bud, he added, "A real fighter, this one. I'd keep her, if I were you."

"I'm planning on it," said Bud with a grin. "It'll be our wedding anniversary in a couple of days. On December 31 we'll have been married a whole year. At one point I wasn't sure she'd make it. And, whatever she says, she's still not one hundred percent. She has to take it easy for a while and there'll be months of rehab. We have to get her walking properly again."

"Hey, come on, I'm sitting right here, you know," I said, "albeit in this blessed wheelchair. I feel fine. You also promised I could have today to tie up all the loose ends here. I can't leave until justice is served."

John tilted his head. His eyes softened with concern. "Cait, Bud made me promise not to talk about any of this until you were out of the hospital, and I haven't. However, despite the fact you're one of the brightest people I've ever met, I know you're not in possession of all the facts pertaining to the matter, so there's no way you *could* know what was going on. We had Patrik Matyas, aka Peter Mezey, in custody for a while, and he gave us some information you don't have."

"Before you tell me what he's confessed, just answer me one question," I said.

"Okay. Shoot," said John. He received a thump on the arm from Bud for that.

"When you searched it, which I'm sure you did, you didn't find any listening devices in my apartment, did you?"

"Correct," replied John.

"That makes sense. And it means that, for once dear husband, I'm afraid I have to acknowledge I made a mistake."

Bud pantomimed a shudder. "No, not a mistake. Perish the thought."

I couldn't help but smile. "Because I was wrapped in a fog of paranoia, I took the message on my bathroom mirror—LISTEN TO YOUR HUSBAND STOP MEDDLING—to mean I should listen to what you'd been telling me during our Skype conversations about refraining from investigating the Seszták case. My fevered little brain was only too happy to believe my apartment was bugged—that the walls really did have ears. But I was wrong. It wasn't that at all." Both men's eyes were twinkling.

"Go on," said Bud wickedly.

"Patrik Matyas was the one who entered my apartment and wrote that message on my mirror, but he did it for an entirely different reason."

"And that was?" said John, goading me.

"He did it because Stanislav Samokhin, the Russian record producer who was so desperate to sign Zsófia Takács to a contract, and whose nose I had put badly out of joint, asked him to. Or told him to. Stanislav spoke to Patrik at the club the night they were both there to see Zsófia sing. I might have interpreted their brief exchange as an innocent one between the only two people over the age of fifty in the place—as Patrik would have had me believe—had it not been for the exact nature of their interaction. Stanislav bent his head to Patrik's ear, an intimate gesture. If they'd really been strangers to each other there'd have remained a distance between them. Not being privy to all the files you can access, I don't know what the exact connection between them is, but it's enough of one for Stanislav to be able to get Patrik to act on his behalf to scare me off being protective of Zsófia. I should have known it was Patrik who did it; no one had broken into my apartment, you see—the front door was open, not forced. It's an apartment held by the HUB for visiting professors, so there's no reason why he wouldn't have access to another set of keys. I'd spoken to him at the St. Martin's Day dinner at the Vajdahunyad Castle about how you have often told me I shouldn't get involved in students' business back at UVan, Bud, so the message he left should have pointed directly to him—I'd told no one else any such thing. But because of my general state of mind, I leapt to a totally incorrect conclusion—that all my conversations were being listened to. However, there were no complex bugging systems, there was just a man taking what I'd said and using it to frighten me when he was required to do so."

John and Bud didn't say a word, then they both grinned.

John said, "He's already admitted what you've surmised. He didn't realize he'd left your front door improperly closed, and threw quite a little tantrum when he found out about that, by all accounts. The plan had been to terrify you with an 'impossible message.' He's also admitted to his various roles through the years as an informant and infiltrator, as you told us in your messages."

"Will you allow Patrik to return to his post?" I asked.

"He's been back at the HUB for three weeks," said John. "His allegiances have changed somewhat, of course."

"His real name is Vladimir," added Bud. "One of the delights of working for a government that has absolute control over all personal records is, of course, that he could become anybody his masters wanted him to be. Happy now?"

I said I was.

Bud sighed. "So, if you got that far lying in your sickbed, how about the Ilona Seszták murder? I'll admit we've spent no time on that at all. The Matyas thing had to be dealt with, and John handled it all very nicely. The death of the Seszták woman wasn't something I was prepared to work on—it would have kept me away from your bedside. So?"

"That's the big picture stuff dealt with," I said. "By the way, did you ever find out if Tamás Örsi entered Canada in October 1976?"

"No one by that name did, Cait," replied John. "But then paperwork is easily created if you work for a government."

"Right then—so now we're left with the family drama. I'm clear about what happened, but getting the truth out into the open won't be easy, I don't think," I said.

"If anyone can do it you can, Cait," said Bud with a truly happy grin.

Echoes from Canada

WE SAT AROUND THE DINING table in our suite with Tamás and Klara Örsi and Zsófia and Alexa Takács, facing a dazzling array of sweet and savory treats and a selection of beverages. The room service people had done an excellent job, and the atmosphere was quite festive. That had been my aim—since I'd told the Örsis and Takácses I wanted the chance to celebrate my recovery and imminent return to Canada with them all.

I allowed Tamás to explain, to my face, how he'd done his best to hit the wolf I was running toward and not me, and how he'd rushed me to the hospital in his work truck, leaving his young colleague to haul away the two sedated wolves alone. He also told me he had resigned from his post, and that he and Klara were now looking for a small home somewhere away from people where they could enjoy his well-earned, and much overdue, retirement. I thanked him for his explanation, and he looked as comfortable as he could in my company after that.

After the small talk about my recovery—and weight loss—had subsided, and we inevitably reached the topic of Valentin's death, I was finally able to tell Zsófia how sorry I was about the loss of her uncle. She'd visited me at the hospital, but I'd held back from saying anything, until I could say everything. This was the time.

"It's unlikely we'll any of us meet again," I began, "though you know, Zsófia, you have a place to stay in British Columbia should you ever need one, so this is the day I must, unfortunately, change all of your lives forever. And it won't be in a good way."

"What do you mean?" asked Alexa, sipping tea. The room was devoid of any alcohol.

"I mean I have to tell you some things about your own family you might not be happy to hear."

"Lies eat at the soul," said Klara sagely. "We know this. Truth is painful, but better. We should be glad we have the chance to speak the truth. It was not always possible."

"Indeed," I replied. "So, I'll get right to it. The night before Valentin died, Klara, Tamás, Zsófia, and I discussed the fact that Valentin was adopted by your parents, Alexa."

Alexa spoke. "Once they told me he wasn't related to me by blood, many things from the whole of my life made more sense. When Zsófia informed me he was the child of a couple killed by their other son, I also understood why my father made me promise I would always look after him—even though he was my older brother."

"For a man who chastised us for our deceitfulness, Kristóf was himself a man who told many lies," said Tamás sadly.

"Indeed he did—and probably more than you think," I said. "Valentin told you he was planning on revealing more family secrets in his final book, correct, Zsófia?"

"He did, though I don't know what he meant. I read the entire manuscript, and I couldn't see what truths he was telling. When you read it, Mama—before you burned it—you said you saw it. Mama will not share that information with us, Cait, and now the manuscript has gone, so we'll never know."

"Yes, it's gone, but, thanks to you allowing me to read it, it's not forgotten."

"I don't understand," said Zsófia, voicing the opinion of four people in the room.

I cleared my throat. "Book six, page 782, paragraph four, line three—I quote: 'The King lay in his chamber, his last breaths rattling the breast that had once been great. Zoth hovered beside his father's bed. Handmaidens bathed the old man's brow with the milk of goats, which the healer said was good for him. Zoth found the stench of death in battle glorious, but the sight of his father dying before him made him feel sick.'"

Everyone except Bud and John looked puzzled. I continued, "Page 823, paragraph two, line one: 'Hailing his firstborn one last time, King Rohan—leader of men, lover of women, demon of the battlefield, now almost deceased—whispered into the young man's ear, "I know you saw me with your sister's corpse, and if I wish to enter the great halls of the afterlife, I must now admit it was I who killed her."'"

For a moment the room was utterly silent.

"How did you do that? I sort of remember something of the kind being in the manuscript, but how can you be so sure of the exact words?" asked Zsófia.

"She's just making it up," said Alexa. "It means nothing. Is that it?"

"No," I replied. "There's more. I won't recite all of the entries, and the page references are moot since you destroyed the manuscript itself, but there were at least seventeen more points at which Valentin addressed matters pertaining to your mother's death, Alexa, hidden in plain sight as references to the death of the princess, King Rohan's only daughter."

"And you remember them all, do you?" mocked the woman. "Did you write down those little bits and memorize them?"

Bud and John sat forward in their seats, allowing them a better view of the faces of our guests.

"No, Alexa, I didn't need to. I have an eidetic memory, often referred to as a photographic memory. I can recall every word of the manuscript, as though I were turning the pages in front of me."

Zsófia grabbed my hand in excitement. "Really? Do you think you could type it all up, just the way Uncle Valentin wrote it so I can read the clues you're speaking of?" I said I probably could, intrigued that Zsófia was choosing to still refer to Valentin as her uncle. "That's wonderful, Cait. I can read what he said properly, and the world *will* get the chance to know how he wanted his saga to end. Uncle gave all the income from the book to me—I'll split it with you, equal shares, if only you'll do it." She dismissed my protests with, "No, I insist. It's only fair. Without you doing all the typing, there'll be no clues, no book. Please say you'll do it?"

"All right, I'll do it." *I hate typing!*

"My daughter will make you a wealthy woman," said Alexa angrily. "Lucky you."

"We are already wealthy, Mama," replied Zsófia. "Neither of us has a care about money, even without the last book, and Klara and Tamás know they are set for life too. So what if Cait gets a share? We'll all have more money than we know what to do with and I will be able to work out who killed Ilona. The public will also get their closure. Everyone wins."

"Everyone except the person who killed your grandmother, Zsófia," I said.

Zsófia's mood changed abruptly. "Yes, of course. I got excited because I thought I could try to spot the clues—but you already know what they are, don't you? Do you know who did it, Cait? Have you found out any more? Uncle Valentin's death has been so hard to bear it's made me almost not worry about the death of a woman I never met. Even if he wasn't my uncle by blood, I loved him as though he was my whole life. But all deaths are sad, and Grandmother's shouldn't have happened. Uncle Valentin took his own life because he couldn't face the future for himself. I—" she hesitated before she added quietly, "I hope he knew he was loved. That we'd have loved him whatever happened."

Alexa said, "He knew, child. He just chose to ignore our love when he killed himself."

Zsófia's sharp intake of breath was followed by, "I do wish I knew what happened to my grandmother. Do you know, Cait?"

"I do."

"Was it Patrik Matyas? I know we talked about how he was in Vancouver at the time. He could have done it."

Without so much as glancing toward Bud and John, I answered, "It wasn't Patrik Matyas who did it. He was in Vancouver for other reasons. He was a watcher. A listener. Not a killer. Did you run into him at all when you visited Vancouver, Tamás?" I dared.

The old man blanched. "I have never been to Canada."

Klara looked at her husband with a curious glint in her eye. "Is that where they sent you? Were you told to make sure your sister kept quiet? I've done some calculations, and the trip you took that really changed you—made you a different person for so long—was about the time she was killed. You should tell us the truth now."

Tamás straightened his shoulders. "I was not in Canada at that time, I was in Italy."

"Italy?" Klara sounded surprised. "Why were you there?"

Shaking his head, the old man replied, "I was sent to take photographs of dead animals, and living people. There had been a terrible tragedy—a chemical accident. Dioxin gas had been released. I was part of the group sent a few months later to document its effects on the animals and people of a place called Seveso. It was a difficult assignment." He looked at his wife with a tortured expression. "I saw things a man should not see. I have never been able to forget them. I am sorry it made me a poor husband when I returned. I could not tell you, my dear. It was too dangerous for you to know." He looked at John and Bud and added, "They'd been using similar types of chemicals to get rid of unwanted vegetation in parts of Mother Russia, then growing food on the land they'd cleared. They were interested to find out what happened if too much of the stuff got to animals and humans. I know no more than that."

"Thank you, Tamás," I said.

"Of course Tamás wouldn't have killed his sister," snapped Zsófia. "Was it Uncle Valentin's real brother? The one who killed his family? Did he somehow find his little brother and kill the woman who had adopted him?"

"No." I shook my head.

"Do you even know what happened to him?" Zsófia looked across at Bud and John.

I, too, looked at my husband for his input. He answered, "There are no records of Edward Cook, of any sort, after he left the hospital where he was treated for schizophrenia. We must assume, therefore, he never connected with his brother. I'm sorry to say our best assessment is that he lived a possibly short life on the streets—maybe having assumed a new name, or a nickname—and has since died."

Zsófia and the rest of her family all looked at each other with apprehension; I'd removed most of their hopes of someone outside the family being Ilona's killer.

The young girl grasped at one last straw. "And you're sure it wasn't just some stranger who did it?" she asked quietly. I agreed. "So," her voice was heavy, "if what you just quoted from Valentin's book is true, then it was Kristóf who killed her. But how did Valentin know about it so he could write about it?"

"I believe your mother can tell you the truth of the matter. Can't you, Alexa?" I looked at Zsófia's mother, daring her with my eyes to not answer.

For a few moments I thought she wouldn't speak, then she snarled, "There is no sense in this. Isn't it enough your grandmother was murdered? What—do you want a grandfather as a murderer too?"

I reached across the table and gently placed my hand on Zsófia's arm. "It's natural for a girl to love her father—as I am sure you loved yours, Zsófia. There are many clues in your uncle's work that your grandfather favored your mother over her brother—twenty-seven in the five volumes before the final one. Even without them, Valentin's own words when we dined together told us he must have felt it to be true, even if it wasn't. Did you feel you were your father's favorite, Alexa? And was he yours?"

All eyes turned to the woman whose face was grim, her fists now clenched on the table in front of her. "I loved Kristóf *and* Ilona—they were both my parents."

"True," I replied, "but you saw how upset your father was with your mother's man-chasing antics, didn't you?"

Alexa glared at the table. "I was too young to really understand, but I knew she did things that annoyed and hurt him. That night—the night she died—she said Kristóf had a man cold and was putting it on, but I'd seen him throwing up, he was so sick. She should have stayed at home to look after him. She was his wife. It was her duty. I know all about wifely duties; I nursed my husband through years of illness, then right through his last months when his body was wasting away. It was awful. But it was my duty. And I loved him, and I loved my princess. Ilona didn't love Kristóf, she just pretended to. She shouldn't have left him that night. She shouldn't have left me. He needed to be looked after. I ran after her and told her so, but she got angry with me. I don't know what happened exactly, but I do know she was surprised when I hit her. I slapped her with my hand. Across her face all covered with make-up. She wasn't listening to me—what else could I do? She toppled over. She hit her head, but she didn't die. She was alive. She was moaning."

I spoke softly, "Everyone was looking for a killer who could have hit your mother hard on the head with a rock—not for a killer who could push her down a steep path, awash in a rainstorm, where her entire bodyweight was behind her head when it connected with a rock in the ground. The torrent would have swept away the blood overnight, so there'd have been no sign of it the next day. But you couldn't have moved her body, Alexa, and we know it was moved. That's what your father did for you, isn't it? You ran off and left her there, dead, and begged your father to help you."

Alexa leapt up. "I didn't *kill* her. She wasn't *dead*. I just slapped her. She just toppled and fell. She *wasn't* dead, I tell you. It was an accident."

Zsófia's naturally pale complexion took on an almost blue hue as she stared at her mother. "An accident?"

Alexa snapped, "Yes, a slap, and maybe I pushed her. A bit. She didn't understand why I was so angry. She thought it was funny when I said she should stay home and look after Kristóf. After she'd fallen I ran home to Kristóf and told him what had happened. He said I wasn't to worry; he would sort it all out. He told me to take a bath and go to bed. I was wet through. I was just a child. *I* didn't kill her."

I shook my head sadly. "But that's not *exactly* what happened, is it, Alexa? Lividity takes time to set in. Valentin told me his mother's face was flushed when he, and you, saw her on the slab. Her body must have lain in one position, face down, for some time before your father moved her. Did you wait before you told him what you'd done? Did you hope she'd die?"

"No! I didn't wait . . . not on purpose. I . . . I was scared. Dad was sick. I didn't know what to do." Alexa sounded like a little girl.

I knew I had to step in before the woman became hysterical. "That's what you have told yourself all these years?"

"It's the truth," she screamed.

"So you believe—what? Your father went out into the storm, found your mother, bashed her on the head until she was dead, then dragged her body to the part of the path where she was eventually found?"

Alexa was biting her bottom lip so hard she drew blood. She nodded stiffly, and looked at her hands as she said, "When Kristóf told the cops none of us had left the house that night I just agreed with him. I had to protect him, or they'd have taken him away. I loved him. He was my father. He never said anything about it to me. Ever. I knew *I* hadn't killed her, so it must have been him. I knew he must have hit her again."

"When you read the final manuscript, you realized something, didn't you, Alexa? You realized Valentin had seen your father moving your mother's body that night."

Tamás let out a little gasp and looked at me astonished. "This was in his book?"

I nodded. "Valentin knew nothing of your involvement, and having seen Kristóf in circumstances he could only have interpreted as meaning his father had killed his mother, his psyche dealt with that information in a way that served to protect him from the terrible truth he thought he knew. The police records tell us he didn't speak to anyone about the events of that night for some time—not until he'd suffered what sounds to me like some sort of psychotic break. I have a suspicion he put the remembrance of his father's actions away from his conscious mind, though the effect it had upon him manifested itself in his turning to drugs—to change his sense of reality. It also allowed him to, eventually, weave a complex mythology based upon a central crime in his saga. You told me he began to write after your grandfather's death, Zsófia. That was his trigger."

Zsófia was dry-eyed and aghast. "You mean Uncle Valentin knew Grandfather had killed Grandmother, and he wrote all his books as a way to allow his subconscious to work through that knowledge?" I nodded. "The stoning of the queen? The king in the final book telling his son he'd murdered his sister? This is what tells you Grandfather killed Grandmother?"

I knew the hardest part was coming. "It tells us that's what Valentin believed." I sighed. "You saw Ilona's body in the morgue, didn't you, Alexa?" The woman nodded dumbly. "Why do you think your father made you touch the wound on her shaved head? Surely you saw there was only *one* wound? Valentin did, and told me so. He believed your father was being cruel when he took you two along and forced you both to examine your mother's wound. Upon reflection I don't think your father was being cruel—I believe it was his way of showing you what you'd done, Alexa. He didn't use words to tell you, he used the evidence of your mother's body to show you. But you didn't see it. You didn't understand what he was showing you. He should have used words."

All eyes were on Alexa. "I don't know what you mean." She was almost whispering.

"There was only *one* wound. Kristóf didn't hit her again. Your mother suffered only one blow to the head."

"You mean it was me who . . . No . . . No, that can't be right." She became rigid, and began to shake. Her mouth moved, but no sound came out. Her eyes spoke of the horror she was experiencing. Her fingers curled as if she was in physical pain. "No, it's not true. I didn't kill her; Kristóf did it. It must have been him. I *know* it was him. Oh, I'm so sorry, my darling," she gazed at her daughter with terror, "I never wanted you, my baby Zsófia, to know your grandfather killed your grandmother. It can't have been me who did it. She was moaning when I left her. How can I have killed her?"

The woman was still denying the facts. "The blow your mother suffered when you pushed her led to her death. It was the only injury she sustained."

Klara stood behind Alexa and held her heaving shoulders. Zsófia sobbed onto her mother's arm.

Minutes passed before anyone spoke.

Eventually Tamás said, "What will happen to Alexa?"

I looked at Bud, who shifted in his seat. "It's not for me to say," he replied softly. "It's an open case back in Canada. When the authorities there hear about this they'll . . ."

"What is the point of them doing anything?" said Klara, her deep voice heavy with the tears she was struggling to hold back. "My sister-in-law died. It is a family tragedy of long ago. Isn't it time for the old crimes, from the old days, to be put aside?"

Bud's furrowed brow told me he was grappling with his emotions. "I'm no longer an officer of the law, but I have a duty . . ."

"If we begged you to say nothing, what would your answer be?" said Tamás, standing behind Alexa and taking his wife's hand in his. "This family has suffered so much. We have many wounds to heal. How would it serve justice to bring this to the attention of the authorities? Look at Alexa. See how she is suffering. She will carry this guilt with her forever. She was a child back then. It was an accident. Justice is more than punishment, it is more than retribution; it is a moral decision, not a social imperative. Her suffering is justice. Can you not see that?"

"Please don't do anything that means my mama will be sent to prison, Bud," said Zsófia though her tears. "Can't you see she's already there? Mama has been so strong for so long, and always for other people. She looked after Kristóf and Valentin, then she looked after my father, then cared for Valentin when he was sick—always keeping her secret for what she thought was the sake of others. Tamás is right. It would serve no purpose to punish her, to remove her from society. You'd only be punishing us. We didn't do anything wrong."

John didn't make eye contact with Bud. My husband stood. "It's not my decision. It is a case that must be weighed by a jury. There are mitigating circumstances, I can see that, but Alexa caused her mother's death. That cannot go unanswered. I have upheld the law my entire life. I have also put wheels in motion that have drawn attention to this case, which means I cannot stand down at this point, even if I wanted to."

I looked at the man I loved, and knew I would never forgive myself if I stood against him on this matter. "I agree with my husband. Facts have come to light that must be passed on to the proper authorities. However, Bud, I would suggest you discuss these findings with that one 'special' person in Canada who has already approached you about Ilona's death. Maybe it should be that person who decides how to proceed."

Bud's brow smoothed. "You're right, Cait." Looking at Alexa's upturned, mournful face he continued, "I must fulfill my professional obligation, but I will say that there might not be the political will to pursue the case."

"Politics might help our family, for once," said Klara heavily.

"It might," I agreed. Bud sat down again, and I could tell he felt relieved he could reasonably pass the decision-making up the chain of command.

Zsófia hugged her mother, whose head was cradled in her arms on the dining table. "Mama, please, look at me?" Her mother raised her head a little. "We can talk about this. We are family. Tamás, Klara, and I can help you. And we can find a professional who will allow you to work out what this means for you. It's a tragedy that Uncle Valentin took his own life not knowing who he really was, and believing the man he thought was his father killed the woman he thought was his mother. But maybe it's better this way. He was able to love you as his sister all these years, and you only have to read his books to know how important that relationship was to him. You must have seen how he wrote kindly about sisters in his books?"

Alexa shook her head. "I didn't see that. I didn't understand what any of his words meant. Ever. I've been an incredibly stupid woman. I'm a killer, and I didn't even know it. I cannot imagine how just talking to someone can ever help me come to terms with that fact."

"Words have great power," I said, "especially when they come from the heart. They can wound, but they can also help the healing to begin. I think Zsófia's idea of finding a professional with whom you can speak, in complete confidence and with absolute openness, is going to be critical for you."

"So says the psychologist, and I agree with her," said Bud.

Final Words

SITTING IN MY WHEELCHAIR IN the exclusive lounge at Budapest Airport the next day—John had arranged for us to fly business class, so we were being treated like royalty—I enjoyed a last cup of Turkish coffee with Bud. He'd taken to it as much as I had, which surprised me.

"After finding out they charged so much for my time here in Hungary, and knowing they don't really want me back, I'm not looking forward to having that meeting with my head of department at the UVan campus in a couple of weeks," I said.

"Tell them to stuff their job," was Bud's very un-Bud-like response.

"Pardon?"

"Cait, my love—you haven't been happy there for months. I hate seeing you so caught up in politics that you can hardly sleep at night. Walk away. Have a fresh start."

"*Walk* away? Hardy-har-har, Bud." I rolled my wheels a couple of inches closer to his toes.

"Too soon?" Bud winked. "Come on, you know you can walk a little already, and it's just a matter of time and rehab before you're able to get about like you always did. We both know you were very fortunate, Cait, so let's try to look on the bright side, eh?"

I grappled with my emotions for a moment then set my jaw. "I know you're right. It'll be hard work, but I know I'll make a full recovery. I'm much more fortunate than many in that respect."

"At least take a leave of absence for a year? The job will be there for you. They can't get rid of you now you're like this."

I rolled my eyes. "Full of wit and pith today, aren't you? This isn't just a job we're talking about, it's my career, Bud. I can't just 'walk away.' What's an academic without an academic post? Nothing. This is my life."

Bud leaned forward and held my hand. "No, it's not, Cait. It's your career, yes, but it's not your *life*. Life should be about more than just a career. I've struggled with that since I retired, but now I'm coming to terms with it. And I can help you do the same. If you're going to get paid for reproducing what you read of Valentin's work, you'll have an income that would allow you to not live off me—which I know is important to you."

I shrugged, rather halfheartedly. "You're right about me wanting to contribute to our financial wellbeing, but I also feel I have something to contribute to the body of knowledge and understanding of criminal psychology. There's so much I could do."

"So do it. Get the book written up for Zsófia, then work on your own to connect with others in your field who think like you do. You don't mean to tell me, in this day and age, that there's no other way you can put forward your hypotheses than with the backing of a university?"

"I wouldn't be able to publish papers."

"But you could offer your services to law enforcement services, right? I know John's spoken to you in the past about working with him."

"Oh no, Bud, I'm not going to get dragged into the twilight world of international backdoor information gathering and profiling. It's just not me."

"You consulted for me, you could consult for others. If you weren't teaching at UVan you'd have the time. You've been moaning for at least a year about how the low-level courses they insist you deliver mean you're grading sub-standard reports from students who are forced to take your classes, rather than working the way you'd prefer, with operational professionals. Maybe now's the time to do it."

"Well, it's rehab and the book first, I know that." I smiled at my husband. "It'll be good to work with Zsófia. Maybe we can help each other through our tough times."

Bud's face told me he was feeling uncomfortable before his words did. "About Zsófia. Now that I've met her I see she's a bright girl, and, yes, vulnerable with it. But what was it about her that made you take all this on in the first place? Was it—I know this is something you don't ever really talk about—but was it because of that business at the start of your relationship with Angus?"

I sagged. "You mean my miscarriage?" Bud nodded. I sighed. "I don't talk about that often because it doesn't frequently come to mind. I'd only found out about being pregnant, and told Angus, the day before I lost it. I know a miscarriage can be hugely traumatic for many people, and I'd never want to underestimate the impact it can have upon some people's lives. But for me? Physiologically, it was almost as though nothing had happened. Psychologically, the main effect it had upon me was that Angus used it against me in every way he could, for years. But, honestly, I'm not lying at all when I tell you from my heart that I don't believe everything is meant for everyone, Bud; I really don't believe I was cut out to be a mother. I'll grant you, when I met Zsófia, who's about the age that child would have been now, and, yes, a bit like me when I was her age—though I was spared all the family drama, I'm pleased to say—something inside me kicked in and I felt a twinge of . . . I don't know what to call it. Sorry, I just don't have the words." I gazed into my husband's eyes. "She's not a surrogate. I'm *not* sad I'm not a mother. I'm going to be just fine working with her. I have no hidden agenda. There's no big child-shaped hole in my life. Okay?"

Bud squeezed my hand. "Okay. So long as you're sure."

Our flight was called, so I was saved from having to say more than, "I'm absolutely certain. From my point of view, the most impactful aspect of having the chance to work on this book with her is that

Zsófia said the advance for the book was half a million dollars. Half of that is a lot of money. So, yes, to be fair to you, and to us, I could at least take a leave of absence and think about doing something other than staying at UVan, I suppose."

"You do that. You're good at thinking things through."

"Sometimes I am."

"You're right about that," said my husband.

Acknowledgments

ONCE AGAIN I SIT HERE with a list of people to thank for helping me with this book, and, once again it includes the stellar team at TouchWood Editions, and a few people who have told me they'd rather remain nameless. So, to Taryn, Frances, Cailey, Pete, Tori, and Renée at TouchWood Editions, and the nameless informants: thank you.

This tale is set in Budapest, a city rich in history, art, architecture, music, food, and contradictions. It's a wonderful place that confounds most expectations, yet delights at every turn. I've spent many months there over the years, and have been fortunate enough to stay not only at wonderful hotels, but also in the homes of people who have lived there through "interesting" times.

To Ilona, who allowed me to use her name; John and Shirley, who spoke with passion about their Hungarian upbringing; Peter, who first invited me to work in Budapest back in the mid-1990s; the members of the Hungarian diaspora here in British Columbia, who have delighted me with their tales of characters from "the old country"—I thank you all.

Thanks to you for choosing to join Cait Morgan as she spends time in Budapest, and to the reviewers, bloggers, booksellers, and librarians who might have helped you find her.

Welsh Canadian mystery author CATHY ACE is the creator of the Cait Morgan Mysteries, which include *The Corpse with the Silver Tongue, The Corpse with the Golden Nose, The Corpse with the Emerald Thumb, The Corpse with the Platinum Hair, The Corpse with the Sapphire Eyes, The Corpse with the Diamond Hand,* and *The Corpse with the Garnet Face.* Born, raised, and educated in Wales, Cathy enjoyed a successful career in marketing and training across Europe before immigrating to Vancouver, Canada, where she taught in MBA and undergraduate marketing programs at various universities. Her eclectic tastes in art, music, food, and drink have been developed during her decades of extensive travel, which she continues whenever possible. Now a full-time author, Cathy's short stories have appeared in multiple anthologies, as well as on BBC Radio 4. In 2015 she won the Bony Blithe Award for Best Canadian Light Mystery (for *The Corpse with the Platinum Hair*). She and her husband are keen gardeners who enjoy being helped out around their acreage by their green-pawed Labradors. Cathy is also the author of the WISE Enquiries Agency Mysteries. Cathy's website can be found at cathyace.com.